Love Most Foolish, Love Most Wise

by
Charlotte Ann Smith

PublishAmerica

Baltimore

For Nancy
& Beth
Charlotte Ann
Smith

First printing

ISBN: 1-4137-1239-8
PUBLISHED BY PUBLISHAMERICA, LLLP
www.publishamerica.com
Baltimore

Printed in the United States of America

This book is dedicated to my husband Russ, whose loving support in the research and writing of this book has made it all possible.

My endless thanks to my sister, Linda Meade, my consultant in psychological insight, and to my cousin Jean Chalk, my cheerleader-in-chief.

Chapter One

Bristol, England. November, 1666

Weaving between heaps of offal that littered the dockside streets of Bristol and dodging slops pitched from upper story windows, Catherine dashed like a madwoman toward the ship bound for Mary's Land, a vessel that was even now abuzz with activity.

If the toothless old man coiling rope in a splintered shed was to be believed, it was ready to sail, and her younger sister Mary, whom she loved like a child of her body, was on it.

"A comely wench, hair like sunlight?" he'd questioned. "Aye, it was but a short time ago I saw her make her X on the papers of indenture. She will be belowships now, held tight lest she change her mind." He'd leaned forward conspiratorially. "It is a pretty price the captain will fetch fer her indenture in Mary's Land."

Remembering those words, Catherine felt the bile rise in her throat as she closed the final distance to the ship's plank and dashed onto it despite the cursing of the sailors, one of whom obviously got his hand caught twixt board and deck as her weight forced the board down.

When she jumped onto the deck, he whipped the back of his uninjured hand across her face. "Filthy bawd," he shouted. "God's blood, ye hev broke my paw."

Even had she known what to say, there would have been no time to answer because rough hands grabbed her arms and dragged her toward the gunnels, obviously intent on throwing her overboard into the evil smelling water that smacked the stained planking below.

"Hold," a voice shouted with authority. "What happens here?"

"It is a stowaway," one man answered, the inaccuracy of his statement no deterrent to his volume.

"She hev broke my hand," the injured sailor complained.

Catherine looked up hopefully at someone who might at least ask her what she wanted.

"Well, explain, woman, and be fast about it. The tide does not wait for foolishness."

"I think my sister has signed an indenture and is aboard this ship ... "

"Thirty souls have signed," he interrupted her impatiently. "Who is she?"

"Her name is Mary Quentin, and she is blonde and most beautiful," Catherine answered, wishing she could brush aside the unruly hair that fell over her eyes and obscured her vision. "She is but fifteen. You cannot take her."

The man – he must have been the captain – laughed as though she'd said something absurd. "Aye, she has signed. Fifteen is enough. An excellent age, in fact. Mary's Land has need of young women, the younger, the better. I *can* take her, and take her I will. Now, off with you." He nodded to the other men. "Walk her back down to the shore, you cut-throats. It is not fitting to throw her overboard."

Tears welled up despite Catherine's attempt to be bold. "Then, will you take me? I will sign the papers. Please do not send her off alone." The tears spilled over, and she couldn't wipe them away because her arms were still pinioned.

"And will you weep your way to the new world?" he asked. "It is a bad risk. Such as you do not survive the trip. You look to be long on bone and short on flesh, half starved already. Neither our biscuit nor our salt meat will fatten you up. You'll likely die from the journey."

New terror coursed through Catherine. Would Mary starve so that her beauty would be tarnished? Would she die?

"I am fit," she shouted defiantly. I have eaten well enough; I am not likely to starve. Take me with you. I will fetch a price to make it worth your while." Desperation made her wrench her arms free. "See, I am strong. I can cook, and I can sew, and I can write."

"You can write?" The half smile she'd seen earlier returned to his face. "And read?" He shook his head no at a man reaching out to grasp her arms again.

"Aye, I can read."

"There be proof?"

"Try me."

"Come then," he told her. "Cast off," he said to the sailors. "Should she be telling lies, she will feed the fish outside the harbor."

Catherine followed the man, sure now that he *was* the captain. A curious mixture of relief and anxiety wracked her. She could continue to stay with Mary and protect her, but the world as they both knew it was swept away in an instant.

She was grateful to the scribe who had satisfied her curiosity long ago about the mysterious letters of the alphabet, who'd read words aloud to her as he traced them with his fingers, who'd encouraged her as she drew words in the dirt with a stick and eventually allowed her to write on the precious paper provided him by his patrons.

That the captain changed his mind because she could write told her she had a skill important in Mary's Land. Perhaps God had a purpose in plunging Mary and herself into something so enormously new, though so completely terrifying.

The cover over the opening above her slammed shut as Catherine stepped down into the foul darkness of the ship's innards. She could hear coughing and squabbling voices as she stumbled down the ladder and then found she could not stand straight because the overhead beams were too low. She stepped sideways and was roundly cursed as her foot came down on human flesh.

"I am sorry," she said, deciding to stand still until her eyes accustomed themselves to the near blackness.

"Mary?" she called. "Mary, it is Catherine. Where are you?" Another surge of terror pulsed through her. What if they were all wrong, all lying? What if Mary were not aboard? What if she, Catherine, were sailing away from her sister forever?

But the other voices quieted briefly as though curious to hear the answer, and she heard a muffled voice. "Catherine, I am here."

Though she felt light-headed with relief, Catherine could make out now the people who sat or lay on the flooring, and there was a figure rising from their midst, holding out her arms.

"Stay, pretty lassie," a wheedling male voice intoned, and Catherine surmised with alarm that most of their fellow travelers were men.

"I am coming," she told Mary.

Moving carefully around the people who were as packed together as pigs in the market, lacerated by the whimper that came from Mary, Catherine finally sank down beside her weeping sister, forcing others to shift out of the way.

"Oh Catherine! Oh, Thank God you have come!" Mary pressed herself into Catherine's arms. The two embraced and held to each other with all possible strength while Mary sobbed out her anguish.

"What have I done?" she cried when her heaving body had subsided somewhat. "It is too terrible a price to pay. It is too ugly!" she wailed into Catherine's shoulder.

"Calm yourself, Mary." Catherine rubbed Mary's back though she wanted nothing so much as to wail herself. But she was not a mere sister. Her dying mother had charged her to become both father and mother to the squalling newborn, and fulfilling that charge had become Catherine's life. She remembered telling herself she could be a child no longer now that she wore the mantle of motherhood.

"We can do naught but bear up," she said to her shaking sister, wondering how she herself could be strong enough to do it.

They were silent except for an occasional sniffle as they continued to cling to each other. Then Mary spoke again.

"Do you remember how we spoke of Mary's Land, that we should travel there some day because I am named Mary?"

"They were magical stories to comfort and amuse a wee child," Catherine replied. "Of a certainty, you know that now. It is not the reason you placed your X on that evil paper. You are not that innocent child."

"No, it is not the reason." Mary went silent again, clutching Catherine's hand as the very planks of the ship groaned, and the surface they sat upon began to heave.

"Nor were the tales your reason, those false stories they told in the Bristol streets of the beauty and wealth and sweet weather of Mary's Land," Catherine went on.

"Nay, not for those, either," Mary agreed.

The man who'd been crowded and displaced from his proximity to Mary by Catherine's arrival snickered. "It is no sweet land," he said with irritation. "The papists there eat young chippies the likes of ye."

Mary shivered.

"What we say is none of your affair," Catherine told the man as sternly as she could.

"It is the affair of all in this fine parlor, for all can hear it," he answered.

Mary shifted to her knees, stretched up, and began to whisper into Catherine's ear. "Goody Menton did not tell me 'til you went to market early this day that Ephraim Tanner would arrive shortly to take me away … that I was to be his … mistress." Her voice broke as she sank back down on her haunches.

"His mistress!" Catherine repeated, aghast.

Mary stretched up again and continued to whisper into Catherine's ear. "Goody said our father had last made payment for our keep two years ago, and now that he was declared dead at sea, Mr. Tanner would pay her the sum that was owed."

Catherine put her hands over her eyes as though she could hide from what Mary was telling her.

Mary continued. "She said I would be kept in comfort with a serving wench and fine clothes, and that all I must do was submit to his demands." Mary choked up again. "Fat old pig with his pocked face and his rotten teeth. Pfagh! He sickened me when he called and hung over me and kissed my hand."

There was a long pause during which Catherine could hear Mary gulping as though to force her gorge back down her throat. "Goody gave me a sack and told me to put my second bodice and skirt into it along with my fancy sewing, but I dropped the sack, took my cloak, and ran from the house…and ran…and ran…until I came upon a man who told me I could go to Mary's Land. He said I could work four years and then be free to find a fine husband, that there were many men in need of wives in Mary's Land. And now I am here in this vile place with these vile people." She sank down and began to cry anew.

Catherine hugged her close again, seething with anger. What Goody had intended was that she, Catherine, be well away when Mr. Tanner came for his purchase, so she had been sent on an errand. Then Goody Menton had lied to Catherine, telling her that Mary had had a fit of temper over a trifle and run away. The 'good woman' had even made threat to get the sheriff after Mary, to make her pay for her tantrums. And, of course, had the plan not been foiled, Catherine, compliant, hard working Catherine, "long on bone and short on flesh," would then be separated from her sister and set to a lifetime of continued unpaid labor in the inn's scullery to repay what her father could not. It was so easy to see.

She felt a wave of hysterical laughter well up and fought to turn it into a cough. "Mary," she said. "It is not the brightest of moments now, but perhaps you chose better than you knew…and Christ's blood, I found you just in time." Catherine had never blasphemed before, but never had she been aware

9

of such provocation.

"Catherine!" Mary exclaimed. "It is a bad word you have used."

"It is a bad thing that overtook us, but the future cannot be worse than the miseries of the past. This could be for the best if only we make it so. We must stay together on this ship. At every moment, we must be together. Promise me now, Mary, that you will never leave my sight."

"I promise. Oh, faith, I promise!" Mary assured Catherine, who laughed ruefully.

"Besides, I did not pause to fetch my cloak, though it is well past Michaelmas and cold already," Catherine said.

"We will share mine," Mary replied. "It will be warmer that way,"

"And little sister," Catherine whispered, "call no one vile. There must be decent souls here among these poor travelers."

Mary and Catherine became silent, wrapping the single cloak tightly around themselves and listening to the rumble of voices that sometimes erupted into quarreling and cursing. Both began to shiver as the ship's motion increased and the cold became more intense. Moving around would have helped, but there was no way to move, nothing to do. Hour followed empty hour, and although Catherine tried to think of a riddle or game they might play to pass the time, her mind had become as numb as her body, and ideas would not form.

The words of Tildy Barrow, fellow servant, fellow sufferer, ran through her mind. "Let the Lord be your strength, child. Let the Lord be your strength."

Presently, Mary began to slap at her legs, and through a mounting nausea, Catherine came to realize that she, too, was suffering bites, first her legs, then her arms. The sounds of muttering and the cracks of hands on flesh told her others throughout the hold were similarly afflicted. She recalled with a shudder her father's words, "I do believe a ship with too many fleas is more like to be a plague ship."

Mary started to cry again. "I will be naught but sores," she sobbed.

"Bites will go away," Catherine comforted her. "I had not thought to long for anything about Goody Menton, but I would give much for her pallet stuffed with pennyroyal for the fleas," she said through clenched teeth.

"Oh! yes that," Mary replied, "and even some of her thin gruel. I am so hungry."

How could Mary be hungry? Catherine's stomach was in such rebellion she wondered if she would ever be hungry again. "If they give us food, you can have mine," she promised.

Scratching, slapping, shivering, the two dwelt in endless black time until the single lantern somewhere off in the distance was extinguished, and sleep pulled them briefly into forgetfulness, prone on the wood planking. Suddenly, though, Catherine awoke. An animal was crawling over her ear. She freed her hand, reached up and swept it overhead, batting aside a furry creature that squealed as it landed nearby, only to create a similar disturbance with another sleeper, who sat up screeching.

"It hev bit me. It is a rat, and it hev bit me!"

Catherine struggled not to cry, not to break down and sob. She owed it to Mary to be strong. Mary's body was shaking again with suppressed weeping, and Catherine drew her sister's head down on her breast and ran her hands over Mary's abundant hair, now matted and stinking of the planks they slept on.

She began to wonder if any of the trials and tribulations of her twenty years had been half so dreadful as this. When her gently bred, loving mother had screamed her way through Mary's birth and then turned all stiff and blue and cold? When her father had gone back to sea, entrusting the wee new babe to her six-year-old self and the pair of them to 'Goodwoman' Menton, the greediest, cruelest female in Christendom? When she was beaten each time she took the blame for Mary's childhood misadventures? When she longed for a father who never came, or when the hour arrived that brought news of the sinking of the ship in which he'd invested all his wealth and, worst of all, his certain death?

Fully awake now, she fought the gorge that rose again in her throat. Mary seemed to have returned to sleep, but Catherine's body had never known such misery.

After what seemed like days rather than hours, the hatch cover was dragged aside, and a thin gray light filtered down over the wretched scene.

"Ye are to come up to deck, eight souls at once," a voice called. Numbers of men arose and scrambled toward the light, but Catherine held Mary close to her.

"We must not vie with the others to be first," she said.

As if to confirm her wisdom, a sharp voice called angrily, "Wait yer turn!" Then the hatch darkened with a bang, and a wail of pain followed.

Avoiding the quarrels that erupted all around them, Mary and Catherine were among the last to climb to the deck. The sailor who had struck Catherine just the day before pointed to several buckets by the rail.

"Fer washing," he mumbled, and Catherine thought that water on her face and hands might quell the sickness a little and cool the itching bites. Still wrapped in their single cloak, the two hurried to the water and threw aside their wrap. Mary was the first to dip her hands in the water and draw it to her face. "Aiee!" she gasped. "It is cold and it stings. Catherine, it stings my face."

Catherine splashed her own face. "It is sea water," she murmured. "It is salty. It will ruin your skin, Mary. Do not wash with it."

"But then my face will darken with black spots like Goody Menton's," Mary wailed.

"Well then, do not do it often," Catherine warned. Her sister's beauty must be protected.

The passengers, who seemed to Catherine to have been treated more like cargo than humans, were next directed toward sailors who held out cups and spoons and pointed to a keg and wooden buckets. It became clear that each person was to fill his cup from the keg, drink, and pass the cup on to another. Catherine received hers, filled it, and stepped aside so that Mary might do the same. She stood holding the brew, knowing she ought to swallow, but unable to force herself to do it. The liquid smelled terrible. Mary took a sip, made a face, and immediately poured it on the deck.

A sailor approached, grabbed the cup, and shouted at her. "Ye needs must drink t' stay alive, silly bitch." He shoved her roughly toward the pail from which another man was handing out biscuit.

Catherine was pulled along because the cloak, restored after their washing, now bound them together again, and some of the liquid in the cup she held slopped over onto her chest. She took the tiniest of sips she could manage, then closed her eyes, fighting not to gag. It was ale, what one usually drank to break the fast, but it was *so* sour. The fact that it was greatly watered helped, but only a little. She handed the nearly full cup to the man behind her and turned her attention to the offering of biscuit, receiving hers just as Mary pulled on their common cloak, tugging Catherine off to the side.

Only too willing to relinquish her portion, Catherine was relieved to see that Mary, at least, was ready to eat. In fact, Mary ate ravenously and accepted Catherine's share, her obvious need to devour it taking the place of a thank you.

Three sailors approached them as Mary finished her dry meal. The girls backed away, but found themselves trapped against the gunnels. Catherine's hold on Mary tightened as she tried to block Mary from the unwanted attention.

"Let us see the wee pretty chippie," one man wheedled. A second reached around Catherine to put his hand on Mary's hair.

"Go away!" Catherine hissed. "Leave us alone."

"We will leave *you* alone, but let us see the fair lassie," came the answer as the cloak was pulled away and Catherine was yanked aside. She and Mary began to scream as Mary was surrounded, and Catherine pounded on broad backs and scratched weathered necks to no avail. An arm reached out and tossed her screeching to the deck. She could no longer hear Mary screaming and looked up to see her sister silenced by the kiss of a ruffian who was pushing her down toward the planking.

"God, no! Stop him!" Catherine shouted with all the strength she had. She perceived dimly that a crowd had formed around the scene, but the onlookers did nothing, merely stared, curious, perhaps aroused. Some were part of the crew, others denizens of the hold.

"Stop them," she begged. "Oh! please, stop them."

"Cease!" a deep authoritative voice roared. Catherine had stopped her beseeching to catch her breath and looked up to see the captain pushing through the rapt group.

"Leave the girl alone!" he bellowed, grabbing two of the offenders by the neck and kicking the third into obedience. They rose reluctantly and turned to face him, their faces mutinous.

"The females below-ships do not make up a brothel for your use." His voice had dropped to quite a sinister whisper. Catherine remained seated on the deck, wiped the tears from her eyes with her sleeve, and viewed the captain with gratitude. She could not see Mary, but could hear hysterical sobs slowly diminishing.

One of the devils must have snickered because the full fury of the captain's voice lashed out again. "You find this humorous? You will have no traffic with an unwilling woman, not crew, not men bound for indenture. Is that understood? Should such a thing as this happen again, you will be keelhauled, and this is no idle threat."

He paused, looking at Mary, who was struggling to stand up, then addressed the culprits again. "Now get about your duties. When food is served, you will report to Matthew Wiggins. There will be two weeks short rations for you."

An unhappy murmur passed among the sailors. Catherine guessed that full duties with short rations must be a heavy price for lust, and she already knew that to be keelhauled, to be dragged by a rope under water along the ship's keel from fore to aft, was surely to drown.

Shaking their heads, the group dispersed as the captain approached Mary.

13

"Where is your cloak, woman?" he asked.

Mutely, Mary pointed to the deck where it lay trampled. The captain picked it up and draped it over her shoulders. She looked beyond the man, her reddened eyes searching and coming to rest on Catherine.

"Come, Catherine," her voice quivered, and Catherine hastened to join her beneath the cloak's folds.

"Have you no other cloak?" asked the captain.

"No, sir," Catherine answered.

"You had not expected to indenture yourself, had you?

"No sir."

The captain turned. "Evans," he called to a sailor standing nearby. "Take these females below and make sure they are placed with the other women." Then, he smiled and put his hand on Mary's head. "Dry those eyes, lass." He reached into a pouch fastened around his waist. "Here are sweetmeats for you," he said, placing them in Mary's hand. "Be comforted. You will be safe."

Thus began the only good thing about the voyage, huddling with two of the other three women aboard. Eleanor, ordered by the courts to depart for the new world, believed herself to be about Catherine's age – she wasn't quite sure – and had had more difficulties in her life than Catherine could even fathom. But for all her problems, Eleanor was generous. She had an extra cloak, an unbelievable luxury Catherine suspected to be stolen. Two weeks into the voyage, Eleanor pressed it upon Catherine, and any doubts Catherine might have had about its origin were buried in gratitude.

Phoebe, their second friend, was somewhat older, a widow left with nothing and seeking to improve her prospects in a society overbalanced with men. She was motherly, helping Catherine to shelter and to calm Mary when circumstances threatened to overwhelm her.

Phoebe boasted about her cooking skill and knew already that her indenture would be served at the scullery fire of a manor. An agent, employed by a landholder named Josiah Hook, carried her signed papers with him on this ship.

A third woman divided her time between numbers of men, muffled moanings and bumpings issuing quite often from whatever spot she happened to inhabit. Once she accosted Mary.

"Should ye once shed yer cloak, ye would be kept warm all the way to Mary's Land by these gents, but ye are too fine fer the likes of us, ain't ye. It is so far into the air ye hev got yer nose, were there any birds about, they would crap upon it."

"We will go our way, and you had best go yours," Catherine warned her. "We have not troubled you, nor asked for your opinion." The slattern snorted in contempt and walked away, but thereafter she taunted the sisters whenever she saw them.

One blessing fell on Catherine six days into the crossing. Despite the ship's violent tossing, her stomach became calm, and her appetite returned. She might have eaten all the scanty fare provided, but Mary was so perpetually hungry, Catherine passed half her own portion to her. After a while Catherine's stomach no longer noticed the loss.

The captain, whom they now knew as Captain Hudgins, began to greet Mary and Catherine during their morning's time in the fresh air. One day, he put a packet of dried figs in Mary's hand, commenting that she'd become much too thin. Mary thanked him coyly and gave him a flirtatious smile, her head turned to the side but her eyes looking toward him, much as the street women of Bristol did when a man might buy their services. How had Mary learned to behave in such a fashion, Catherine wondered. Was one born with these wiles?

"Mary, you behaved in a most unseemly way," Catherine admonished her later. "You must not do that. Be careful how you use your eyes and your smile. It was like an invitation to the captain to take liberties…"

"Fie, Catherine," Mary interrupted. "He has taken care of me…us…and see how he gives us treats."

Us, thought Catherine angrily. The *me* before Mary caught herself was more accurate, for she rarely thought to share. Catherine had seen few children who shared; most hoarded what little came their way. *Mary is really but a child*, she told herself as she forced her anger to go away.

As the finish of the endless voyage finally loomed, the captain began to press large portions of both figs and sweetmeats on Mary. Catherine wondered whether these acts had been born of kindness, lust, or fear that Mary's indenture price would fall with her weight.

Catherine pretended she considered the impulse generous, and though it was obvious that he sought only Mary's thanks, Catherine behaved as gratefully as she knew how. She had a special reason.

Taxing her courage to its limits when land was in sight, she said to him, "If it please you, sir, I have a request."

15

He raised his eyebrows quizzically, as though she had no right to such a thing, but he would listen nonetheless.

Catherine took a deep breath. "I would ask that when the indentures are sold, mine and my sister's might be sold together, that we might be two to the barrel, so to speak."

His eyebrows went up again, his narrow face seeming to become even more narrow. "You would make that request, would you?"

"Aye."

He looked down at Mary. There was pleading in her eyes. "Oh, please," she said. "Without Catherine, I think I will die of fear."

He hesitated, cleared his throat, and looked out to the horizon. When he returned his gaze to Mary, he answered. "We reach Mary's Land later than I had hoped, and bidders might be scarce. I must see how many there are. I cannot promise, but I will do what I can." He put his finger beneath Mary's chin. "Let me see your smile, good lass. I have given you an honest answer."

Mary's smile was as weak as his promise, but still it was a smile, and he seemed satisfied.

Catherine wondered if Mary, young as she was and only seeming to get more beautiful, would always smooth the path for both herself and her older sister with her winsome smile, curls of sunshine, and beguiling green eyes. Even as a young child, Mary had captured attention wherever she went. She'd known since infancy how to charm, and now that her body had matured into curving, graceful proportions, she was even more able to do so. But her capacity to seem fetching had lately become dangerous where men were concerned. Even tattered and dirty as she was now, her allure still shone through.

A cold March wind blew in from the sea as Daniel Falconer eyed the other men who'd come to St. Mary's to bid on indentures when the ship arrived. The vessel was too late for the court and council sessions that would have brought crowds into the small town, so there were only a handful of other bidders. This meant that prices would be low, Daniel told himself with mounting optimism. Acquiring one more manservant would guarantee him extra land as well as labor for his freehold, and he desperately needed another woman to oversee his two children, to assist in all the household chores, and to aid at peak season in the time-consuming growing of the tobacco so prized in Europe. He'd just released a most cantankerous maid a year early from her indenture so that she might marry the swain who'd filled her belly and take her shrewishness to his poor hut.

Daniel's optimism dimmed, however, when he saw only four women, one obviously a trollop and a second previously bound to the manor of Josiah Hook. A third was so thin and pale she'd not live out the year, but a fourth looked sturdy enough. Unfortunately, she would therefore be in demand by anyone who needed female labor or wanted a hard working wife.

Invited to examine any of the prospective servants more closely, he approached the two available females with reluctance. He'd been indentured himself, had stood in their shoes, having his muscles squeezed by bidders and his intelligence questioned. He knew what it was like to be a piece of human chattel, one's fate entirely in the hands of another for the foreseeable future. He would certainly not insult the women by opening their cloaks to examine the heft of their bodies as others were doing.

He regarded the thin, tousle-haired girl from a courteous distance and saw on her face a look of gratitude for his reticence and a yearning so naked in one who held herself proudly that he was tempted to bid only for her. Then he told himself not to allow foolish notions to interfere with his determination to prosper in this difficult land.

The bidding started on the men whose contracts were held only by the captain, and for two thousand pounds of tobacco, he bought the papers of a short, stocky man with a face that was deeply pocked. The man seemed bright and willing enough.

When the women's papers were offered for bid, the strumpet walked away with a man Daniel didn't know, a man grinning lasciviously, well pleased with himself.

The bidding on the likeliest unclaimed maidservant went to fifteen hundred pounds of tobacco, and though Daniel could have gone higher, he perceived already that he'd be outbid. Josiah Hook's agent won her indenture for the great manor in addition to the indenture already secured. The two women were hurried away.

The small crowd now began to disperse. It seemed no one wanted to bid on the girl so near death, the human stick. Daniel had nothing to lose; her indenture would cost next to nothing. If she survived, long suffering Martha would have the assistance she required. And if the girl did not survive? Well, he would not have lost much.

"Two hundred pounds tobacco," he called as the ship's man offered up her indenture. A ripple of laughter went through the group of men.

"This girl can read and write," said the auctioneer. "That be of value to ye."

Daniel had no need of such a skill. He could read himself and needed only a hard worker.

"'It would be but a nuisance," someone called.

"'It would give her ideas I would not want her to have," another answered.

"Afore she died," came a third comment as the general exodus continued. It began to appear that the bid of two hundred pounds would stand.

"Spare me a moment!" Captain Hudgins stepped up beside the auctioneer pulling a hooded figure behind him. This was the selfsame captain who had brought Daniel to these shores. He had sailed here many times and was well known.

"I wish to offer these two female servants, these two sisters, together," he said, motioning toward the thin one and patting the hooded one on the back.

Daniel groaned inwardly. Damn the man. What was his object? Daniel had just convinced himself he'd pay the two hundred pounds and fatten the girl up, and now Hudgins was throwing complications in the way.

Then the captain pushed back the hood and pulled the cloak from the girl's shoulders, and a collective gasp traveled through the gathering. She was beautiful, the most entrancing thing Daniel had ever seen. It was impossible to believe the two women were sisters. The girl shivered in the cold and bit her quivering lip and then smiled a tentative, frightened little smile as those who had meant to depart turned back and clustered close to the captain to stare at the beauty and at the walking skeleton who could read.

Daniel was thirty-two and healthy, but had already decided that to need a woman was hell on earth. There flashed through his mind times he had wished himself castrated like the bulls not fit for breeding. When he had bowed to his need and married, so angry had he been at his wife's demands, at the way she had sabotaged his every plan, that on her death he had vowed never to marry again.

Afterwards, he had avoided the all too available chippies for fear of disease, and since there were precious few females available for marriage, none of whom had come his way, his vow had been kept.

Today, his body awoke in reaction to the vision before him, and such was the silence of his neighbors he was certain most of them were similarly smitten.

"God's wounds," he swore to himself. He'd now have no servant at all; he'd never make the bidding. And he didn't like the jolting of his body into an awareness and a need he'd not be able to satisfy.

But the words of many of the other men surprised him.

"Too rich for my blood," one man commented.

"Have not food enough to feed two useless females," another added.

"She will be naught but trouble," a third mumbled.

"Pretty faces do not last long, nor trim the tobacco neither," still another said as he made it clear he was now just lingering to see what the outcome of this interesting diversion would be.

One by one they turned away. It was a shame, Daniel reflected, that no manor lord was present, but now it could be said the game was to his own advantage. When the auctioneer opened the bidding again, Daniel had a brief internal debate over purchasing possible untold anguish and bid five hundred pounds.

"One thousand," a voice answered him. The man was Giles Watkins, whose cruelty to a servant had once been brought before the court. Furthermore, he was increasingly a madman as all could see. He came to drink with other townsfolk at the Ordinary, and they said he spoke nonsense, threatening to fight opponents who weren't there. People said he had gone mad from the harlot's disease; the sores on his body bore out their opinions.

And he looked to be the only other bidder.

Daniel shuddered. He believed the man's holdings were larger than his own, ably worked by an assistant, a man called Amos, who'd soon inherit them, thus profiting by his master's death and his own simple diligence. Daniel would never be able to meet Watkin's bid, but even though his common sense whispered he ought to stop, he had to try.

"Two thousand," he shouted.

"Three thousand," Watkins countered.

Daniel hesitated. A year's progress would be lost if he continued on this path. "Three thousand, five hundred," he said nevertheless.

"Four thousand, five hundred." Watkins wasn't going to give up.

"Five thousand," Daniel said, his voice almost dying in his throat. If he went higher, he and his household would be unable to buy the basic goods they needed to survive the next winter, nor could he repay the debts he'd incurred just to get his freehold established.

"Six thousand," Watkins screamed in glee, already sensing his victory.

Daniel was silent. The auctioneer had pointed to Watkins and opened his mouth as though to confirm the sale when the captain stopped him. At that same moment a stranger sidled up to Daniel. "Cap'n say raise yer bid e'en though ye need pay but five thousand pound. They must na go to Watkins."

It could be a trick to ruin him. The captain could deny he had sent any such message, but Daniel doubted it. He thought rather that Hudgins knew of Watkins and would not set him upon the pretty maid. If Daniel were wrong, he could lose his holdings. If right, he would live with a body in torment until her indenture ended or she looked favorably upon him. He liked neither prospect, but still felt compelled to bid.

"Seven thousand!" His words were more an eruption than a shout.

"Eight thousand," Watkins growled, obviously angry that it was not over and insulted that the auctioneer had hesitated.

At ten thousand, Watkins' man Amos tapped his master on the shoulder, and the two began to argue.

The auctioneer took advantage of that interval to award the sale to Daniel. Watkins then aimed a punch at Amos, missing by a wide margin, and stomped away, cursing loudly.

"Let the buggering spawn of Satan hev the bitches. He will not hev 'em long," were his last intelligible words.

Catherine opened her eyes. When the vile man — she had warned Mary against calling anyone vile, but sometimes there were no other words — when the vile man had seemed to outbid the other, she had closed her eyes and begun to pray. And God had answered her prayers. The one man who had granted her a measure of dignity would own their labor for the next four years. Though he did not appear to be particularly happy about his purchase, in most ways she liked the looks of him. He was of a middling height, a little taller than herself, well muscled, robust, and without fat. His dark hair was pulled back in the customary queue, but portions of it had escaped as though he had been running his hands through his hair. Curly strands hovered over eyes that gleamed with intensity, and accentuated a nose that had obviously been broken.

"My thanks to you, Captain," he said with dignity.

The captain laughed. "'It was not for your benefit I lost all that tobacco. It was for these young women. I could not sell their services to that madman." He turned to Mary. "You see, I kept my promise. I kept you and your sister together," he said as the new master arranged with the ship's steward for his payment.

Mary's hand shook visibly as she wiped tears from her eyes.

"You have been so kind. I thank you."

Daniel beckoned to the three servants whose services he had bought and bade them follow him.

"God go with you," the captain said.

"Blessings on you, sir," Catherine answered before turning to follow her new master.

Struggling to keep pace, she thought again about the mixture of generosity and self-serving with which the captain had treated Mary. He had given her extra food fearing he would receive lower bids had he not done so. For the same reason, she suspected, he had searched through the clothing packed among the cargoes destined for the wealthier of the settlers, selecting garments to enhance Mary's beauty. Then he had instructed her to use his cabin to wash in clean fresh water while he stood outside to guard the door.

He had promised to try to sell their papers together, but kept the promise only after it became clear that Catherine would fetch a lower price than a mutton chop. That was when he had stepped in to ward off separation. One could not overlook, however, that he had lost five thousand pounds of tobacco by refusing to sell to the madman. Catherine was sure that if one were to weigh his generosity against his selfishness, generosity would tip the scale.

Chapter Two

The new master set such a pace as he led his hirelings to their new workplace that Mary was almost running to catch up, and Catherine had to lengthen her stride in a most unaccustomed fashion. Having given his name as Edwin and then lapsing into silence, the new manservant strode easily along, but Catherine was beginning to feel quite dizzy. She'd eaten only scantily for months now, and had done nothing to push her body into maintaining its strength; there'd been nothing *to* do but take one daily turn about the deck.

Mary started to puff as she ran toward the master's side.

"Sir," she began to address him.

"What?" His voice almost snapped, and his eyes when he turned to look at her showed the intense quality Catherine had seen earlier. He seemed quite angry, and Catherine was not sure why.

"How far must we go?" Mary asked, obviously struggling to hide her breathlessness.

"It is about five miles, and we must be there before dark," he replied, his voice curt.

Catherine's hopes that Mary might be able to persuade him to slow down faded, and she found she could scarce drag one foot after the other.

"What manner of freehold have you?" Mary asked.

"It is thirty acres planted with tobacco, but it will soon be larger," he replied, "and do not trouble me with further questions." His voice was not merely sharp now. There was something close to rage in it. Mary had never before seemed to elicit anger from a man, and she was obviously startled, but she was so certain of her charms that she turned and opened her mouth to speak again.

"Mary, enough," Catherine hissed.

Mary threw her a look of irritation, but spoke no more, falling back into step beside her.

Catherine became increasingly oblivious to her surroundings. Every ounce of concentration went into keeping up with the others. For a time, the wind off the water whipped the dust from the path into their faces, but as the sky darkened into dusk, the wind dropped, and the walk became a little easier.

Not for long, though. Presently, a deeper blackness than that of the dying light moved into the edge of her vision and then blanketed her eyes, and Catherine felt herself falling helplessly to the earth.

Daniel strode along relentlessly, trying to decide what he could eliminate from the list of needs for his freehold now that he had spent so much tobacco on an ornament and a dying girl.

Suddenly, a shriek from the 'ornament' startled him out of his reverie.

"Catherine!" she wailed.

He turned to look and saw the new manservant and the ornament, but not Catherine.

"Where is she?" he questioned. "Has she run away so soon?"

"She is there beyond that tree...on the ground." The ornament turned and ran back, kneeling beside her sister.

"God's wounds!" Daniel swore as he turned back. Was she dead already? Movement as the pile of bones tried to push herself to her knees told him she wasn't, though he feared her continued presence among the living was probably no blessing. Now he was faced with the inconvenience of getting her back to the house in what would soon be darkness.

Rejecting the idea of leaving the girl where she was as too barbaric even given the cauldron of temper that boiled up in him, he stood over her and watched her struggle to rise. Obviously, she could not; she would have to be carried.

"Whore's breath," he muttered to himself as he leaned down to reach beneath her arms and throw her over his shoulder.

She jumped, startled, as he touched her, and as he slung her over his shoulder, he heard her whisper, "Please, pardon me this weakness."

He did not trouble himself to reply. Instead, he muttered to Edwin, "You will take a turn with this burden later, though by the virgin, it is not much of a burden." He turned to Mary. "Did they feed her nothing on the ship?"

"It was her stomach, sir. It was unsettled. She gave much of her food to me."

So that explained why one had thrived and the other shriveled. To let his eyes linger for even a moment on the face that looked so prettily up at him was to feel desire tearing through his body again. He wished the starving and the feeding had been reversed so that the tall one had become strong and the little one less lovely. Then he would not be so sore troubled.

The whip lashed Catherine's legs again and again. Its cruel edge dug gullies in her skin and sent blood coursing down to her ankles. *I will not cry! I will not cry,* she told herself.

"Steal the milk would you? It is not meant for the likes of you." Goody Menton examined Catherine's eyes for tears, and Catherine knew the woman would thrash away with the leather until tears appeared or there was danger she would be rendered incapable of the morrow's work.

Goody Menton must have seen that danger approaching because abruptly, she turned and hung the whip by the door.

"See that you sin no more," she rasped as she left the skullery.

It was no sin, Catherine knew, no sin at all, to get milk for Mary. She would never stop stealing milk for Mary, but now the tears were free to come, and when Tildy Barrow stooped to wash away the blood and bind the legs, her sympathy only increased the flood.

"Let the Lord be your strength, child," Tildy said.

"Mary will die if I do not feed her. She will die!" Catherine was sobbing.

"Here, here," a stern voice said, and Catherine felt her shoulders shaken. "Wake up, girl. It is a bad dream. Wake up."

Catherine opened her eyes again. Where was she? It was so confusing. Then she remembered she had been on her way to the house of her new master. On a previous waking, she had found herself slung over someone's back like a sack of flour, yet been powerless to halt such an affront to her dignity. This time she was lying on a bed softer than anything she had ever known, one redolent with the sharp scent of the pennyroyal she had so desired, to combat fleas on the ship. A heavyset woman, who had graying hair but did not look otherwise very old, was muttering to herself.

"He hev not the sense of a turkey hen, that man. What am I to do to care for a starveling and all else besides?" she was asking. Then she addressed Catherine. "Now that ye hev woke, here be corn cake, and there be stew if ye can eat it."

Catherine felt no hunger, had felt none for a long time, but knew she must eat. She pushed herself to a sitting position and put her feet on the floor, waiting for the wave of dizziness to pass.

The woman eyed her questioningly as she stood and walked unsteadily to the table. "I can eat but a little I think…for now." Sinking onto the bench, she was grateful to be able to relieve her legs of their burden. As she spooned the stew from the wooden trencher and sipped the ale that had been set before her, she smiled at her reluctant benefactor. "This is most good," she said, "and as soon as I have any strength at all, I will prove to you that I can work hard. You will not rue the night you first saw me."

"Fore God, I do hope not, but ye needs must eat more than that." The woman eyed the spoon that now lay on the table.

"If I eat more, it will come right back. Pray, what is your name?"

"It be Martha."

"I am Catherine, and I will eat more very soon, especially this strange looking bread."

"It is from corn," Martha said, "and grows mightily here when wheat will not." She paused and then continued. "Ye fuddle me, for ye do not speak like a worker, but more like a lady fit to lie abed at the manor."

"Do not be fooled. I have worked harder than a six-armed scullery maid. My labor will suit you, I think." Catherine looked around. "Martha, where is my sister?"

"Above in the loft with Daniel's two children. It is where ye and me will sleep as well when ye can climb the stair. Daniel sleeps with the working men in their dwelling across the field this night, but most nights he sleeps here." She indicated the bed Catherine had just vacated. "It is a fine bed, ye see, wi' a frame and ropes to tighten and hold the pallet firm, and since the pallet is large enough fer all of ye, yer bum does not hit hard wood." She leaned over. "I lay upon it once when Daniel was away," she whispered.

"It was most pleasant," Catherine agreed. "Will there be such beds in heaven, do you think?"

Martha laughed. "Be the Lord willin'." Her expression changed, and she pointed to the food again. "Soon, ye mought watch the children afore yer strength is full back, and should ye be hearty by the month o' May to help transplant the tobacco, it will be to the good."

Catherine began to nibble on the corn cake, willing it to stay down. She must get strong quickly. She liked Martha already. The woman was forthright, but not unkind, and Catherine already longed to be a help to her rather than a burden.

* * *

The sounds of voices were an affront to Catherine as she tried to snuggle

25

more deeply into the warm, soft bed. She was experiencing the most contradictory sensations, feelings of well being at war with apprehension.

The voices were those of Daniel and Edwin and one other man, their words indicating they'd be mending fences at first light.

Catherine opened her eyes to flickering firelight, ashamed now to be a slug-a-bed in this busy household. She must rise and help, she decided. She could see Martha moving about by the fire and contrived to pull a blanket around herself as, her back to the men, she sat up, carefully swinging her legs over the edge of the bed and feeling the shock of the cold wood on her warm feet.

Martha saw her. "Yer clothes an' all be in the shed." She nodded at the door. "Can ye get yerself there alone?"

Catherine clamped her teeth together though they felt loose in her gums and shook her head yes. Clasping the blanket with one hand and supporting herself on a shelf and then on the rough wooden wall, she made her way through the door and painstakingly pulled on her skirt and then her bodice, tightening and tying it. When she sat on a stool and leaned over to put on her shoes and stockings, she almost pitched to the dirt floor in a fit of dizziness, but she sat very still for a short time, and it passed. How could she have gotten so weak in one day? She had not stumbled about so badly yesterday on the ship, though she had been terribly dizzy. She supposed the long walk to this dwelling had weakened her more than she knew…but then she had not even walked all the way to the cabin. It was frightening, this lack of control. Quite frightening.

Martha came in and put her arm around Catherine to walk her back to the table. Catherine smiled weakly. There was something about Martha's strength that flowed into Catherine, and she felt much better as she sat down, nodded to the men, and began to spoon up the porridge Martha put before her.

After only a few mouthfuls, she had to stop. Daniel looked at her with what seemed to be contempt. "Why are you not eating?" he asked, nay demanded to know.

"I can eat but small bits, though I will continue as soon as I can." She felt ashamed for the second time this morning. She could not even take her food adequately.

"Eat little bits all day, if you must, but eat," he ordered.

Martha nodded toward an unfamiliar man. "This be Catherine," she told him. To Catherine she said, "That great smiling rogue with no hair be Ezekiel."

"It is a poor sign when a captain can no feed the poor wretches he carries on his ship," Ezekiel said conversationally, if not quite tactfully.

Catherine supposed her emaciation must be something to behold. "It was not the fault of the captain," she said. "It was my own stomach and my sister's need." Daniel was gazing at her, frowning. Catherine looked at him, and he turned his eyes away.

Ezekiel leaned toward her and said in a tone that was anything but gloomy. "Well, ye will na starve here. It is a goodly household."

"I can see that. I am most grateful..." Catherine's words were interrupted by the clatter of feet descending the stair. She looked up to see a boy and a girl seeming about the same age, perhaps four or five. They ran to Daniel and clambered onto the bench, one on each side of him.

"Good morrow, Father," they said in unison as they settled themselves.

Catherine watched him reach out to hug them both. "Good morrow, my little elves," he answered. His greeting struck a note of pain as Catherine remembered a father who had gone away and not come back.

Daniel became silent as the children bowed their heads, mumbled a blessing whose words Catherine could not hear, and made the sign of the cross. The family was papist!

Catherine and Mary had been forced to Puritan practices by Goody Menton, and then restored with the death of Cromwell to Anglican ways, but all of it had been merely confusing to Catherine in her childhood, empty of any real meaning. In fact the only heartfelt prayers she could remember were those offered at her mother's side, and it was that little flame of faith, fanned by Tildy Barrow, that she had tried to pass on to Mary. Would they now be forced to pretend to be papist, something about which she had heard only scorn? It had the feel of something alien.

"What is your task today?" Daniel asked the children.

"To write our letters five times and to help Martha plant potatoes," the boy replied as though this question were routinely asked and answered. The tie between Daniel and his children comforted Catherine a little. There seemed to be love here.

"Where is the young woman?" Daniel asked.

"The pretty lady must be sore tired," the boy answered again.

The girl giggled. "She did not wake when we cut her sunny hair."

Catherine choked on the mouthful of porridge she had just forced herself to take.

"You what?" Daniel responded rather like a musket firing.

The girl looked frightened and repeated more softly, "We cut her hair."

The statement hung in the air interwoven with a silent question. *Was that wrong?*

"Martha cuts our hair," the boy defended. She says hair too long is troublesome. We thought to help."

Catherine wondered how much had been cut and what Mary's reaction would be. She gasped as the boy fished a long tangled mass of golden hair from the top of his breeches.

"Judith! Jonathan! You have done a bad thing," Daniel admonished them sharply. "There will be no supper for you tonight." He got up and beckoned to his workers, who rose as well. Both children put their heads down contritely.

"It is your sister's fault," he said to Catherine, "and yours as well, Martha. She should be awake by now. Did you think to let her lie abed all day?" He took his coat from a hook by the door, but turned back again to Martha. "All who dwell in this household will make contribution."

"Aye, Daniel, she will," Martha placated, "but I hev give her this day to gather strength. She will earn her keep. Fore God, she will."

Daniel harrumphed and swept through the door, slamming and securing it behind him.

"He hev got the devil on his shoulder," Martha said to Catherine. "The dear Lord knows why." She took the mass of hair from Jonathan and looked at Catherine. "Will she want this or does it go to the midden pile?"

"No, do not throw it away. Let me have it," said Catherine. But when she found it in her hands, she did not know what to do with it. She was still clutching it when Mary, in a fit of tears and temper, charged down the steep narrow stair, almost falling, but catching herself. She saw what Catherine held and stomped over to her.

"How dare you!" she screamed. "My beautiful hair! Why, Catherine, why?" She stood tugging at the short strands of hair that hung raggedly over her ears. Her face was now twisted with rage.

"Calm yourself, Mary, I did not do this. I cannot even climb those stairs. It was the children. They sought . . ."

"The children!" Mary now directed her fury to the two small culprits. "You should be beaten. What foul brats you must be to play so obscene a joke..."

"Mary, listen to me," Catherine said softly. "They thought to help you since Martha has declared their own long hair troublesome."

"Help me! Help me! Help *them* to be less stupid." Mary ran the back of her hand across her eyes to wipe the tears away.

Catherine stood, swaying a little and put her arm around her sister. "Come and eat. We will trim your hair so that it is not jagged. It will still be pretty and full of curl, and it will grow."

"It will take years," Mary wailed. She turned to the children again and spat her words at them. "You are devils!"

Knowing that part of the task she and Mary faced was to help care for the children, Catherine saw this as a bleak beginning. They huddled together now at the table. Judith's face seemed drained of color, but Jonathan's dark eyes, so like his father's, flashed with defiance.

"We be not devils," he argued, "and you be not a pretty lady any more." He slipped from the bench, took his sister's hand, and pulled her up the stairs.

Martha was shaking her head, her lips pressed firmly together. "They be Daniel's twins," she told Mary, "and he be your master. It is a fool thing to fash them so." She paused, but then added softly as she placed a trencher of porridge before Mary, "They be full of mischief, though. I will wager it was indeed deviltry they was about." Suddenly, she sucked in her breath. "God's blood, there must be a knife o' mine up there, them imps." She turned and ran up the stairs, and Catherine could hear the scolding she administered. *It must be acceptable for Martha to 'fash' the children, but not Mary,* she thought.

"I cannot eat this porridge," Mary complained. My stomach is twisting. You may eat it, Catherine." She pushed her trencher toward her sister.

"Thank you, Mary, but I cannot even finish my own. There is food aplenty in this place." Catherine pushed the food away, reflecting on the strange twist of fate. Now that there was no need, Mary was offering her food.

"It is most odd, this taste," Mary commented.

"It is made of corn," Catherine told her. "You must accustom yourself to it, for Martha says it is what grows best in this land."

Mary was still glowering over the breakfast when Martha returned.

"Be ye finished with yer meal?" she asked, and added as Mary nodded yes, "Then fetch the sleeping pallets down, take 'em out, and beat 'em on a tree. Soon there will be sun enough to plant potatoes."

"But I am not…" Mary began, stopping when Catherine kicked her foot.

"Go now, Mary," Catherine said, and Mary reluctantly rose from the bench to approach the stair.

When she had disappeared into the loft, Martha asked, "What age is the girl?"

"She is but fifteen," Catherine told her.

"It is old enough to fashion her ways to this place." She shook her head.

"Fifteen year! It will be no easy thing, but she must learn." She looked at Catherine wonderingly. "She has the face of twenty year or more. What of you?"

"Twenty-one," Catherine answered.

" Yer journey hev added years to ye. We will aim to take 'em off again," Martha said.

The sound of quarreling erupted in the loft, then ended abruptly as a pallet flew down the steps. Martha raised her eyes to the ceiling and shook her head.

Because she wanted so badly to make amends, Catherine stood up quickly to assist Martha in the clearing and straightening, but so sudden a movement made her head spin, and she sank back onto the bench.

"Not yet, lass, not yet," Martha cautioned. "God's truth, ye should be back abed. Let us get ye there."

As Catherine sank down onto the bed, she remembered the children's prayer at breakfast. "Tell me truly, Martha," she said. "It is a papist household. Are you papist, too?"

"Nay," Martha answered.

"Need you observe their custom?"

"Nay," Martha repeated. "Lord Baltimore – he be the master of this colony – he ordered that all be free to choose their own way, and Daniel abides by that. And it is strange, but Baltimore tells papists here to follow their way quietly without show to the rest. I think we that are not papist hev the greater numbers, and he does not want popery to rile anybody."

At those words a tension in Catherine eased, one she had not even known was there. It was strange not to have to follow the religion of your master, but she was grateful for that.

Daniel was disappointed in himself when he realized that he had half hoped to see the "pretty lady" this morning and that his disposition had suffered when she failed to appear. He glanced at Edwin, who now broke his silence.

"Methinks yer two women be gentle bred," he commented. "They talks like it, and on ship they kept away from the rest."

Daniel had been himself gently bred. The plight of the two girls reminded him again how useless such distinctions were now.

Edwin continued, "'Course, that tall one would blather on an' on should a man look crosswise at the little one. She be but fifteen, ye know."

Fifteen! She looked so much older, and she had Daniel so stirred, his dreams had already filled with sensuous images of her. Many men had married females so young, indeed considered those tender years ideal, but to Daniel the age of fifteen was but a year or two beyond babyhood. He had thought at first that marriage to her was a possibility; now it seemed preposterous. He had to get her away. He would sell her indenture. That was what he would do. Perhaps she would suit the fancy of Josiah Hook at the manor. He would throw the tall one into the bargain, which would not be much of a bargain, given her present state. A little later perhaps.

He wondered idly how Mary would look with her hair lopped off, but decided that, short of shaving her bald, the damage could not mar that beauty. He shook his head to clear it of untoward thoughts and told himself to remember that beauty was short lived. The only valuable quality in this Mary's Land was a determined will to do hard work.

He struggled to bring his focus back to the old fences to be mended and to the tree girdling that must be done in the days to come to prepare new land for the tobacco. Already, his earliest fields were yielding poorly. Tobacco wore them down quickly, and to use manure, which was, at any rate, not in great supply, was to affect the taste of the burning leaf.

Suddenly, all thought of Mary was driven from his head. He saw that great sections of fencing had fallen, the upright posts either broken off at the base or heaved from the dirt as though the ground did not want them.

"Great Mother of God," he gasped on first view. It occurred to him that the task on which he had planned to spend only a few days would take much longer. This would postpone the tree girdling, which in turn would mean fewer fields available next year.

Now, anger gripped him. "Who has done this?" he bellowed.

Edwin, startled, was quick to deny wrongdoing. "We was with you all night," he reminded Daniel.

"I am not accusing you," Daniel shouted, watching with increasing ire as Ezekiel patted the man on the shoulder as though to tell him not to be alarmed.

"Whoever did such a thing, I will boil his liver for him!" Daniel raged. "I will shoot his animals! I will use his hair for rope!" He picked up one of the fallen posts and slammed it against another, which had been leaning crazily and now crashed to the ground.

Released by the violent action and the stab of pain the sudden twisting had brought to his back, Daniel's fury began to ebb. He realized that wasting his strength on rage would not help him. He needed instead the will to repair the damage and to escape the despair which seemed to be settling on him.

It was Giles Watkins," he concluded, his voice low, but shaking. "A madman who would avenge his loss at auction. God's wounds, he could ruin me completely did he so desire…and I would have to kill him to stop him." He put one hand over his eyes, shaking his head, and stood thus for a short interval. Then he looked up.

"Ezekiel," he said. "Fetch the mule and haul as many posts from behind the barn as you can drag. I will start to root out these broken bases."

He was aware of a weak winter sun climbing over the horizon as he shook off the morning chill and began to dig. While he worked, his thoughts returned to Giles Watkins. Daniel was momentarily puzzled. If Watkins were getting even, why were the damaged posts the greatest distance from Watkins' land? To avoid suspicion he concluded.

A clear mid-April day sent shafts of sun and crisp air though the open shutters. Catherine had been grinding corn, but, overtaken with weakness, had been bidden rest a bit. Obliging because she had no choice, she watched Martha, who seemed exhausted already though it was only mid-morning. Catherine knew she must soon be working at full strength because Martha needed her so badly. It was torture to feel so useless.

Mary had taken the empty buckets to the well and not yet returned. The good Lord alone knew what was keeping her. The children sat at the table in one of the rays of light and repeated their letters, tracing them in little piles of corn meal. They would form one letter, smooth it out, and form another, saying each aloud. If they hesitated too long or fell to giggling or conversing on some extraneous topic of greater interest, Martha would remind them in a weary voice of their task. Judith would obediently print and repeat another letter, but Jonathan would purse his lips in frustration.

It was too easy for them, Catherine realized. They were ready for the next step, which whoever was teaching them, their father probably, must have been too busy to initiate. It became clear that the greatest help she could provide would be to take the children outside and, tracing letters in dirt, help them begin to learn whole words.

"Come, children," she commanded. "Get your cloaks, and we will do wonderful things with those letters."

Judith looked inquiringly at Martha, who nodded assent, while Jonathan jumped down readily from the bench, relief written large across his features…relief and something else. Mischief probably. Catherine would have to watch him carefully.

32

Soon the three were settled comfortably by the door, seated on sections of logs. The children had proudly written their names with sticks on the ground, although Jonathan complained at first that his was much too long. Catherine was now helping them add simple words to make sentences. They learned very quickly.

The crunch of slow footsteps drew their attention as Mary approached, two buckets of water hanging from a wooden yoke that went unsteadily over her shoulders.

"It is about time," Jonathan said in imitation of Martha. "Did you drink the well dry whilst there?"

Mary did not answer him. Instead, as she neared Jonathan, she pitched forward, feigning a stumble, hitting him in the shoulder with one of the buckets, which tipped over, dumping the water all over him.

Gulping in surprise and fury, he jumped up. "Ugly sow!" he shouted as he lowered his head like a bull and ran forward, aiming for Mary's stomach. "It was on purpose..." His words were cut off as skull met midsection, and Mary fell to the ground with a grunt, the other bucket tilting its contents into her lap. She burst into noisy tears.

Catherine, who had risen, but not in time to intervene, felt the world go gray again just as Daniel came running around the side of the house, shouting. What he was saying was lost on her as the blackness she was trying to fight triumphed.

Daniel surveyed the scene in dismay.

"I stumbled, sir. It was an accident," Mary managed to say through her tears.

"That is a lie. It was intended that she spill the bucket on me," Jonathan said, his voice quivering with a combination of rage and fear. "She that took half the morning just to go to the well."

"And you have attacked a woman," Daniel said through clenched jaws, bringing Mary to her feet as quickly and with as little physical contact as possible. "Go and get dry," he said to Mary. "Leave the buckets. I will fetch water." He turned to Jonathan. "Dry yourself. Before God, you will feel the strap before this day is out."

Then he turned to his daughter, who was bent over Catherine's still form, grasping her wrists and calling her name in alarm.

Daniel's first reaction was disappointment at this sign of Catherine's continuing weakness. She had gained weight, and color had returned to her skin, but he could not hope to sell the two indentures until she displayed more strength.

"Here, Judith." He put his arm around his worried daughter and gave her a hug. "She will recover. You will see. Let us take her in to bed."

Catherine was not the feather she had been when first he had needed to lift her, but she was still not solid enough to suit him. As he placed her on his own bed, he told himself how absurd it was to be carrying about a faint servant as he had done too much recently.

"She has taught me to write my name, Father, and to write 'Judith loves Father' on the ground. Come and see."

"In a moment, little one." He watched as Martha ran a wet cloth over Catherine's face, and she began to stir. He took her hand in his, finding it cold. When she looked up, her eyes widening, he said sternly, "You must take care of yourself."

"Faith, you must," Judith echoed. Daniel smiled at Judith and then looked back at Catherine. "Thank you for teaching my children. I would be well pleased should you continue." As soon as he had said it, he wondered at himself. Why had he made such a request when he intended to sell her service away? Perhaps he would sell only Mary's service, but then he would have less of a bargain to offer. He closed his mind to the confusing possibilities. It was not something to be decided now.

As Catherine became more fully aware, she realized Daniel had said something kind, but the expression on his face was not kind at all. She knew she was no asset to him and was not surprised that his brows were knit in a frown. What surprised and confused her was that he was holding her hand, and it sent a sensation pulsing through her unlike anything she had ever experienced.

Chapter Three

Her skirt hiked up and secured to free her knees, Catherine crawled along the broken earth, planting rows of onion bulbs. She had insisted on being allowed to do it, but of necessity, she worked slowly, longing all the while to be her former agile self. Mary grumbled along in the next row, accomplishing even less than Catherine.

"The onions must be a little deeper," Catherine reminded Mary for the third time.

"I know. I am sorry. Fore God, how I hate these tasks and this place and that wicked boy."

"Mary, it is not wickedness, merely childhood…and it was so obvious you had wet him deliberately, a drooling lunatic would have seen it."

Mary stood up defiantly as though to deny the charge, but obviously thought better of it. "He sore provoked me," she claimed. "It was no more than he deserved." She stood still, seeming to expect Catherine to argue.

With difficulty, Catherine got to her feet regarding her sister sadly. "Mary, you have a beautiful face. It is time to become beautiful all through."

Mary frowned. "I do not take your meaning."

"You should be beautiful within as the dear Lord commands, kind and forgiving. You should not fash a little boy forever for his pranks. He has been chastised, gone hungry, felt the strap. It is enough. You need not punish him more."

"He need not insult me more, but he does," Mary retorted.

"You must be quiet with him, remind him gently it is not seemly to talk thus, show him small special kindnesses."

Mary's lip trembled. Her face became red, and her eyes filled with tears. "You have taken his side against mine. I have not even you as friend in this devil's land!" she accused with a sob as she dropped her sack full of onion bulbs and ran across the newly planted rows toward the woods.

Catherine wanted to comfort Mary, but she had not the strength to follow. Instead, she sighed and finished the planting, both her rows and Mary's, and then walked in the high warm sun to meet the children for their lessons.

Under Martha's watchful eye, they had been using corn kernels to practice numbers at the table, and when they saw Catherine, they hastily drank the last of their watered breakfast ale and stood to accompany her. Catherine remembered her frustration years ago at Mary's refusal to discipline herself to these learning tasks and was happy to have willing students in the twins.

She reached out to put an arm around the shoulders of each child. Judith responded with her own arm around Catherine's waist, but Jonathan shrank from her touch. When they had settled outside on their log seats, sticks in hand, Catherine asked, "Jonathan, do your shoulders hurt from your punishment? May I see them?" She reached out to loosen his shirt.

"Do not touch me!" he fairly hissed. It was as though he had forgotten his anger for a moment because he was eager for the lesson, but now was filled with it again. "Do not touch me, not you or your evil sister. I wish you away." He ran the back of his hand across his eyes as though hoping his sudden tears would not be noticed. "She tells lies, she does, and I am beaten with the strap." He jammed his stick at the ground until it broke, then picked up the pieces and hurled them away.

"Jonathan, she is not yet a full woman like Martha. She has scarce left childhood..."

"That is another lie!" he shouted. "You lie...you, too. Her body swells and curves like a woman grown. She is no child, but a wicked witch!"

He had not seen his father come around the corner of the house, and when a big hand clamped onto his shoulder, obviously causing him pain, his anger seemed to turn to despair.

"When such ugly words pass through your lips, it will be days before any food will go in it. Stand up, errant pup and tell this good woman you are sorry for your words!" Daniel's voice rose so alarmingly, it came close to frightening Catherine, though she was not its object.

She watched Jonathan begin to tremble and could stand the injustice no longer. "Please, sir," she managed to choke out. "Please, let me explain."

Daniel looked at her in surprise, but she could see his grip on Jonathan's shoulder loosen somewhat. Judith stood horrified, her eyes wide with fear.

"He must not talk thus, but he feels himself ill used, and there is good reason." Catherine had to pause to gather her courage as the three regarded her quietly. "I should have told you yesterday and did not. It was with purpose

Mary pretended to trip and spill the water. Jonathan should not have punched her, but it was malice on her part, and he knew it."

Daniel put his hands on Jonathon's shoulders, turned him, and looked him in the eyes. "This is not the last time you will face a woman's malice, but it is the last time you will attack her for it or call her names! Do you understand?"

Jonathan nodded.

"...because if you do not, the next I hear of it, you will eat naught but porridge for a long time. Do you hear?"

"Yes, Father," Jonathan whispered.

Daniel looked at Catherine, his face stern. "And tell Mary..." His voice softened on the word *Mary*. "Tell Mary she will work no further misery on Jonathan or...or the same will go for her."

"I will." Catherine felt her knees weaken as Daniel turned and strode away.

What further proof do I need that the wench is but a child, Daniel asked himself. *A troublesome child at that.* He wondered again at the possibility of selling or perhaps swapping Mary's indenture, hers alone, but feared now he would be offering no bargain. Moreover, to separate the sisters would be too cruel. The memory of his separation from his brother William was still so painful he had to set himself to some labor that required all his strength whenever it wanted to take hold of him.

No, it would have to be both sisters, or neither. He saw in his mind's eye the image of Mary in all her seductive force and knew that should he sell neither, he would have to marry the girl despite her age. He shuddered in the bizarre grip of desire and apprehension.

When his father was but a speck across the fields, Jonathan stood up. Dropping his new stick and leaving the word "love" half written, he scampered into the house. Catherine wondered what his intentions were, but did not call to him. Instead, she continued the lesson with a smiling Judith, who had declared herself glad Jonathan was not to be punished.

Presently, he returned, walking to Catherine and taking her hand, into which he pressed an object. He sat down, and she looked at his gift. There on her palm was a small blue stone washed smooth and shining by the sea. He had given her a token of thanks, a peace offering.

"Thank you, Jonathan. I shall treasure this," she said, smiling at him and receiving a smile in return.

Daniel approached the house with a feeling of accomplishment. Fences now enclosed the new fields he had created by girdling the trees last year, and newly girdled pines promised an additional field for next spring. With the help of the new man, he had been able to realize, bit by bit, a little more of his dream.

Mary came near, her gloved hands holding a basket of young nettles, which would become fresh vegetables for the evening meal. What had been a scowl turned to a smile when she saw him and had its usual disconcerting effect.

Instead of entering the house, she bent over to place her basket on the ground, deliberately it seemed, giving him a view down the front of her bodice.

"You are very happy this evening," she said, straightening and pulling off her gloves. "Something good came of the day, did it not?" She raised her arms to run her hands through her cropped curls, drawing his eyes again to the contours of her breasts.

"Ah…yes…we finished much work," he answered lamely. A knot formed in his stomach. A few words, a single gesture from her, and what had felt like an expanding world had constricted to a narrow channel filled with burning need. It would not do. There was no other choice. She would be sent away, she and her sister with her. He would tell them all tonight before he lost resolve. In all fairness, the two had to be informed before he approached Josiah Hook.

Mary entered the house, but instead of following her in, he grabbed the axe, wresting it from the stump in which it was embedded, leaning a plump log on the stump, and beginning to split the log, working as if demons were chasing him, muttering to himself as he worked. He did not see Catherine go past.

Catherine was deeply troubled. She had just witnessed Mary's brazen behavior and was appalled. Why was Mary so intent on playing the temptress? She gained nothing, only angered Daniel. Catherine wondered what she could do to put a stop to these worsening ways.

As she went through the door, she heard Martha fussing. "Save the smiles and charms for Daniel," she was saying. "They will not work on me. Be yer work not done, it will mean sore distress for the rest of us…and it would not hurt ye none to smile upon the twins now and again."

Catherine said nothing as Mary stomped up the steps to the loft. "Neither do smiles work on Daniel," she hissed.

Martha shook her head disdainfully, and Catherine was grateful for the distraction when the twins came clattering in. She spread some dry meal on the table so that they might practice their writing. Then, she hastened to assist Martha, hoping to make up for the chores Mary had left undone again. She washed the nettles, unaware that they were stinging her hands, and plunged the young plants into the pot of boiling water. Presently, because she realized that the twins had quieted, she looked up to see them gazing at her expectantly. Jonathan had written "I see you Judith," and she had written, "I see you to Jonathan."

"What fine scholars you are," she praised. As she spoke, Daniel entered and surveyed the twins' work.

"I see you both," he told them, "and I see a clever lad and lass." He looked up at Catherine. "And a fine teacher as well."

Catherine felt herself blushing with pleasure, but his gaze turned suddenly stony. It was the second time he had praised her – oh yes, she was counting; it meant so much – and the second time he had become suddenly cold. She wished she could understand what was wrong.

Martha announced that the stew was ready, so Catherine summoned Mary, who would never miss a chance to eat, and then swept the corn meal from the table into a wooden bowl for later use. She was placing the trenchers when Mary appeared and pretended to be helping.

The preparation complete, Martha called Ezekiel and Edwin, who waited outside. First stomping their feet, they came in and sat down on the benches. Catherine noticed that Daniel waited for Mary to sit and then positioned himself in such a way that he could not see her. *He must be so disgusted with her,* Catherine thought. *Is that why he is so cold with me,* she wondered. *He treats the twins and Martha and the men with warmth and acts like we are vermin about to bite him.*

He had seated himself across from her, though, the twins beside him. The household became quiet as he and the twins said the blessing and made the sign of the cross. He reached out to ladle the nettles and the stew into trenchers, and Catherine found herself wanting to run her hand along his arm, to do something to make him smile at her. Then a wave of anger at herself passed through her. *What foolishness,* she told herself. *What perverse nonsense to long so to touch him.*

When the last of the simple fare had been consumed, Daniel drained his tankard of ale and directed the men to return to their dwelling and the women and Jonathan to remain at the table. Martha was quite nonplussed. Daniel knew she wanted to complete her evening tasks before her strength was gone. He felt ashamed at what he was about to do, and to look at Catherine made him doubly so. She did not deserve to be sent off, but a mere glance at Mary strengthened his determination. He could not afford to be overcome with softness, to waver as a woman would do.

"My words will not take long," he said. "You have no doubt seen that there has been a lack of some goods we are accustomed to. There is no new cloth this year, and the much needed tools of iron must wait for replacement, even for mending." Although he hated his dishonesty and the sanctimonious ring of his words, he forced himself to continue. "It is because of the high price I paid for the papers of Catherine and Mary, and I must sell those papers."

Catherine sucked in her breath, straightened, and put her hand across her mouth.

"No, Father, NO!" Judith wailed, her face reddening.

Jonathan, in a motion that astounded Daniel, shifted closer to Catherine and threw his arms around her waist as though to hold on to her so she could not leave.

Martha stood abruptly. "It is not to be believed," she moaned. "I ferbid it!"

Daniel remembered the ready obedience of servants in England and reflected that it was vastly different here with laborers always in short supply and able, when their terms of service expired, to become one's equal. He himself had descended to servant-hood and risen back to equality.

Martha covered her face and groaned. She realized, he thought, that what she forbade did not matter.

Catherine now had her arms around both children, who were crying quite openly. He could see no change at all in Mary's demeanor.

"Can we not mend our old clothes and our old bedding?" Judith asked. "And I will sew 'til my fingers are sore."

"I will work hard at the tobacco, Father, I promise," Jonathan declared. "Please, do not send Catherine away."

"Away where?" Catherine asked.

"I had thought to Josiah Hook," Daniel answered. "His need for servants is constant."

"Because they are poor treated," Martha snapped, and for the first time, Mary looked frightened.

"I will go with you, Catherine," Judith sobbed.

"I, too," Jonathan echoed.

When Judith's sobs rose to wails of mourning, Daniel wondered if he could do it. He had come reluctantly to realize that he had a valuable asset in Catherine; she worked skillfully, efficiently, and uncomplainingly. Now he saw how much the children loved her already. Certainly, there was more show of feeling than they had ever given their unhappy mother.

"I do not wish to be the cause of hardship," Catherine said to the children, her voice cracking. She hugged them closer.

She cares for others more than she cares for herself, Daniel told himself.

And though all the while he had been asking himself why not send Mary alone, he knew the answer would continue to be that he could not do such a thing to the sisters. Even now, the memory of his own brother made his eyes sting, a weakness he strove to hide.

Where was that armor of toughness one needed to survive in this harsh land? Indeed, where was the strength to withstand the devilish promptings of desire?

Suddenly, he was angry that he should be faced with such a dilemma and angry with all of the people in the room, himself most of all. The only remaining alternative would be to marry a girl he could not love or to take to his bed out of wedlock a gently bred virgin, even one whose behavior suggested she was little more than a hoyden. And by Christ's wounds, he would surely burn in hell if he did that.

He threw his leg over the bench and stood. "My word is final," he said before he crossed the room and left, slamming the door as he went.

It had rained for two days, and today was still gray and gloomy. All work preparing the fields, now awash in mud, was at a standstill, and Daniel was frustrated. Each day that saw no progress in expanding the tobacco fields was a loss. Then, too, he found himself postponing a meeting with Hook, telling himself he was just too busy. Now, he had no excuse.

Adding to Daniel's sour mood were his children's failure to speak to him unless forced, Martha's frowning and grumbling, and the puzzled expressions Ezekiel and Edwin turned upon him until he asked what was troubling them.

He was about to enter the lean-to by the house to fashion new axe and plow handles, something to use up his too abundant energy, when he saw a man and woman approaching. She was wearing clogs to protect her from the mud and stepped carefully along. The man held her hand, seeming to steady her, although this would not have been necessary and seemed to be only an excuse to touch. Daniel envied them the simplicity of the mere holding of hands.

As they came nearer, he recognized Hook's overseer, Hammet Sadler, and reflected on Hammet's good fortune. His indenture over, he had found so much favor with Hook that he had been given, not only land in addition to that promised by Lord Baltimore, but also tools, animals, seeds, and a dwelling in exchange for an agreement to continue to oversee the manor. Now it looked as though he had also found himself someone to take to wife, a woman Daniel did not at first recognize.

"Good day, Daniel," the man called as he and his companion made their way across the last sodden stretch of yard.

"Good day, yourself," Daniel replied. "Though the day would benefit from an improvement in the weather."

"Ah, well, it is good to take rest when ye can." Hammet turned to his companion. "Daniel, this is Eleanor I want ye to meet. We two plan to wed soon as she be spared fer a day or two from Hannah's clutches."

"Congratulations, then," Daniel smiled and nodded at the woman. She began to look familiar, and he knit his brows trying to fathom why.

Hammet laughed. "It is a frown ye are casting on this star of my good luck," he claimed. "Is it because ye know Hannah to be so hard a taskmaster? The household work be always well done, but it is a high price the other servants pay."

Daniel reeled within against the vision of cruel treatment for the sisters. He remembered that Martha had said the same thing. When he brought his attention back to Hammet, he realized the man was regarding him quizzically. The frown, oh yes, the frown. "It is not that I am casting disfavor on your happiness," Daniel hastened to say. "It was that I tried to recall when I last saw…"

"Eleanor," Hammet supplied.

"Eleanor," Daniel repeated. "I think it was the auction for the indentures. She is as newly arrived as my own servants, is she not?"

Hammet laughed again. "It is surprising you remember the others at all when you were the one who carried off the beauty."

Daniel started to comment, but Hammet interrupted. "Do not deny it; I was not there, but all of St. Mary's has heard the story. Come, Daniel, let us wade through the mud of yer freehold to let me see your progress. We have come that Eleanor might see her old friends from the journey, but I would not want to sit and listen to females chatter."

Hammet had been merely an acquaintance, and Daniel wondered at the words "see your progress," since Hammet had never before visited and had nothing against which to judge the progress. Nevertheless, he was proud of what he had accomplished and happy to have an opportunity to show it off as well as to take his mind off his present dilemma.

Catherine was on her way to respond to a tap on the door when it was thrown open, and Daniel ushered Eleanor in.

"Someone to visit you," he announced abruptly and departed.

"Eleanor!" Catherine cried, the bleakness of her mood banished. She rushed forward for an embrace. "Oh! it is good to see you again. You look well. How have you been, and how is Phoebe?"

"Me and Phoebe, we be fine," she said. "But ye are the surprise, Catherine. Ye were near dead when I walked away from ye at the dock, and now ye look hearty, praise God." She paused to pull the cloak from her shoulders and to smooth her carrot colored hair. Catherine took the garment, hung it on a peg by the door, and bade Eleanor sit down.

"And Mary...prettier than ever," Eleanor commented. Mary smiled a greeting.

Catherine nodded at Martha, who was mixing cornbread at the end of the table. "Martha, meet Eleanor, our kind companion and friend aboard ship. Eleanor, this is Martha, who has taken good care of us...and who truly knows how to make good food even better."

"Ah, then ye must needs meet our Phoebe," Eleanor replied as she slid onto the bench. "Phoebe be likewise gifted."

Martha looked pleased as she took the wooden box containing apple tarts from the shelf. She placed the box in the center of the table and fetched tankards for cider.

"You two are happy, then, there with Josiah Hook?" Mary asked, sliding closer to Eleanor.

"Ah...well....Truly, I can no say that." Eleanor held out her hands to show scars. Catherine observed them with dismay, and Mary sucked in her breath.

"Chilblains?" Catherine asked.

"The rod," Eleanor answered. "Be the hearth not cleaned proper. Be the Turkey rug on the table spotted, be there dust on the chest, it is the rod. And be there a spill, it is the strap on the back. Turn yer head the wrong way, and she is on ye."

"Phoebe does that?" Mary was amazed.

"No, no, not Phoebe. She suffers, too. It be Hannah, the housekeeper...the witch." The last words were a whisper. Eleanor's good-natured face darkened; her eyes flashed defiance.

Mary covered her face. "Our indentures are to be sold to Hook," she groaned.

"Never!" Eleanor looked indignant. "Why?"

"We are too costly," Catherine said. "Our indentures came at too high a price. The freehold cannot prosper."

Martha reached out and touched Catherine's arm. "It is a mystery to me. This girl be sore needed here. She lightens our burdens as nothing else hev done."

Catherine hoped Martha would say something good about Mary, but could not imagine what that might be.

"The fact be," and here Martha leaned forward, her words clipped and emphatic, "the fact be that should Catherine leave, I will not be far behind."

"But the children…" Catherine burst out, stiffening with shock. "You cannot leave the children."

"I am a free woman," Martha said angrily. "I hev refused four offers to be wife that I might care fer the children. Fer pay, I take scant tobacco. I ask only that my work no be killin' me. It is that much care I hev fer the children. And what does Daniel do? He gets help, the best there is, and now he will not keep her. "It is too costly," she mocked. "Well, then I am too costly. I will not hev it."

Through her distress Catherine heard a sob at the top of the stairs. The twins were there; they had listened to Martha's outburst, and Catherine's heart bled for them. For a moment she could say nothing. Finally, she managed a faint, "Surely you do not speak truly."

"I speak true," Martha said. "And I will tell Daniel so. It will be on *his* head should he so hurt his children."

"And to send us where we will be beaten," Mary moaned. "Oh, Catherine, He cannot! He cannot!"

Eleanor sat quietly, looking from one woman to another. "And I thought to bring ye such good news," she murmured.

Catherine longed to run up the stairs and comfort the children, but what comfort could she bring them? And it would be rude to leave Eleanor when it had been so long since they had last been together. She tried to break free of the ideas that had been set to boiling in her head: the notion that Daniel for some reason did not like her; a pain, which was quite odd in the face of his dislike, that she would not see him again; the suspicion that Mary had angered him with her behavior. She seized on Eleanor's words. "What is the good news? We seem to be much in need of good news at the moment."

"I am to marry Hammet Sadler," she said. "It is the best fortune as ever fell on me. He be a free man with his own land and pay from Josiah Hook on top of all."

Catherine brightened. "Then he will buy your indenture?"

"Oh no," Eleanor said. "Hook will no allow it, but I can live at Hammet's and walk to the manor house each day as long as I do it faithful...and Hammet told Hannah he would sure break her neck do she beat me more."

Catherine took Eleanor's hand between both of her own. "I am so glad for you," she said. "You have a good heart. You deserve good fortune."

"And when will we have good fortune?" Mary wailed, but it was a question no one could answer; no one even tried.

Instead, Martha began to question Eleanor about the other servants on the manor, and Catherine, knowing none of them, took that opportunity to climb to the loft where she found the twins huddled together, a most uncharacteristic pose, their faces bleak, their eyes red. When they saw her, they rushed to throw their arms around her.

"Not you and Martha, too," Judith whispered.

"I will run away," Jonathan declared. "I will 'denture to Hook, me and Judith, too."

"It has not happened yet. We are all still here," Catherine comforted. "Let us wait to see what will come about." She hugged them close and tried to use the scant comfort of her own words to keep tears at bay.

It was thus that Daniel found the three when he came up to fetch the twins, to show them off to Hammet.

Chapter Four

Spring came to Mary's Land with the soft, moist touch of a lover. Evenings were fragrant with a quality that made Catherine want to smile and weep with longing all at once. And mornings were so vibrant with birdsong she wished she could sing along. She also wished she could reach up and smooth the lines of care from Daniel's face as he broke the fast with his children, tender with them as always and rock hard in his treatment of both Mary and herself.

His attitude toward her as she waited for him to make the intended negotiations with Hook was becoming increasingly painful. She alternated between anger that he should be so unfair and desire to ease his dark mood and change his mind by her diligence and her thoughtfulness.

This morning he had reminded the women that soil in the kitchen garden was now prepared for the planting of corn.

"We know, Daniel," Martha told him. "Did ye think us blind? We will start the work when ye hev taken yerselves out of the house and we hev done the chores."

"Eat that porridge fast, Edwin," Ezekiel joked. "She wants us gone."

Edwin laughed, but chewed a little faster nonetheless.

Later, with the men departed and indoor tasks hurriedly completed, the three women and the twins carried the seed to the field, spread themselves out side by side, each at a different furrow, and began to plant. At first Catherine found it pleasant, done to the accompaniment of sea-scented breezes, the chattering of squirrels, and the songs of mockingbirds. Soon, however, the sun rose high, the breeze dropped, the songsters quieted, and what was left was burning sun; hot, humid, clinging air; muscles beginning to ache; and the feeling that the field was growing larger even as they toiled.

"It is so hot," Mary complained. "Can we not stop and work again tomorrow when it is cooler?"

"We hev other work fer tomorrow," Martha reminded her, "and all must be done in time to plant the tobacco." She stood to watch Mary's motions. "Not so deep," she warned. "It will sprout late and weak or not at all." Bending back to her task, she commented, "It is but a child's play we hev this day compared to planting the tobacco. The sun be hotter, the rows be longer, and ye must do it day after day. It is when the days are near their longest, and ye wish the sun would hide, never to show its face again. Mary, now it is too shallow. Set yer seed somewhere between."

Catherine held her breath lest Mary loose an angry tongue on Martha, but Mary's movements became exaggerated as she expressed her ire only in the way she worked.

As they neared the end of the field, Martha straightened again. "Look there ahead." She pointed at the plants growing at the edge of the woods. "Ye see that vine with three leafs together and a fair shine upon it? Do not touch it with yer bare skin lest ye want to itch fer two weeks and break out in great watery bumps."

"Does it kill you, that touch?" Mary asked.

"No, but it is a misery should ye come afoul of it. Make certain ye stay well away. Ezekiel was so bad hit last year he could not work fer near two weeks."

Catherine stood and looked at it carefully so that she might memorize its appearance, the better to avoid it in the future. Then she reluctantly resumed her task. They were all moving to new rows now. The twins would probably need to stop soon, and Mary was slowing considerably. Catherine felt grateful she now had the stamina to be of real help to Martha.

When Martha had gone well ahead of Mary, Catherine turned back to speak to her sister briefly about the continual flaunting of her body in front of Daniel. "Mary," she said softly. "I must remind you to mend your ways with Daniel. I have seen you behave with him like the street women of Bristol…just as you did with the captain on the ship, but worse. You bend and stretch to show off your breasts; you hike up your skirts to show your lower legs; you speak coyly and with much batting of your eyes. It seems to anger Daniel, and it certainly does no one any good."

Mary stopped working and straightened, her face distorted with fury. "I cannot plant properly. I cannot move properly. I cannot speak properly. I anger Daniel. I do nothing right." Her voice became louder. "Why, then must I do these hellish chores when I do not do them well enough?" Her voice rose still higher. "Well, I will not do them at all." She dropped the stick she was using to make holes for the seed and ran to the forbidden plant at the end of the field. She grabbed great handsful of the shiny green leaves, rubbing them on her face and arms.

"See!" she shouted as Martha watched, aghast. "See, now I will not be able to plant the tobacco. Like Ezekiel, I will not be able to do any work." She threw the leaves back upon the ground, turned, and ran along the field toward the path that led to St. Mary's.

"She be in need of a good strapping," Martha declared angrily.

Catherine wanted to cry, but the relief of tears would not come. She had eased Mary's pain when she could. She had protected her from amorous sailors. She had done her work for her. She had protected her from Goody Menton's punishment. She had protected her from a long painful voyage alone. But she did not seem to be able to protect Mary from herself.

The sun of May burned more hotly than any Daniel could remember. Already, the ground seemed to steam as it usually did in midsummer. He wondered if he was more affected by the heat this year than he had been in the past because of the boil of uncertainty within. He had still not "found the time" to approach anyone about selling the indentures, and to be honest with himself, the memory of Catherine hugging his children in the loft during Hammet's visit made his stomach burn every time he thought about the sale.

He thought of the man Hamlet in the play by Will Shakespeare. He was like that Hamlet, unable to make himself do what he knew he must do. Of course, Mary's ungodly attraction was greatly diminished just now. Her face was all swollen and red with the itching, oozing blisters that made him want only to look away, and to glance at the beautifully shaped body was to see instead hands with fingers spread wide by large seeping bulges. She could not even open her mouth to eat and had to suck broth through shore reeds. One would have thought she would avoid complaint since, according to Martha, she had brought the misery upon herself, but she whined nevertheless and demanded service from her long suffering sister. She had been a drain on the freehold and now could not even earn her keep during this crucial stage of its labor.

He turned his attention to the twins, who worked in the rows next to him to plant the tobacco seedlings taken from the woodland beds and now ready for sunlight. The entire household, with that one notable exception, was moving along the rows, creating hills three paces apart. The twins had insisted on helping, and he had deemed it well for them to begin early in such endeavors.

Last evening, he had made them practice with him until he was sure they would not ruin the tender shoots, and now he watched to be sure they did not tire and slack in their new skill.

Her clothing already obviously clinging in wet swaths to her body, Martha worked on his other side and beyond her were the men. Catherine labored just beyond the children. He occasionally heard her encouraging and praising them.

"Ye have brought us a fine girl," Martha told him. "She does great heaps of work now that she be stronger."

But Daniel's mind had swung back to Mary again. "She is too pretty," he commented before realizing he had not heard Martha correctly, that he had just made a fool of himself.

"Nay, not Mary!" Martha was vehement. "She be as useless as a shoe without a sole. It is Catherine I speak of. Hev ye eyes fer naught but the comely lass? I wouldna hev thought it."

Suddenly, she stopped working and stood, her hands pressing against the small of her back as though to push away the ache. Her eyes were wide, her mouth open in astonishment.

Daniel raised his eyebrows quizzically.

"It is Mary ye needs must banish from yer sight!" Martha asserted with the force of her realization. "It is because of Mary's pull on yer body ye must sell the indentures."

Daniel could not answer.

"Yes, by Christ's wounds, it is Mary. I hev been blind." She shook her head. "Mary," she said. "Feckless Mary, whose thoughts be fer naught but herself, and the dear Lord laughed at us all and made her pretty."

She bent over to continue her planting, and Daniel, still speechless at her understanding, unable to give it the lie, to contradict her, stooped to the seedlings in his row and resumed his work.

"Daniel," Martha said as she moved beside him. "It is a harsh problem fer ye, should what I know of men be true, and I am full sorry fer it, but I hev been here well past my indenture for ye have been a kind master...'til now...and yer children hev needed me, but do ye send Catherine off, do ye do that to yer babes, it will be the end of me. I will say yes to the offer of marriage that still stands, and I will leave as well."

Daniel stopped working, sank down upon the hill in which he had just planted a seedling, put his arms over his knees and his head down on his arms. He was left without an option. He would try as long as he could to avoid it, but some day, all too soon, he would have to take Mary to wife. The odd twist that to wed someone with the sacred name of Mary should fill him with such foreboding brought a wave of unholy laughter to his lips.

Martha grabbed him by the arm. "Be ye well?" she asked anxiously.

He looked up at her, and when another peal of laughter escaped him, she backed like an animal shot.

"Well?" he asked, choking down the next bubble of misplaced mirth, clenching his teeth instead. "Am I well? What is the meaning of 'well'…or 'unwell' for that matter? There is but duty. Only duty. Do not leave, Martha. I will not send the women away. I will do what I must."

Chapter Five

It was the sixth day of the planting. Each day had been hotter and more hellish than the one before. Mosquitoes had begun to bite early in the morning, and everyone had rubbed exposed flesh with the 'tea' of pennyroyal to ward off the troublesome attacks.

There had been times when Catherine feared she would drop to the ground and need again to be carried ignominiously back to the house, but she prayed for strength and pushed herself as hard as she knew how, willing herself to bend and plant, bend and plant, bend and plant.

She knew now that she and Mary were to stay, that the twins were not to be deserted, that she would continue to see Daniel, however briefly, every day. This knowledge gave her strength and made her present efforts worth the struggle.

Today, she worked in the row next to Daniel and found that it required extra effort not to glance continually in his direction. He had just sent the twins to the shade at the edge of the forest, deeming their efforts enough for one day.

Catherine wiped her brow with the back of her hand and commented, "I have always had much work and thought it difficult, but this is the hardest thing I have ever done, this planting."

"You work very well, Catherine. I am grateful for all that you do," Daniel replied, and then, instead of turning to stone as he had done after past compliments, he smiled a warm smile that pierced Catherine with pleasure. "Thank you, Daniel," she responded. "Of course, yours is the greatest labor. You set the example for the rest of us."

"I have the most to gain, have I not?" Daniel worked silently for a time. Then he said, "Tell me, Catherine. You speak in a gentlewoman's fashion that does not match your servant's role. Where do you come from? What of your mother and father?"

"They are dead," Catherine answered. "My mother at Mary's birth and my father at sea, sunk in his own ship that carried all his wealth. Though I was but six at my mother's death, I tried to keep speech and manners I had learned from her and to teach them to Mary…and Tildy Barrow, a fellow servant, fallen from high estate, helped me to remember."

"Ah, that explains it." Daniel smiled. "Your history is like mine. I was a gentleman's son forced into indenture."

In surprise, Catherine stopped working and stood straight. "You were indentured?"

"Aye, at sixteen. It has been a difficult road to the making of this poor freehold, but it will be a better property, or I will perish in the trying."

"Better? How?" Catherine asked.

"It will be bigger." Daniel's movements became more forceful as if to accentuate the *bigger*. It will have more workers and ship more and more of the tobacco to England." He lowered his voice and leaned toward her. "Or elsewhere," he added.

Catherine found this a little frightening. Martha had told her it was forbidden to ship anywhere but to the heavily taxed English ports.

"…And," he added. "I will have a cow and a house of brick with windows of glass and Turkey rugs on the tables." He chuckled. "You will think me a dreamer."

"Nay, Daniel," Catherine was quick to reply. "How can there be any gain without dreams? And while you dream, could you not remember it would give the children such pleasure to read from a book – a Bible would be best – or to have their writing preserved on paper. How I wish we could give them those things."

He glanced again in her direction. Her face had become animated as though she had caught some of his fervor. He was no longer a villain unable to converse with her or even to look at her because he planned to do that which would hurt her. Odd that now the barrier was down, he found something in her that made talking about these plans comfortable. Odd that he did not feel a fool for speaking of hopes which might never come to be. Odd that despite the smudge of dirt streaking the perspiration on her forehead beneath the shade of her bonnet, he could see a blush on her clever face, a face somehow appealing despite its lingering gauntness. He did not know why, but her very attitude made him feel sure of himself, gave him an unaccustomed measure of contentment as he continued to work silently beside her.

Catherine and Martha left the fields as the sun began to dip in the sky. The men would continue to work, but the two women would prepare the night's meal.

Catherine was elated. "Martha, rest a little when we reach the house. I will do the work. You can scarce put one foot before the other. See how you stumble."

"Catherine, be ye certain ye can do it, I think I must rest…and how is it ye still hev strength in yer bones when mine hev quit?" Martha looked at Catherine and frowned, a gesture that did not match the next words she had to say. "Even a bloom on yer cheek. It is a wonder."

She shuffled along a little farther and then said suddenly, sharply, "By Christ's wounds, Catherine, it must not be Daniel that puts the bloom on ye."

Catherine could feel her face warming, a confusion overtaking her.

"Oh no, sweeting," Martha persisted. "Do not let yer hope on Daniel rise full high lest ye be hurt. He will do naught but dash ye down. He is not fer you."

Catherine sucked in her breath. She was not yet ready to admit, not to herself and not to Martha, that it was indeed Daniel who "put the bloom" on her. The question *why not* died on her lips as did the pleasure in remembering his kind words. Was there a woman he planned to wed? If so, why had she not heard about it? The strength she had had to begin the meal preparation without Martha ebbed away, and when they reached the house, and Mary began to complain through swollen lips of her discomfort and of the long day alone, Catherine snapped, "None of that, Mary. We are too tired to listen to such whining."

That night, when Catherine dragged the collective aches her body had become to her pallet in the loft, she found that the children had rearranged their 'beds' to place them one on either side of hers. As she lay down, each sleepy child reached out and took her hand. Though she could not situate herself comfortably with her hands thus captured, she remained in the position that would maintain the contact.

How touching it was, how rewarding, their response to her. It almost, but not quite, took away the pain of Mary's behavior and of Martha's words. Eventually, caught somewhere between delight and despair, she drifted into an uneasy sleep.

The day had been long. The night was scented. The strawberries were sweet and ripe, the new lettuce and tiny onions succulent and crisp. Most important of all, the planting of the tobacco was done.

Edwin and Ezekiel had moved trestles, tabletop, and benches from the house to the yard where a full moon was so bright Daniel and Catherine could play scramble stick and hunt-the-stone with the twins.

Trenchers now emptied of strawberries, honey, and cream, lay scattered across the table, and the children's laughter rose above the night sounds of frogs and insects. It was the first time Catherine had seen Daniel looking happy.

"There, Catherine, I have won again," Jonathan shouted. "I am that good, am I not?"

"Oh, you are most good," Catherine assured him.

Daniel, sitting beside her, chuckled. "You have let him win three times," he said softly. "Mayhap he should meet his match in his father."

Catherine pushed the sticks toward Jonathan. "Give your father proof you are best," she said.

Jonathan began gleefully to arrange the sticks, set to defeat Daniel, and Catherine watched Martha as she played the same game with Judith. Martha's work-stiffened hands were no match for Judith's dexterity, and each game was followed by a shout of triumph.

Edwin and Ezekiel smoked their clay pipes as they played at draughts on a checkered cloth with wooden rounds carved with Xs and Os. As they moved their pieces, they sipped the prized apple brandy reserved for the most special of occasions.

It was time for the children to be abed, but they had been allowed to remain and celebrate. After all, they had participated in the planting.

There was just one person missing. Mary, still swollen and disfigured by the potent leaf, had retreated to the loft when the celebration began. Her absence was a sadness sitting on the edge of Catherine's pleasure. She worried about Mary's self inflicted unhappiness, troubled that every effort to point out the errors in the girl's ways led only to greater error.

Let go of these thoughts tonight, she told herself as Jonathan proposed a tug-o-war.

"Oh, no, my bones will not allow it," Martha groaned.

Catherine wondered how they could play such a game when there was no possibility of equal teams; she could see that Edwin was similarly puzzled. She soon learned that it was but a joke, that the teams moved back and forth to shouts of delight from the twins, that the falling down was soft and deliberate, that the teams took turns winning.

For the final tug of the game, Edwin and Ezekiel pulled behind Judith, and Daniel and Catherine pulled behind Jonathan. Catherine was somewhat distracted as Ezekiel yelled, "Are ye ready?" Her arms were around Daniel's waist, and she felt an absurd urge to pull his body full against hers and kiss the back of his neck. Too preoccupied with that desire, she forgot to let the game take its customary course and tugged instead with all her strength, throwing Daniel off balance and breaking Jonathan's hold on Judith. She fell back, Daniel on top of her, Jonathan on top of him. For a time, the breath was knocked out of her, and she struggled to recover,

Daniel, who had scrambled immediately to his feet, knelt down beside her. "Catherine, are you all right?" The concern on his face was genuine, and as her breathing returned to normal, Catherine was almost sorry. She would liked to have been the object of his attention just a little longer, but she smiled reassuringly.

"I am fine," she said, "but the fall fair took my breath away. It is back now, and I think my own foolishness caused the fall. Will we try again?"

"I think not," said Daniel. "The hour grows late, and the children seem tired. Let us just sing."

Everyone gathered around the table again, and Daniel led the singing. At first there were several ditties Catherine didn't know. Unable to join in, she listened to Daniel's beautiful voice so mellow, clear, and true that a longing for something undefined came over her. Then, he began a song she did know, one that she'd heard at the inn, surprisingly enough a country song. Now, she sang along.

When the moon glows
When the crop grows
When the cold goes
Ah 'tis spring
'Tis spring
'Tis bounteous spring

When the ice flees
When the tree leaves
When blows soft breeze
Ah, 'tis spring
'Tis spring
'Tis bounteous spring.

When the birds sing
As they take to wing
Then we're all kings
Ah, 'tis spring
'Tis spring
'Tis bounteous spring

As the song came to an end, Catherine found herself crying. Brushing a few tears away with the back of her hands didn't work. The tears would keep coming despite firm orders from herself to herself to cease this nonsense at once.

Daniel sent the children off to bed, Edwin and Ezekiel carried the crude furniture back into the house, and Catherine stood still, trying to bring herself under control before she joined the children in the loft.

"What is amiss?" Daniel asked.

She was startled. She had thought herself alone.

"Oh, Daniel, do not bother about these tears. I do not think I could even tell you what is amiss…only perhaps that I have not seen such happiness since…since…my mother died."

"How old did you say you were then?" he asked.

"I was but six."

"And all happiness died then? There was naught else to bring joy?"

"There was Mary."

Daniel was not surprised. He waited while Catherine continued.

"Mary was in my keeping, but also in the keeping of a greedy tradeswoman my father left us with when he went back to sea. She had pretended to him to be kindly when she was not."

Daniel was beginning to understand. "You cared for Mary and shielded her from harm, did you not?"

"As best I could."

An utterly bare existence save for the child, Daniel thought. *Thrown in an instant from childhood into the cares of a grown woman.* He struggled to put aside the thought that the object of her loving – and of his need, come to that – was as spoiled as bad meat. He sought instead to say something comforting.

"At least you have her with you. I have not been so fortunate."

Catherine looked up at him questioningly.

"I was separated from my own brother William at the time of indenture. He was sent elsewhere, and I do not know where."

He could say no more. The moment had become charged with pain.

"Oh, Daniel," Catherine said softly. "I am so sorry."

The tears in her brown eyes spilled over again. Daniel could see their gleam on her cheek in the bright moonlight and found himself wanting to kiss them away.

"Dear Lord, I meant to give comfort, and I have given only more pain," he said instead.

"Perhaps it is good to be reminded that I am not the only one who has suffered," Catherine replied.

Chapter Six

Her face, hands, and arms still streaked with red, but otherwise back to normal, Mary had resumed half-hearted attempts at her duties, complaining loudly over grinding corn, fetching water, or stirring the wash pot. She had also resumed the flirtation that seemed so troublesome to Daniel. Today, Catherine had been particularly dismayed when Mary "performed" in the presence of a friend of Daniel's, a priest, who had just blessed the crops.

It was because of Mary's behavior that Catherine followed her down the path toward the well and halted her in her journey. Catherine knew that what she had to say might deflect Mary from her task and that she might have to haul water in Mary's place, but she felt that she must speak nonetheless.

"Mary," she called when the two were well away from the house, and Mary was only a short distance ahead.

Surprised, Mary turned, dropped the yoke and buckets to the ground, and waited while Catherine hurried to her side.

"I was sore distressed today to see your behavior with Daniel. It was made worse because of the visit of the holy man, an old friend of his."

Mary's face went blank. "I do not know of what you speak." She sounded so innocent Catherine was led to wonder if what Mary did was not deliberate at all, if there was something in her that made her a coquette. Were that so, the child had to be made aware of what she was doing. Thinking of Mary as a child, though she was certainly of marriageable age, made it easier for Catherine to speak.

"I have told you before, Mary. You must be careful not to…to *display* your breasts by the movement of your arms. You must be sure your bodice is full closed. You must not wink, nor peer sidewise seeming to part the harem veil.

"But, Catherine, I do not do…"

"Yes you do," Catherine insisted, "and you must stop it. Stop it Mary!"

Catherine's voice was rising. "Do you not understand? Daniel dislikes it; he avoids you."

Mary picked up the yoke and settled it across her back, the buckets swinging against her hips. A contemptuous smile flitted briefly across her lips.

"It is himself he avoids," she said as she began again to walk toward the well.

Frustrated, Catherine watched her go. She was at a loss to speak further, deciding she must not have heard Mary's words correctly. They made no sense.

A visit from Father Thaddeus was a comfort. Daniel's ties to the good father went back to his childhood, and the priest had attended Daniel's mother in her last illness.

After blessing his crops, Father Thaddeus was now off to visit several other friends and would come back to dine and stay the night. This morning's conversation had been all too brief, and because Daniel was in need of the counsel of his old mentor, he would be grateful for his return.

As he approached the corner of the house, Daniel could hear Mary's voice, shrill and angry. Was she talking to the twins? He stopped just out of sight to hear what it was that disturbed her.

"You think you have a blessing, but it is a curse that Father Thaddeus has laid upon your crops. Papists are the tools of Satan! Do you know that? The crops will shrivel and die, and we will all starve. And where will you bad children be then?"

Daniel could scarce trust his ears. He rounded the corner from one end of the house just as Catherine came from the other, her face white where her lips were pressed together in consternation.

Mary saw Daniel, and the fury so obvious in her voice only an instant ago died, a look of confusion briefly taking its place, to be followed by an innocent smile. It was all too clear she was wondering how much he had heard.

"Yes, Mary. I heard your cruel, false words to my children." He stepped between Jonathan and Judith and put an arm around each. Luckily, Mary's effect upon them had been only to arouse defiance; he could feel that their bodies were rigid with anger. Her opinions had made precious little influence on them in the past, but this was the first time she had expressed hatred of their faith.

He pictured himself using a whip on the girl, stripping her bodice down and adding streaks to her back to match those from the poisonous weed that still appeared faintly on her face and hands. If anyone was in need of physical punishment, it was she. But as fast as it appeared, the image of whipping became something else, a tantalizing, arousing picture of Mary with her breasts bared.

A wave of shame followed such wayward thoughts so that he found himself stammering, his anger drained away. He attempted to resurrect it, however, as he spoke to the girl, whose smile had faded. Her head dropped so that she appeared to be properly contrite.

"There are many paths to God, Mary," he said as firmly as he could. "In England kings and princes forbid those separate paths, but here in Mary's Land, we have leave to follow what we choose. Hatred is the tool of Satan. Lies are tools of Satan, not a faith that asks only that you love and trust God." He paused to give strength to his voice and to his resolve. "Now you will spend the rest of the day, no supper, mind you, in the loft…"

"But it is hot!" Mary wailed.

"All the better to remind you that Satan's kingdom, the kingdom of liars, is hot." He stopped again, attempting to make what he was about to say as firm as possible. "Should you leave the loft, you will be whipped." (*If Martha will do the whipping*, he thought to himself.) Aloud he continued, "Now go. Take a jug of fresh water, and get out of my sight."

Mary ran into the house, crying now.

"Pay no heed to her words," Daniel said to the twins. "They are false, all of them." He then entered the lean-to trying to remember why he had approached it in the first place.

The door was open, and he heard Judith speak, her voice tremulous.

"Catherine, do you believe the words that Mary spoke?"

"No, Judith, of course not. They were nonsense. I cannot think what made her speak thus."

It is the devil in her, Daniel thought, *the same devil that clamors for me.*

But perhaps there was salvation for him after all. The vision of her spiteful behavior might help keep that devil at bay. It was something to store away to use for armor against future torment of the flesh.

The evening meal was over. Daniel and Father Thaddeus smoked their pipes as they strolled along the borders of the freehold, Daniel regarding with affection the small wiry man whose white hair surrounding his tonsure, was as wiry as his body.

"Have you heard ought of my brother William?" Daniel asked.

"Nay, I fear not, but there are few English Catholic missionaries, so our scope is narrow. He could be anywhere in these Americas, and we would never find him. All I can promise is that I and my old colleagues from St. Inigoes will continue to ask. For all the reverence I had for your saintly mother and all the affection I have for you, I pray to find you an answer.

"I know, Father, and I am grateful. When I have more wealth, I will send searchers myself, men who will have wider range. Daniel looked out across the horizon as though to search it for his brother. Then, he asked, "How does the mission prosper, Father? You have been there, what, two years now. Is that not so?"

"It is so, Daniel, to answer the second question. To the first, I must say I do not know. Sometimes it is hard to preach the faith to these native people. They are not so simple as we supposed at home in England, and they have a gratitude for the gifts of the forests and fields beyond that of any Englishman I have known. What's more, they seem to have an understanding of spirit. As you know, it was telling my superiors how I value this that set them against my thinking and forced me to find a new path to a new mission."

He sighed. "So now I am a maverick, wandering in the wilderness like John the Baptist, if I may be so bold as to make that comparison. Or perhaps I am a wayward child shouting to the trees, never certain whether what I do is obedience or disobedience to God himself.

"Of course, I describe the sacrifice of the blessed lamb and am grateful that many of my flock have responded, though not as many as I would like."

He chuckled and drew on his pipe. "But it grows. Slowly, surely, St. Stephens grows, though not with the backing given St. Inigoes. We do not have the wealth gotten from a plantation thriving on slaves, who, like my native congregation, are seen to be doomed souls, not the rightful heirs of the very earth they inhabit."

Father Thaddeus stopped walking and turned to face Daniel. "I will tell you something," he said. "I am grateful for the huts built in the forest by the Piscataway that a weary traveler might rest or take shelter. I tell you, Daniel, there have been times I have misjudged my strength and my food supply and found within one of those simple structures a place to rest and dried meal for sustenance. When I am able, I say thank you to my unknown benefactors by leaving provisions of my own."

He shook his head in an expression of wonder as he and Daniel took several more steps. "Most think the native a savage, yet his generosity can be most surprising as the first settlers of Mary's Land learned. But enough of my doings. What of you, Daniel? Your holding seems to prosper. You have managed it well. How do you do otherwise?"

"Otherwise?" Daniel repeated, halting and turning to lean on the fence. "Otherwise, Father, my soul is in danger."

"How so?"

"In shame I say this. I have conceived a passion for Mary, though I know she is a woman – nay a child yet – full of female wiles and not worthy to be wife or mother."

Father Thaddeus put his foot on the fence and stared at the field. "Mayhap she is but a woman ripe for marriage. I thought this to be true as I watched her this morning."

"Nay, Father, it is not so easy. She quarrels with the twins and shirks her duty and has regard for no one's needs but her own." Daniel turned to face Father Thaddeus, feeling like a child tattling.

Father Thaddeus continued to regard Daniel quietly for a time, then sighed and spoke somberly, "Could it be that you not only lust, but you also judge?"

Father Thaddeus didn't understand. Daniel pondered how to make it more clear. "There is judgment to be sure," he told the priest, "but the problem is that I like…her body…." He paused to recover from his own shock that he had just spoken those words aloud. "I like her body," he repeated,"but I dislike her soul. I dislike it mightily."

The priest went silent again, frowning in concentration. Finally, he said, "Perhaps, should you wed the sister, thus satisfying your needs, this unholy desire would leave you."

"Wed Catherine to quiet my desire?" Daniel recoiled at such an idea. "Marry Catherine and long for Mary? It would be like Jacob who married Leah when he wanted Rachel. It would be a cruel thing to do to Catherine."

Father Thaddeus continued to frown, turned from the fence and walked slowly forward. Daniel followed. "Catherine certainly seems worthy enough, and should her bearing in your company be a true picture, I predict she would welcome such a thing."

Daniel shook his head sadly. "Ah, were that so, it would be so much to the good, but again, Father, it is not so simple. "Perhaps my appetite for the flesh would grow on that which feeds it, and Mary would still torment me."

"By the virgin, then, Daniel, send the girl away." Father Thaddeus sounded exasperated. "Get her out of your sight. That is simple enough."

"You must know above all men I cannot separate the sisters."

"Then send them both away, and be done with it." This was said angrily.

Daniel had not seen the appearance of anger in his friend before, but he pressed on with the nature of his problem. "I had planned to do just that, but the children love Catherine, and Martha threatens to leave should I do so." Daniel looked at the priest, his eyes asking for understanding.

Father Thaddeus just gazed at his pipe, which had gone out. "You have built yourself a prison with stones fashioned of excuses, and you have chained yourself within it. It is obvious I cannot guide you, Daniel. Only the dear Lord will be able to do that. You must pray hard and often, but keep several things in mind. As husband, you would have authority to insist on more virtuous behavior, perhaps even to bring your wife to faith. There are too few of the faithful in this land. The fruit of your union and the winning of your wife would bring blessed increase…though you must bear in mind a forced conversion is no conversion at all."

He paused again, then teased. "And there is the whip for difficult females."

Daniel laughed at the jest. The good priest would never ever have advocated beating anyone, but Daniel remembered the last time whipping had crossed his own mind. *How could I whip Mary?* he thought. *I would end by mounting her like a crazed stallion.*

This consideration left him momentarily without further words for Father Thaddeus, and the two became quiet as they turned back toward the house.

Chapter Seven

Catherine looked up from her concentration on the new words the twins were tracing on the ground to see Daniel swooping down on them from the western fields. In a customary gesture, he put one arm around each child, but today the embrace was heartier, his smile broader.

"Can you write tobacco?" he asked Judith.

"Oh, yes, Father," Judith answered and began immediately to prove it.

"And can *you* write tobacco?" he asked Jonathan.

Jonathan smiled and nodded and had traced a 'T' and an 'O' before Daniel looked at Catherine. "Can you smoke the tobacco?" he asked, his eyes twinkling.

Catherine was nonplussed for a moment before she laughed and answered, "If it became a requirement of my indenture, I would try."

Daniel spread his arms as though embracing everything. "We should all write it, all smoke it. It does better this year than I have ever seen."

That, of course, explained his jocular mood. His joy infectious, he grabbed Catherine's hands and whirled her around in a dance of triumph. When his feet went still, he continued to hold her hands. To look into his laughing brown eyes with the touch of his hands on hers was to drown in a wave of forbidden feeling. She was quick to push such a reaction away so she could joke lightheartedly.

"You see! I arrive in Mary's Land, and the tobacco grows better. What other benefits would you require of me?"

Daniel chuckled. "Well," he said, rubbing the stubble on his chin, "let me consider it. Ah, yes, thirty new acres under cultivation even as we speak and a plague on Virginia tobacco so that ours will be in demand and fetch a higher price."

"It is done! You shall have it. A plague of locusts…even as we speak." Still smiling, she said, "Tell me, Daniel, why has the crop done so well?"

She was sorry she had asked because the jubilation disappeared from his face to be replaced with a look of great seriousness. "The rains, gentle, but long lasting, have come at night, and the days have all been sunny. It is the best weather I can remember. I think I will be able to repay my debt in full."

"Then if all continues to go well, the freehold will prosper this year." Catherine was anxious to have some reassurance that the price of indenture, hers and Mary's, would not be the breaking of Daniel's venture.

"There is but one cloud hangs over us," Daniel told her. "The Virginia planters want us to join them in refusing to sell tobacco. The price is too low, and they seek to drive it up. If the landholders of Mary's Land do not do it, neither will they, but our assembly has been squabbling like a pack of dogs over the decision. I intend to go tomorrow to let my wishes be known..." Daniel laughed mirthlessly, "...Though my wishes will not matter a whit to the rest."

Catherine shook her head as a wave of foreboding washed over her. It would be so painful should Daniel's dream be swept away. She looked down at the children, who had not listened to the conversation, but were busily tracing sentences containing the all-important name for the crop that dominated the colony.

"What a difficult path to follow, this planting," she said. "If the weather is right and the crop abundant, the price is too low. If the weather is bad, there is not enough crop to sell."

"You have the meat of it, Catherine. It is the farmer's lament." He looked out toward the edge of his greening fields. "If I must choose, it will be the perfect weather every time...even when it means hoeing out the weeds earlier than ever."

He went into the lean-to, came out with three hoes and a coil of rope, and started off briskly for the eastern fields.

Catherine and the twins had settled pleasantly into a lesson on numbers when there came from the field an agonized shriek that sounded very much like a man was being murdered. The three dropped their sticks and ran in the direction of the sound, which had now become a medley of tortured shouts.

"God damn him to hell," they could hear Daniel cursing as they neared. Breathlessly, she and the children approached the scene, Catherine fearing that someone would lie injured or dead. But there was not one soul on the ground. That which was prone was the fence with its posts dug from the ground and its cross pieces broken and scattered. A huge portion of the tender green plants in the field, as far as the eye could see, were trampled as though someone had gathered all the animals in the area – horses, cows, mules, pigs, anything – and set them to milling about. Mixed with the animal prints there were boot prints to announce that human malice was the cause of the destruction.

"I will kill him! I will send him straight to hell!" Daniel was shouting. He saw Catherine and the twins. "Get the children away from here," he shouted at her as though not wanting them to see his rage, though in an instant he had forgotten their presence and was shouting again. "I will pluck out his fingernails. I will tear him limb from limb. Now! See! It is the land closest to Watkins'. It is his revenge that I have Mary." He brought both fists against a leaning fence post. "Mary!" he groaned. "Naught but trouble." He glanced murderously at Catherine as though the destruction were her fault.

Catherine was not hurt by his demeanor. She wanted only to calm him and tell him that all would be well. But she knew it would not be well. She thought of the agonizing hours it had cost all of them to plant. This was no small loss.

Suddenly, he shouldered a fence post and a rope and began to charge off in the direction of the Watkins freehold. Ezekiel ran to him and grabbed him from behind, taking Daniel's arms in one of his own and placing his other arm around Daniel's neck. The post fell to the ground.

Daniel's rage was evident though he was choking, and he broke away, racing again toward Watkins' land. Edwin ran after him, dived, and caught an ankle throwing Daniel heavily upon the ground. Both Edwin and Ezekiel leaped upon him, lying atop of him, holding him immobile.

"Let me up, you sons of Satan," Daniel shouted, thrashing and twisting, but to no avail. "I'll have you pilloried," he bellowed.

Catherine stood horrified as gradually Daniel quieted a little.

"Dan'l, Dan'l, ye cannot kill a man with a stick o' wood," Ezekiel insisted. "Fact be, ye cannot kill a man atall lest ye wish to die yer own self. Calm yerself, man. Take it to the court. It will do ye no good to go off like a mad bull."

"All right, all right," Daniel said, the fight gone from his voice. "Let me up now. The mad bull is tamed."

Gingerly, the two men got up, obviously ready to grab Daniel again should his words be untrue.

Shaking, Daniel got to his feet. He stood still, his eyes closed, his head bowed. "You are right," he said again. "It is a matter for the court, though that court has scarce punished Watkins for his many misdeeds." He looked at the ruined field, at Catherine, at the twins. "Damn the man, what are we to do? All those days of labor gone. And even if it were not too late to plant again, I have no more seedlings, nor, I would guess, has anyone else."

Catherine realized that the children were crying and wondered if they had ever seen their father so angry. She stooped to put her arms around them, to draw them to her. Daniel seemed unaware that they were there, that they were frightened. He just stood now and shook his head.

It occurred to Catherine that the only thing stranger than servants attacking the master was that the master was not even angry with them. He had just treated such behavior as one might that of brothers – and the two men would be worthy brothers. They were both good men; Daniel was lucky to have them. She began to wonder what manner of man Daniel's lost brother actually was.

Catherine had to resist another one of her urges, this time to draw his head down on her shoulder. She continued to hold the children, whispering, "Sh…sh…it will be well. Do not fret. It is not so bad as it seems."

Finally, Daniel began to walk slowly toward the house. He had gone from jubilation to despair in the blink of an eye, Catherine thought as she stood up and took the children by their hands. "How could anyone have done it and we not hear?" she said wonderingly to Edwin and Ezekiel.

"It was a bad night's work," Ezekiel said sadly. "A bad night's work."

The summer's heat had descended with fury. Daniel had left his household members sweating and toiling with the hoe and had come to St. Mary's to gather with other freeholders at what had once been the home of Leonard Calvert, but was now the government house.

The assembly would meet today to discuss and possibly vote on joining the Virginia planters in withholding tobacco in order to drive the prices back up. The time for the appraisal and delivery of last year's crop fast approached, so the decision must be made now. Daniel hoped to hear what the other planters had to say and to state his own views.

Hook's man Hammet joined him just as the town came into view.

"Greetings," Daniel said. "Have the nuptials occurred yet? Do I address a new bridegroom?"

"Ye do, indeed," Hammet answered. "A happy man, but I was very sorry to hear of your loss."

"It was the crop on my newest land, my best soil," Daniel said. "It is bad enough to be flummoxed by wind and weather, but at the hand of man when I have done no one harm that I know of, faith, it is too ugly, too ugly by far."

"Do ye think ye will replant?" Hammet asked, squinting against the sun. His eyes moved to the steps of the government building and then back to Daniel. "Ye might still hev something to show fer that land."

"Not if the Assembly votes to withhold the crop, of course," Daniel said. "And even should it be prudent to try again, I have no seedlings. We used all that we had."

Hammet glanced again at the steps where men were gathering and scratched his chin beneath his beard. "Ye know, there be a new widow at Tanner Creek, oh say ten mile from here, who has seedlings but no one to plant. Could ye not fetch the seedlings from her? She might take promise on the crop in payment."

"Thank you for the suggestion, Hammet, but for now, it is not an idea that tempts me. I will think on it, though, and I am glad you have given my mishap some thought."

Hammet had obviously not listened to Daniel's words of gratitude for he had spotted the man he wanted, one about to enter the building.

"Beg pardon," he said. " I hev to talk to Robert Vaughn afore he gets too busy." He hurried off just as a stranger approached Daniel.

The man was well dressed, his linens white, his breeches of fine cloth, his boots well shined, and his hat made sporting with a jaunty red feather. "Greetings," the man said. "My name is Holden Black, and I am from Virginia."

"Daniel Falconer at your service, sir," Daniel replied.

"Methinks it is a fiery session you will have today," Black said. "And I desire to talk to you about your vote."

"I have no vote," Daniel said. "Only an opinion."

"Your influence, then."

"God's truth, I have precious little of that," Daniel admitted.

"Are you not like to the governor in your faith?" Black asked. "Are you not papist?"

"I am that," Daniel admitted, "but decisions here are not made in the interest of papists; they are made in the interests of all. You hope the council will back Virginia's plan to withhold tobacco, and it is quite possible, but..." He shook his head. "...I must tell you, it will near ruin me should it do so."

"But it will ruin us all if it does not," the man persisted.

"I worry that scoundrels will jump into the breech, and we will gain nothing, only lose," Daniel said. "I think I must hear the arguments in assembly before I make my opinion public, for what it is worth, but tell me, sir, I search for a brother sent in indenture to another settlement, I know not where. Have you heard anyone speak of a William Falconer?"

Black frowned. "I think it is not a name I have heard, but I will inquire. It is a sad thing to mislay a brother." He raised an eyebrow. "Was it the court's doing?"

It was a rude question. Daniel did not want to respond to such prying. He hesitated, and Black spoke again. "The courts have sent us many a good man. To know the truth of it is not to stand in judgment. And if I know that truth, I can make a better inquiry."

Daniel did not see what difference it would make to the search, but what did it matter if he admitted to arrest in another time, another world.

"It was the court," he answered, his face heating.

"You see, should he have been sent to Virginia by court decree, there will be court record of who bought his indenture." Black smiled reassuringly.

"Truly?" It was the first hope Daniel had ever been given. "Would that be true in other settlements?" he wondered aloud.

"I cannot tell you that. All I can say is I will ask in Virginia. That name again is…?"

"William Falconer."

"Ah, yes. Now let me see. A hook to hang the name on that I might better remember it. A falcon sitting on the shoulder of our old William of Normandy. That should do it. I will make inquiry and ask that for your part, you ponder well before you clamor to break with Virginia's plan."

"That I can truly promise," Daniel said, smiling. "And I thank you." It was not really a lie, Daniel told himself. He did intend to listen to all sides, although he intended also to speak against the plan.

Black hurried on to talk to other men approaching the building, and Daniel commenced a stroll toward the door.

Suddenly, Giles Watkins was beside him, the hair that encircled his baldness as wild as the look in his good eye. "It was a great bad fortune, yer tobacco field," he dared to say.

Daniel had assumed Watkins would be here today and promised himself he would remain calm, no matter what. He would make a formal accusation to the court and request repayment for himself and punishment for the culprits. But simply seeing the man immediately weakened Daniel's resolve, making him want to shout about the crime to whoever would listen. And to have the misbegotten wretch throw his evildoing in his face! This was too much! No man with any pride, no one worth the land he farmed would let this pass without consequence.

Daniel's rage rose so quickly he felt as though his eyes were bulging. "What do you mean, 'a great misfortune', you devil's goat?"

Watkins' eye widened. "What..." he began.

But Daniel interrupted him bellowing, "Do not raise your brows in innocence, you stinking whore's issue!" With this, as though egged on by his own cursing, Daniel lost all control. He leapt forward to pound the false look of astonishment from Watkins' face with a fist and felt the satisfying crunch of the man's nose with the impact.

Watkins fell backward with a howl of pain, his hands before his face, and began a kind of bubbled cursing through the blood that ran into his mouth.

Daniel was about to leap atop him to continue to pommel him, but strong arms, many arms, grabbed him and pulled him back, holding him immobile. Watkins' man Amos, who guarded his master against the consequences of his own behavior, bounded into the fray with a knife and sank it into Daniel's shoulder before anyone knew what he was about. Quickly, he yanked the blade out, turned it in his hand, and swung his arm low to come at Daniel again and thrust into his thigh. The attacker was about to stab still again, but other men who had been passing by were able to surround and subdue him.

Someone eased Daniel down to the ground as he pressed one hand over the shoulder wound and felt blood trickle around it. Watkins' shouts faded into the distance, and the bright sun turned into a dark circle as a figure leaned over Daniel pressing something over the wounds. Fear that he would be unable to tend to his remaining tobacco overwhelmed him. He pushed the helper aside and tried to stand up to prove to himself that he could do it, but his head was spinning, and someone was saying, "Nay, Falconer. You need to lie back to get the blood stopped. Wilkin will fetch cloth to bandage you, and I will send you home in my cart."

For a moment Daniel had the bizarre feeling he was looking into the face of his father, but told himself he was unsettled by his wounds. His father had died when he was but four. He realized then the man was Josiah Hook, the wealthy neighbor he seldom saw.

Obediently, he dropped back down upon the ground. Somehow, it had become easier to let someone else make the decisions for him, especially now that he'd begun to feel pain.

While Daniel was gone, all the other members of the household were working their way along the rows of tobacco, hoeing away the weeds. Catherine was beginning to see that the misery of planting had been only the smallest hint of what was to come as the summer progressed. When she pushed her straw hat forward to protect her eyes from the glare, the sun beat down unmercifully on her burning neck. When she pushed it back again, the sun in her eyes made her head ache. Her skirts stuck to her legs and became so twisted, she had to stop periodically to wriggle and tug like a woman demented to get them free. Her hands were blistered from the hoe, and her feet bathed in fire. Everything was so sticky. She had never before felt so covered in sweat. She tried to forget such discomfort by sending her thoughts to pleasanter topics: Daniel singing, Daniel swinging her around in an impromptu dance, Daniel, Daniel, Daniel. Oh! that would not do, either. She must try not to think about the man.

Mary, chopping ineffectually at the ground with her hoe, kept up a continuous litany of complaint. Torn between the desire to relieve Mary of such misery and the temptation to shout, *Be quiet! You are not the only sufferer*, Catherine abandoned her daydreaming altogether. There was only the present filled with fear for Mary, unholy discomfort, and the memory of Martha's warning, "He is not fer you."

With all of this in her thoughts, Catherine barely noticed a cart rumbling in from the distance until she heard a voice shouting, "I am needing yer help!" Edwin, closest to the path, suddenly threw down his hoe, shouted, "God's blood; it be Daniel!" and ran toward the conveyance.

Catherine came to feel that every motion of her body was slowed to a crawl. No matter how she tried, she could not get to Daniel fast enough, but she was fast enough to be just behind Edwin as he reached the cart.

Daniel lay upon straw, his face pale and twisted with pain, his shoulder and thigh bandaged in blood-soaked cloth.

"Wh…wh…what happened?" Catherine stammered as she walked beside the cart toward the house.

"He hev a quarrel with Watkins, and Watkins' man Amos stabbed 'im…stabbed 'im when t' others was holdin' 'im back."

"They held him so he could be stabbed?" In Catherine's mind, disbelief went to war with the fear that Daniel had more enemies than he knew.

"Nay, nay," the man hastened to say. "It was to keep him off Watkins they grabbed 'im. They did not see Amos 'til it was too late."

Judith, who had just caught up with the others, was whimpering, "Father," while Jonathan marched stoically along the dusty road, his frightened eyes closing tight every time Daniel grimaced with pain.

Catherine saw Ezekiel following behind and Martha hurrying ahead to the house to prepare it for what was to come. Mary, just behind her, was objecting loudly to Martha's even louder voice ordering her to fetch the pails and get fresh water.

The cumbersome journey completed, Edwin and Ezekiel climbed into the cart to help Daniel down. Catherine wanted to assist, but knew she would only get in their way.

"Nay," Daniel was saying as he waved them away. "I can manage." But he couldn't. He tried to push himself up, but the effort ended in a groan as he sank back down on the straw, the bloodstain on his bandages spreading before Catherine's horrified eyes. She watched as the men carefully maneuvered him from the cart and carried him into the house, laying him down as gently as one might lay a newborn babe.

Now Martha made it quite clear she was in charge. "Ezekiel, get the kettle boiling to make a brew fer the pain! Edwin, fetch clean cloth from the lean-to! Catherine, pick comfrey and chamomile and lemon balm from the garden! It is good fortune that it thrives now; the fresh plant be best. Daniel, lie ye still; when ye move, ye bleed."

Mary appeared and set the pails of water on the hearth. As she approached Daniel and saw the blood, she threw her hands over her eyes and bolted through the door.

"Where will she go?" Catherine muttered to herself as she took a basket down from the wall and started for the door.

Martha heard and answered, "Wherever it is she takes herself when there is work to do."

Feeling that for once Martha's disapproval was somewhat unfair, Catherine did what she could, but knew herself to be of little help to Martha, who worked swiftly and efficiently. It was surprising how much Martha knew about the healing plants, and Catherine decided that she would start to learn about them as soon as she could. In the meantime, her assigned tasks done, the children comforted and sent to play, she could only stand next to Martha to fetch and carry as Martha stanched blood, laid on poultices smeared with the root of the comfrey, bandaged the wounds, and brewed a healing tea of lemon balm and chamomile.

When the tea was ready, Catherine pushed her arm beneath Daniel's upper back, lifted him from his bed, and held the liquid to his lips. He winced as she moved him and made a wry face on first taste, but obediently swallowed it down before dropping back onto the bed with Catherine's arm pinned beneath him. She slowly pulled back the limb that had been privileged to hold him, and he took her hand as it passed by his good arm.

"Thank you, Catherine," he said, smiling. "You are a comfort." Then he closed his eyes, and Catherine was able to pause and look down at a face that had become boyish in repose, its mask of worry gone for now. She found herself looking at a body whose firm muscles were greatly apparent because in the heat of the house, he wore only his breeches with one leg cut away. She wondered if a man could be called beautiful because if that were true, Daniel would surely be one of the beautiful.

She felt an urge to run her hand over his chest and along his arm, and though she had no intention of satisfying that urge, she looked around as though to see whether there was privacy enough to do it.

Martha was casting a troubled gaze upon her.

Catherine blushed.

Chapter Eight

It was the third day after Daniel's injury. The sun was clearing the horizon, the morning heating as Catherine and Martha stood next to the shed with Ezekiel and Edwin. Catherine watched Martha frowning as Ezekiel spoke softly lest he disturb the sleeping Daniel.

"Methinks ye can spare me 'til sunset on the morrow," he told them. "And it would boost Daniel's spirits could we but fetch the seedlings he was blathering about. I know the way to Tanner's Creek, and the crossings be less blessed with water now. I could take the donkey and cart if we all agree, and we could plant again. With watering, there would be a crop, though not what comes from planting sooner."

Catherine realized that she was nodding her head in agreement. Should Ezekiel's enterprise be a success, she would worry a little less that buying the indentures, hers and Mary's, had been too ruinous for Daniel.

Martha, however, was shaking her head. "It is too late to plant, Ezekiel. Ye be dreaming."

Running his hand over his shiny head, Ezekiel regarded Martha with what Catherine saw as a bemused kind of affection. Odd she had not noticed before.

"We can but try," he said patiently, "and do we fail, what is lost?"

"Sweat," Martha declared promptly.

Catherine looked at Edwin, who remained quiet. Like herself, he knew too little to have an opinion.

Ezekiel turned to the two quiet ones. "Hev ye objections to my going?"

"I do not," Edwin responded.

"Nor I," Catherine said.

But Martha looked worried. "It is a long journey to go alone, and with Daniel abed, we need ye here, Ezekiel." She pursed her lips and shook her head again. "But I see ye are bound to do it." She turned abruptly and entered the house.

"And will ye not wish me Godspeed?" Ezekiel called softly after her.

She poked her head out of the door. "Godspeed, ye big fool," she said before withdrawing again.

Ezekiel strode purposefully toward the shed where the cart was kept. Edwin followed, and Catherine entered the house, wondering once again where Mary was now.

Martha's back was turned to her, so she glanced quickly at Daniel. He was looking at her, and she smiled.

"Good morrow, Daniel. How do you feel?"

"There have been better days," he answered, "but I will not perish yet. I hope to be up and about before the sun gets much higher."

"Oh! but you cannot, not today," Catherine hastened to say.

"Do not fret yerself," Martha grumbled. "Do he rise from the bed, he will fall flat upon his face, and we will leave him there."

"You would, you wretch," Daniel teased, "but Catherine would pick me up. Is that not so, Catherine?"

Catherine raised her brows. "No, I would not," she countered, "but I might turn you over and put a blanket beneath your head."

Daniel gave a laugh, which ended in something between a squeal and a hiccup. It sounded so ridiculous Catherine almost chuckled before she perceived that pain had brought it about. She walked to his side and asked, "Would you like a brew to ease the pain?"

"It is not so bad..." Daniel started to say.

"Nor will be when ye keep still," Martha interrupted.

"You are full shrewish today, Martha," Daniel accused. "Does something bite you?"

"People who take small care for themselves," she snapped. "That bites me."

Daniel's mouth twitched in amusement, but Catherine wondered what had soured Martha's good disposition. Was she frightened for Ezekiel? That must be the problem, she concluded. Martha has feelings for Ezekiel, and she is worried. She would not be concerned for Daniel. He is quite safe unless his wounds putrefy. Suddenly, Catherine felt a new wave of apprehension as she realized Daniel was not yet safe, not until his wounds healed more.

She hastened to join Martha in preparing the cornbread and completing the morning chores. The two worked swiftly, silently, a glance or two at Daniel telling them that he slept again.

Martha prepared a bundle of salt meat, cornbread, meal, and dried apples, and walked to the door. "For Ezekiel," she mouthed before she left.

Catherine nodded and took cornbread and ale to Daniel's side. Though she said nothing, his eyes opened as she approached.

"Are you hungry?" she asked.

"Yes, I am." He frowned. "Though it only just occurred to me that it is so."

Catherine reached behind him and lifted him, pushing a blanket beneath his back to support him. When she saw him grit his teeth and grimace, she looked away. It hurt to watch such a reaction. As she completed the task and glanced at him again, she noted with pleasure the gaze that was fastened upon her.

"You have a gentle touch," he said. "It is a far cry from Martha's rough ministrations."

Catherine handed him a spoon and put the trencher on his lap. Every contact with his body made her want her fingers to linger, to soothe and caress, so she avoided touching him as much as possible.

"Martha," Catherine said. "What a jewel she is, rough or not, and you are fortunate in the service of Edwin and Ezekiel as well, are you not?"

"Very much so, and in you also, Catherine. Tell me, how did you learn to labor so long and so well when Mary will have none of it?"

Catherine became uncomfortable. Though she worried about Mary's tendencies and cajoled her constantly, such criticism from Daniel was painful. She focused her eyes on the burning embers in the fireplace as she spoke. "Mary was required to work when she was much too young, so I did her tasks as well as mine, and then, somehow, even when she was strong enough, I continued to do them." Catherine had not seen it so clearly before; the knowledge had lodged deep within, covered in darkness, but now in response to Daniel's question, it had been ushered to the sunlight and been spoken aloud, and God help her, she saw that she had failed the little sister who had been the center of her life. She had spoiled her for the work the child needed to learn to do. Surely, Daniel must see her error and disapprove.

But there was no sign of disapproval when she looked down at him. Instead, he was regarding her solemnly. "You were too young to be responsible for another child," he said. "You cannot blame yourself."

"Oh, but I can…" Her voice broke, and she fought to control it. "And I do." She hesitated. "But it is done, is it not?" She had to get away from the subject. His personal questions about Mary led Catherine to feel that perhaps she could satisfy her gnawing curiosity about him.

"Tell me, Daniel," she said. "You told me you were a gentleman's son forced into indenture and separated from your brother. How did that come about?" She wondered if he would chide her for unwelcome prying, but he answered her without irk.

"My father was disinherited when he married my mother, who was papist. Then, when I was but four, my father was killed fighting for King Charles against the Puritans and parliament. My mother's family had a tannery and a town house in Bristol, but the Puritans seized it all when they were told we were papist."

Daniel paused to concentrate on spooning the food into his mouth. He was awkward with his left hand and smiled apologetically when cornbread dropped on the bedding. After attempting more successfully to get the food to his mouth without spillage, he continued.

"My mother was the last survivor in our family because, even though her brothers had not at first sided with the king, they did so after their possessions were taken. It was a deadly alliance. They were killed, she became ill, and we had nothing left. William and I worked where we could, but as often, we stole food."

Daniel saw Catherine's hazel eyes widen. "We were accomplished thieves, Catherine. Would you believe that?"

"But you were caught, anyway."

"Yes. However, it was foul play that did it. Once we stole coins, but that is a hanging crime, and we vowed not to do it again." Daniel saw Catherine's lip quiver and hastened to add, "After that we took only food and then only in desperation when the cold hovel where my mother lay was bereft of anything at all to eat."

Catherine's hands were shaking. "It was too awful," she murmured.

Daniel began to doubt the wisdom of his confession. "Perhaps my story is too harsh," he said. "I will say no more except that I have survived."

Her head snapped up; her expression altered. "You cannot hang the story there. That is unfair to me. Tell me the rest," she demanded.

He chuckled at her sudden show of spirit, handed her the spoon and empty trencher, and took a sip of his ale. "Well, if you insist so strongly, I suppose I must."

"You must."

"There was one merchant in the market who went to war with all the petty thieves who plagued him," Daniel went on. "He watched closely and soon saw what we were about. Seeking to rid himself of our activities permanently, he hid coins in a bunch of grapes, made certain the opportunity to steal those grapes was too good to resist, and set the law on us when we succumbed to the temptation."

"Then it was a hanging crime." Catherine's voice had become brittle.

"It was indeed," Daniel admitted, "but the courts decreed indenture instead. They did it often, for high crimes and low. It is a wonder the whole of Mary's Land is not a lawless, violent place…"

"Not if the servants were like you," Catherine interrupted "…or like Hammet's Eleanor."

"Or Ezekiel," Daniel added, watching Catherine's look of surprise.

"Why were you not sent with your brother?" Catherine pursued. "Was it a deliberate cruelty in punishment?"

"Only confusion," Daniel answered. "We were both chained and unable to avoid being herded onto two different ships. Though I shouted and called to learn where William's ship was bound, either no one knew or no one cared to answer."

"What was your age then?"

"Sixteen years."

They fell silent. Daniel was glad Catherine did not overflow with sympathetic words. He wasn't sure whether he would have found it irritating or too burdened with emotion for his present condition. He knew only that as the two of them sat in a kind of unspoken bond, a feeling of peace stole over him, a peace that remained even when Catherine asked him why he did not attend mass at the chapel at St. Inigoes.

"I find myself in agreement with Father Thaddeus," he answered. "Father Thaddeus has opposed the Jesuit view that the black man is somehow unworthy of ordering his own life, that it is natural for him to be a slave." Daniel glanced toward the window as though to clear his thoughts and then looked again at Catherine. "I have known bondage of a sort, and the idea of lifelong bondage is too harsh, so I am most uncomfortable with the church at St. Inigoes."

"It must be difficult to find yourself in such a position," she said.

She understands, Daniel told himself. *She seems so often to understand.* His feeling of wellbeing deepened.

But this was short lived. The stair squeaked, and Mary descended. She walked over to him, tossing her growing blond curls. She stood over him, her smile eclipsed in his awareness by the show of bosom, which increased as she bent over. "Are you better today?" she asked.

"I suppose I must be," he told her as, despite his injuries, the torment she brought overtook him again. He bent his knees, raising his legs to hide the telltale sign of his reaction to Mary, but could have sworn she knew exactly what was happening. This girl's awareness of certain matters would have astounded Catherine, he was sure. He glanced at Catherine's face, saw it frozen and grim, and suddenly wanted to be quit of them both.

"I am quite tired now," he announced, draining his ale as he watched Catherine take Mary's arm and pull her toward the door. It was a good thing they were leaving because there was such tension in him, he had to force his eyes to close. Shortly, he heard the sound of Catherine's angry voice and Mary's quarrelsome answers. He could not make out the words, but the content was obvious. *It is a battle Catherine is going to lose,* he thought to himself a little later as he drifted into slumber.

Catherine was scattering corn to the chickens as evening began to close in. She heard hooves along the path and looked up to see Hammet approaching on a small gray horse.

"Good evening," he called as Catherine let herself out of the enclosure and saw Martha straighten from her work in the garden.

"Evenin' to ye," Martha replied.

"Does Eleanor fare well?" Catherine asked.

"Very well," Hammet told her.

"And what of the assembly today?" Martha enquired. "I am full sure ye hev been there."

"It is why I hev stopped. It isn't good." Hammet leaned forward and lowered his voice. "Methinks I have need to speak to Ezekiel."

Catherine filled with apprehension. What had happened in the town today? She had scarce thought about the fight or that Daniel might face punishment.

"Whatever it is, ye best tell Daniel," Martha answered. " Ezekiel hev taken ye at yer word and gone to Tanner Creek fer seedlings."

Hammet smiled. "He has, has he. Afoot?"

"We have no boat," Martha told him.

"It is enterprising," Hammet commented. "He must give good service to Daniel."

"He does. Oh, indeed he does," Catherine said.

Hammet dismounted, tying the horse to a post that held the chicken fencing in place. He walked toward the house, Martha and Catherine just behind him. The women paused at the door, however. Catherine was reluctant to seem too curious about whatever information Hammet had brought and suspected Martha felt the same. The two could hear, though, every word.

"Assembly voted with Virginia," Hammet was telling Daniel. "We are to hold back our tobacco."

Daniel groaned. "I will not survive," he said softly. "I will lose it all."

"I am afeared there is more, Daniel," Hammet said more softly still. "Watkins accused ye of the attack, and witnesses said ye started it."

"I did," Daniel admitted. "The man damaged my crop and had the gall to offer his sympathy."

"The reason why was not mentioned. The justice hev fined ye five thousand pound tobacco and Watkins' man not an ounce. They said he was defending his master."

Catherine grabbed the door frame to steady herself and stopped short of gasping out loud.

"I am done for," Daniel croaked.

Catherine glanced at Martha, whose expression was stony, and put her arm around the older woman's waist, an offering of support in this time of despair.

They heard nothing further from Daniel, but Hammet said, "Since I hev fair took yer speech away, I will be off. Sorry to be the messenger of gloom." He left the house, nodding farewell to the two women, untied his horse, mounted, and rode down the path.

Catherine felt as though she had not breathed from the moment Hammet entered the house to the time he departed. She released her breath in a long sigh.

"I will make a brew to help him sleep," Martha whispered, and Catherine marveled at the way Martha always seemed to be able to push herself to action in time of trouble.

The two entered the house.

"We heard Hammet," Martha informed Daniel. "We are full sorry for such misfortune."

Catherine wanted to express her feelings, but there seemed nothing more to be said. And Daniel did not answer Martha. Instead, he turned his head toward the wall and kept silent.

"Would ye like a sleeping draught?" Martha asked.

"No. Nothing," Daniel mumbled to the wall. "Leave me alone."

Martha beckoned to Catherine, who followed her back into the yard where they sat on the stumps and stared out across the greening fields. There was work to do, Catherine reflected, but there seemed to be no reason to do it. A dull apathy stole over her. It was tinged with the pain of watching Daniel withdraw. Wishing they could all just sleep for days on end, she closed her eyes.

Things did not seem much brighter as morning dawned, but sleep, even the fitful variety Catherine had experienced during the night, had given back her resolve to do what she could for as long as she could. Was it possible that all would end with the freehold abandoned, its members going their separate ways, the indentures sold to other buyers? She shuddered and pushed such wayward thoughts away.

No. Morning chores done, she, Martha, and the twins would work at the weeding in the hope that such labor would be of value after all. Besides, laboring at something normal might be the only way to keep gloom at bay.

"Mary, you stay here with Daniel today," Martha said, and while Catherine felt uncomfortable with such an arrangement, she knew that Martha was only being logical in making it. Mary accomplished less in the fields than six-year-old Judith, who worked only short periods with rest between lest her health suffer.

The problem was that Daniel still faced the wall, unwilling to talk or eat or drink. Catherine wondered if he had simply willed himself to die. She did not want to leave him, and she certainly did not want to leave Mary with him; he did not even like Mary. But Martha's authority was not to be questioned, especially now.

"Mary, do not go away from this house," Catherine warned. "Be sure you are near Daniel at all times. Do you understand?"

"Of course," Mary snapped. "Do you think I am dim?"

"No, just selfish," Martha muttered as she went past Catherine and out the door.

Catherine looked up to see if Mary had heard, but the girl was staring at Daniel and seemed not to have been listening.

Daniel lay still as Catherine and Martha left. At any other time, he knew he would have done something to keep Mary at a distance, but now it did not matter. Nothing mattered. Years of hard work were now all in vain, his holdings all but gone. Would his children be reduced to servitude as he had been? Why had God visited such disaster on him? He had practiced his faith and upheld its laws. He had dealt fairly with others, asking only for some measure of decency in return. He knew he had too quick a temper, but was it not unleashed by injustice?

And now here he was, a ruined man with the temptation of Satan at his bedside. He remained still for a time as all this roiled repeatedly through his head. Presently, he decided he must get up. Yes, he would feel better somehow if he could just move around. He lowered his legs to the floor, not heeding the accompanying pain, and pushed himself slowly to a sitting position. His head spun, but he remained as he was until the spinning stopped. Then he stood and walked to the door. Gazing out across the fields, he could see Martha, Catherine, and Edwin working in the distance. *Where is Ezekiel?* he wondered. *And why should any of them bother at all?* A feeling of affection overtook him briefly, but he fought it back. Such a thing was too laden with fear for the fate that might await them.

He turned to go back into the house, but Mary had been just behind him, and he collided gently with her. He tried to move around her, but she remained in place, the tips of her breasts moving against the bare skin just above his waist, seduction painted on her upturned face. He did not back away, and neither did she. Desire swept through him as he looked down at her plump, rosy lips. He was inflamed by the wish to taste them, nay, to taste more of her, all of her. She was a trollop, a bold trollop, who knew exactly what he wanted and was offering it freely to him.

It was overwhelming. Suddenly, he found himself with his arms around her, his mouth and hands busy where they did not belong.

I will burn in hell, but what does it matter? And she cannot be a virgin. She is too knowing, too compliant. The thought released him to forage still farther on her person.

There flashed through his mind the realization that he was moaning, but that she was silent. However, that thought was gone as swiftly as it came, for now he was steering her toward the bed and pushing her down. He saw very briefly a startled look on her beautiful face, but it passed so quickly, he had no need to pay it attention. He had need only to find release.

It was wrong, but he did not care. The only thing of importance now was surcease of desire, and when it came, when he was spent in mind and body, when he had committed a sin he abhorred, he realized she was whimpering in pain.

She had been a virgin. He looked at her taut face and her eyes closed tightly against the distress. *What have I done?* he asked himself and answered as quickly. *In anger and despair, I have raped a virgin.*

He became aware of the pain, now much increased from his wounds, of his complete exhaustion, of the blood that seeped onto the bed from both thigh and shoulder and from Mary's maidenhead as well. It was diabolical that after all the weakness from his injuries, he had still been capable of this abomination.

Mary breathed deeply and opened her eyes, looking into his in something akin to trust.

"So that is what it is like to make love," she said, and Daniel almost told her that it had nothing to do with love.

"And now we will wed, will we not, Daniel?" she asked.

"Now we will wed," he answered. Too late he realized that she had sought and suffered through his attack, and now she wanted her reward. Why had he not seen that this had been her goal all along?

Chapter Nine

Catherine followed Martha as they trod wearily toward the house, the twins following, still energetic enough to frolic. Suddenly, Martha stopped so quickly that Catherine almost bumped into her.

"I do not believe it!" Martha burst out.

"What?" Catherine asked.

"It is the bedding. Mary hev washed it and with nary a request from me." Martha shook her head in puzzlement. "I wonder why."

As they came closer, however, Catherine could see why. The blanket and the linen bore the trace of reddish brown stain, of blood.

"Daniel's wounds opened again," she moaned. "Oh Martha! he has bled again."

"A man is a want-wit," Martha muttered. "He can do naught so simple a task as keep still 'til he heals." She started to move angrily toward the door, but Catherine grabbed her arm and shushed her. "Daniel might be asleep," Catherine cautioned.

"Half dead, do the stains tell a tale," Martha answered.

When they entered the house, Daniel did indeed look more pale than when they had left. Catherine watched as, eyes closed, he moved listlessly about in the bed. Mary sat beside him with an air of ownership. She was sewing, stitching a seam in a shirt that had lain in the basket for several days. *It is exceeding odd*, Catherine thought. *Mary never sews unless forced. Washing. Sewing. Has she finally grown closer to womanhood?*

Catherine looked again at Daniel, his bandages on both thigh and shoulder revealing the seepage of fresh blood.

"What has Daniel been doing, Mary? Why is there so much new blood, on the bedding and now on his bandage?" she asked.

She noticed that Daniel's eyes flew open and then dropped shut again and that Mary appeared to be startled by the question.

"He has done nothing," Mary answered. "He just bled."

Catherine knew her expression must have been one of disbelief and looked up to see distress written on Martha's face. What did Martha know that she did not? Was there some danger to Daniel that she did not understand? Was he going to die? Her stomach began to ache with panic.

She walked to the fireplace where Martha was feeding tinder and fanning coals to force them into activity.

"Is Daniel in danger?" Catherine asked quietly.

"Aye, there be danger," Martha said slowly, "but not what ye fear. He will not die, but, fore God, the devil rode my shoulder when I left Mary here alone with him."

An absurd thought passed through Catherine's mind, but she pushed it away. "What do you mean?" she enquired.

"Pay me no mind, Catherine. It is nothing I can explain. Maybe it is nothing to bother about at all. Let us get this meal on the table and into our gullets afore I turn into a heap of bones."

Martha's vague answer served only to unsettle Catherine anew, but knowing there was nothing that could be changed, she, tried to overcome her worry with activity. Only when the twins entered softly and went to peer at their sleeping father were a few words spoken. Then they left, and everyone became silent again.

Edwin brought freshly caught, cleaned fish into the room. He, too, went to peer at Daniel once he had handed Martha his contribution to the meal and nodded at Mary. After that, he approached Martha again. "He do not look so good," he whispered.

"Hush," Martha chided him. "Maybe the fish will help build his blood and bring his color back."

Edwin went outside to join the children. Whiffs of smoke from his pipe floated into the room and filtered in around the silence.

Presently, Martha walked to Daniel's side. "Yer meal be ready, Daniel. Will ye partake?" The sound of her voice at its normal volume seemed somehow inappropriate to Catherine.

She saw Daniel's eyes fly open again, then close as quickly. "No," he mumbled.

"No?" Martha repeated, surprise clear in that one word.

"No," Daniel repeated.

"It is fresh fish Edwin has caught," she coaxed.

Daniel did not answer. Martha pursed her lips and walked to the door to call Edwin and the twins while Catherine placed the platters of food on the table.

Mary lay aside her sewing and came to the table, her mouth twitching in self-satisfaction. Catherine had seen such an expression before. Mary is so proud of herself to have done a chore without being asked, she thought. If only Daniel could see this and realize that the girl is growing up, perhaps he would not dislike her so much.

When the blessing had been said, platters of food passed, and trenchers filled, Mary smiled a rare smile and said, "I have something of importance to tell you."

Utensils hovered in mid air. Mouths stopped in mid chew. Mary paused quite lengthily, raising curiosity to a high level. Daniel pitched restlessly.

"Daniel and I are to be wed," she announced.

Edwin laughed. "Ye jest," he suggested.

"It is true," came a faint voice from the bed.

No one moved. There was not a sound. Of the time that followed Mary's incredible words and Daniel's even more incredible confirmation, Catherine later remembered only a glimpse of the legs of the work shelf as she crumpled sideways onto the floor.

* * *

She opened her eyes and saw Judith kneeling over her, crying. Shame made Catherine's face burn for she had thought herself over such weakness, and now she had obviously fainted again. Martha appeared above her, handing Judith a wet cloth, which the child placed on Catherine's forehead.

With the coolness of the cloth came the memory of what had just happened. Catherine felt a tear run down her cheek and wondered whether it was Judith's or her own. How painful that Daniel had shown her such friendship and then chosen to wed Mary, whom he had seemed to shun. How confusing it was. How it hurt that Mary should have come so far as to announce plans to wed with nary a word to Catherine. The memory of Martha's words, "He is not for you," made Catherine wonder how Martha had known while she herself had been so blind, so foolish, worrying all along that Daniel disliked Mary.

She pushed herself to a sitting position, though she didn't want to. She wanted to do nothing so much as to disappear. For an instant, she wished herself back in Goody Menton's scullery where, though life was cruel, it was somehow predictable and dull. Then she looked at the concerned faces of

Judith and Jonathan, and of Martha, stooping to help her up, and knew that such a fancy was nonsense.

"I am fine," she assured them as she was pulled to her feet. "It was the shock, I think, together with the day in the hot sun." She glanced at the table where supper lay untouched and at the bed where Mary was pushing Daniel back down to a reclining position, telling him to keep still.

A feeling of rage and jealousy suddenly pierced her like the strike of a snake. All the years of love and sacrifice, and Mary had not even hastened to her side or shown any concern whatsoever. Instead, she hovered over Daniel, whom Catherine wanted for herself, wanted, oh so terribly she realized now, as Mary occupied the coveted place by Daniel's side.

She could feel tears of fury rising, ready to erupt into a torrent, so she broke from the arms that supported her and ran from the house into the kitchen garden where she could not be seen. Throwing herself onto the ground, she sobbed, something she could not remember ever having done before.

After a long time, the sobbing subsided, and she lay still, conscious of the damp and of an unusual chill, but she paid it no heed. When the night had turned almost full dark, she sat up, clasped her hands beneath her knees, and put her head down, trying to pray that she might forgive Mary and never again experience such wrath. But prayer did not seem to help except that she realized she did not want to let go of her fury, not yet. And when she prayed to be able to face Daniel without revealing her disappointment, it occurred to her that she must avoid him as much as she could.

Presently, outlined by the faint moonlight, a dark figure approached.

"Catherine, ye must come in now." It was Martha. "Ye will start to ail should ye stay out longer. It will not help what ye feel to be sick in body as well as heart."

"As must be obvious to all," Catherine said, rising stiffly to her feet.

"It is the last thing ye need fret yerself about." Martha put her arm around Catherine, an unaccustomed gesture that almost sent her into another flood of tears. "Edwin is a kind sort. Daniel is too awash in misery to notice, the children too young, and Mary too pleased with herself ...."

Catherine sucked in her breath. Those last words were like a whipping.

"Ye hev got to face it," Martha chided. "Ye have set a fine example, but the girl is well past the age when she ought to see there is others in the world beside herself. I would wager she never will."

"If that is true, and I am so blind to it, why does Daniel not see?" Catherine struggled to control her voice.

"Oh, he sees; he sees, but she hev used her body to trap him."

"What do you mean?" Despite her wrath at Mary, Catherine felt the need to defend her sister. She had an inkling of that to which Martha referred, but found it almost impossible to believe.

"Ye must face the truth full front, Catherine. Mary has taunted Daniel with a strumpet's ways. It was why he wished to sell your indentures. Today, she got his needs to flame and offered her body to put them out, though God alone knows how it happened after such wounds as he had." Martha shook her head sadly. "And I am to blame. He did all he could to keep her away, and then I played the hen wit and took us off, leaving her by his bed."

"No! No!" Catherine wailed. "Mary could not have been so wicked." She grabbed Martha's arm. "Why are you so sure? You did not see it happen!"

"It is the bedding, Catherine. It tells all. Daniel's blood and Mary's, too, be it her first time. And now, good man that he is, he must take her to wife." Martha freed her arm from Catherine's grasp and took her hand, leading her toward the house. "Ye did not see the truth, Catherine, because ye did not want to see. Now come in afore ye get a fever, and then there will be three of ye to plague me: you, Daniel, and Ezekiel."

The memory of Ezekiel's journey penetrated Catherine's misery. "He has not returned, has he?" She felt she could not bear another tragedy.

"No, and it was not so long a journey. He should be back long since."

"Oh Martha! What could be wrong?"

"'Fore God, I wish I knew." Martha's voice broke, and Catherine saw she had been correct about Martha's attachment to Ezekiel.

"What can we do?" Catherine asked anxiously.

"Edwin and meself, we will walk the path he took, and we will hunt for him."

"Tonight? Martha, you cannot go tonight. All the animals of prey are out at night." Catherine shivered at the thought.

"All the more reason to go now. Be he in trouble, tomorrow might be too late… "

"Perhaps if I went also," Catherine suggested, "it would be safer…three of us, not just two."

"Edwin will take the musket, and ye must stay with the children and also with Daniel lest his needs not be well met. Come, love, come and get warm. The children hev been fretting since supper. They hev asked for ye. Let their need comfort ye, if only a bit."

Edwin was already seated on the bench, musket in hand and a pack by his side, when Catherine and Martha returned to the house. He and Martha left quietly, and Judith and Jonathan threw their arms around Catherine and drew her to the hearth. Mary had brought her pallet downstairs and laid it beside Daniel's bed. Still seated by his side, however, she dozed over her sewing as Daniel slept, more quietly now, it seemed. As Catherine sat on the bench, the children beside her, and fanned the embers of the fire, she wondered if Martha had finally persuaded Daniel to drink a sleeping draught.

"Mary will be our mother now," Judith said mournfully.

"She will not be mine! I will not let her!" Jonathan retorted.

"No, she will not be your mother," Catherine soothed," but she will be your father's wife, and you must show respect and do what she says."

"But she will say wrong things," Jonathan argued.

Afraid that he might be right, Catherine said only, "Wait and see, Jonathan. Do not fear what has not yet happened. Now, let us stay here for a little while, and I will tell you a story."

"Yes, yes," said Judith, "the one about the wicked stepmother."

Their fear could not be brushed aside so easily, Catherine saw. "Nay, not that one, a fresh story for tonight." She began to create a tale about a pair of twins who sail from Mary's Land to England, but she soon found she could allow her listeners to fashion the tale. Their story ended with the fictional twins finding their real mother, who had not died as everyone thought, but been stolen away, all the while longing to see her children. As they described this real mother, they made it plain that she resembled Catherine in every respect.

When they began to nod, Catherine lit a candle, led them upstairs, heard their prayers that their father would change his mind, and watched their faces shed signs of worry as they fell asleep. She leaned down to kiss her slumbering charges, so beautiful in their innocence.

Then, she carried her own pallet down the stair, lay upon it, and pulled her cloak over her to await Martha's return. Fighting the knot of worry in her stomach, she dozed and woke, dozed and woke again. Dawn tinted the windows, and still Martha and Edwin had not returned. It began to rain, and Catherine grew more anxious. There would be no work in the fields today, she decided, not even if the sun shone. There was no one to do it. Fear brought her to full wakefulness, and she rose to begin the day's chores.

She glanced at Daniel. Suppose he wakes before they return, she thought. Then, I must tell him about Ezekiel; another worry to add to all that plagues him.

Daniel did not wake, however, until the morning was well advanced, until the twins and Mary sat at the table over breakfast. They knew he was stirring when they heard him move and groan faintly.

Catherine realized that she had worked without wishing Mary good morning, that she had not even looked at Mary. She could not. And now she could not look at Daniel, either. She filled his trencher, slid it before Mary, and nodded in Daniel's direction. Mary took the food, went to Daniel, and spoke softly to him. He did not answer, nor, Catherine saw as she looked quickly at him, did he accept his food. Mary brought it back to the table, but no one else wanted it either. None but Mary had been a bit hungry this morning.

Catherine scraped the uneaten porridge into a tin to be mixed with salt pork and sizzled in fat later. As she worked, she felt the anxiety for Martha and Edwin and Ezekiel build steadily. Reassuring the children that everything was fine despite the three missing people, she spread dry beans on the tables so that they might practice numbers.

"Mary, which would you prefer, to fetch water or feed the hens and collect eggs?" she asked.

"I must stay with Daniel," Mary answered. "I am to be mistress of this house now. I will do neither task."

"Everyone works in this household," Jonathan said, repeating what he had heard his father say so often.

"Do not answer me back," Mary scolded.

"Are you Queen Mary?" Jonathan asked, pride in his cleverness written across his face. "Queen Mary," he repeated. "Bloody Mary."

Mary reached across the table, slapped him, and immediately cried out in pain. Obviously he had kicked her.

"Your father will strap you for that," Mary hissed. "Is that not so, Daniel?"

A weary voice from the bed said, "Jonathan, come here."

Jonathan rose and gave Mary a look of hatred as he passed her. Catherine could hear the faint rumble of words, but not precisely what Daniel was saying. Jonathan came back to the table hanging his head, and Mary gloated.

It was all so ugly. Everything was turned upside down, and soon became even worse as Daniel spoke the words Catherine did not want to hear.

"Catherine, it is raining. Where are Martha and Edwin and Ezekiel? I have heard naught of them this day."

She could not answer.

"Catherine, come here," Daniel commanded.

To go to his bedside was to push through a barrier of her own resistance.

She stood next to him, but could not look at him.

"Answer me," he said.

She closed her eyes and took a deep breath. "Ezekiel went to Tanner Creek to get more seedlings," she managed to say.

"Why?" Daniel shouted. It was his greatest show of spirit since Mary's announcement yesterday.

"He thought…we thought…it would cheer you to have more tobacco planted."

"When did he go?" Daniel's voice had now taken on an unnatural calm.

Catherine could not speak the answer.

"Catherine!"

"Two mornings ago," she whispered.

"So he should have been back long since? And Martha? Edwin?"

"They have gone to look for him."

Daniel groaned. "They left last night?" he asked.

"Yes."

"By Christ's wounds", he said bitterly, " I was not meant to farm this land. I am a poor sinner doomed only to perdition, I and all whom I love with me."

Catherine looked down at him to argue, but his head was turned away from her, and she did not know where to start. He was a sinner, she had to admit. He had sinned with Mary.

The room fell into a gloomy silence as she took the bucket, pulled her cloak around her, and went to get water.

It was while she was in the hen house that Catherine heard the creak of approaching wheels. She dropped the bag of corn and knocked over the basket of eggs as she ran out into the rain.

Martha and Edwin were dragging one foot behind the other, moving slowly toward the house, pulling the badly leaning cart on which Ezekiel lay. Catherine ran to them, peering anxiously at Ezekiel for signs of life.

"He be alive," Martha said through teeth clenched to stop her shivering. Catherine could see that her cloak formed a makeshift shelter to keep the worst of the rain from Ezekiel. "It was a blow on the head that hurt him, and the mule is gone, the seedlings destroyed, the cart broken. If it is Watkins as Daniel believes, he should be drawn and quartered."

Edwin halted before the little dwelling he shared with Ezekiel.

"Nay, he must be put in the house," Martha said, relinquishing her hold on the cart to Catherine, who helped Edwin pull it to the door. "Fetch his pallet,

Edwin, and then we will carry him in."

"I will get it," Catherine hastened to say. Edwin and Martha looked as though they would not be able to take another step. Edwin nodded assent, and Catherine ran back, bundled the pallet into her arms and returned as quickly as she could.

It took four of them, Edwin, Martha, Catherine, and a reluctant Mary to carry the big man inside. Once he lay on his pallet on the floor, which was now quite crowded, Martha and Edwin stripped his wet garments from him and wrapped him in a blanket. Mary left the room, a whiteness around her mouth showing Catherine how frightened the girl was of even the sight of injury. Daniel rose from his bed.

"Daniel, you must not…" she started to say.

"It seems I must," he said as he limped painfully to Ezekiel's side. "Has he spoken at all?" he asked Martha.

She shook her head no.

"It was a kindness he set out to do, but I would not have let him go," Daniel told her. "Pull the bench closer to him so that I may sit with him while you go get dry, both of you." He sat, reached down, and ran the back of his hand over Ezekiel's forehead. "It is feverish," he said to Catherine, "and no wonder. They will have a fever, too, his brave rescuers." He let out his breath and shook his head. "God above, do they really deserve all this misfortune?" he whispered.

Catherine became aware that the children had approached and stood on either side of her. Jonathan had taken her hand, and Judith clung to her skirt.

"Is he going to die?" Judith asked, her voice unsteady.

"I think he is too strong for that," Daniel answered.

"He had the seedlings," Catherine said. "They were trampled, and the mule is gone. Daniel, you cannot blame yourself for that."

"Watkins' revenge may go on and on," he mused sadly.

Catherine thought he was better angry than so dispirited. "Revenge for your attack on him?" she questioned.

"No. Revenge that I obtained Mary's indenture at the auction."

"Oh!" Catherine gasped. She wondered how she could have forgotten about that. The real blame, that which had started all of this, was the need to save Mary from Watkins, and Catherine was just disturbed enough with Mary and all she had done to think fleetingly that Mary and Watkins deserved each other. Then she felt ashamed of such a thought and began to move about putting things in order.

Daniel sat gazing down at Ezekiel, shaking his head and speaking softly to the unconscious man. Catherine could hear an occasional snippet of his speech. "…poor fellow, caught up in my transgressions…deserves better…there's none finer….It is an abomination what Watkins has done." On these last words, Daniel's voice was beginning to rise in anger, which Catherine considered an improvement in his mood, but when Martha returned dry clad, Daniel seemed to realize that he was actually talking to himself and so became quiet.

A knock heralded an unusual occurrence, a midmorning visitor. Hammet stood at the open door, hat in hand, and Daniel stood to greet him.

"Come in," Catherine said. "Sit down. Can we get you some ale?"

'It would be welcome." Hammet smiled a friendly smile as he sat down by the table. "Daniel, I see you are back on your feet, but who…" He stood again to look down at the unconscious Ezekiel. "It is yer man Ezekiel, is it not? What happened?"

"He went to get seedlings and was attacked as he returned."

"Who…" Hammet started to ask.

"Who, indeed. I have my suspicions, of course, that it was Watkins, but must hear from Ezekiel himself …if he wakes."

"He is a good man. Such a pity." Hammet accepted a tankard of ale from Catherine. "Thank ye," he said as he took a sip. "This is uncommon fine ale," he commented, smiling at Martha and eyeing the brewing vat in the corner. "Ye are fortunate in yer people, Daniel."

"Yes," Daniel agreed, "and have brought misfortune on them all."

"I would not know about that, but I hev welcome news fer ye. Yesterday, Governor Calvert vetoed the tobacco vote. We will not be holding back our tobacco in Mary's Land after all. If the Virginians hold theirs, it will be to our advantage."

"They would be fools to do it now, would they not?" Daniel commented.

Hammet nodded as Daniel sat heavily down on the bench by the table.

"I will not stay," said Hammet. "I only wished to bring ye the message." He drained his ale. "Thank ye fer the refreshment. It was most needed," he said as he put on his hat and then went out into the rain.

Daniel started to laugh. News of the veto might have lifted him from the pit of despair yesterday, might have preserved his sanity and protected him from Mary's wiles, but it had come too late. Life was so odd, was it not, that some people should be singled out for blow upon blow and others prosper so fully. Why had the Lord given him the trials of Job and none of the steadfastness to withstand them? God was a prankster, was he not, and he must laugh at God's antics or die. Laughter welled up and threatened to overwhelm him until he glanced at Catherine's horrified expression. Then the insane glee turned into an embarrassed groan.

Catherine stirred to hurry to Daniel's side. *He must have a fever himself,* she thought. Then she remembered that she did not want to get near him at all, and she wondered that he had not been more civil to Hammet. After all, the man had gone out of his way to bring information of importance.

When Ezekiel stirred and moaned, Martha hurried over to him and took his hand. "Ezekiel, can ye hear me?" she asked.

Daniel walked back to the bench and sat down upon it, looking into the face of his battered servant.

"Ezekiel," he said quietly.

Ezekiel's eyes opened and fastened on Martha, then shut again as a spasm of pain crossed his face.

"Ezekiel, talk to me," Martha almost whispered. "Who attacked ye?"

"Do not know." Ezekiel's speech was so low and indistinct that Catherine could barely make it out.

"I was coming from…little Indian hut…bending to untie…mule…then black."

"It is the back of his head that took the blow," Martha said.

"He did not try to fight anyone," Daniel concluded. "He was attacked stealthily from behind."

"And the devil that did it stole the mule, stole poor old Maxim," Martha added. "The harness was not ripped from the cart. It was removed careful. Could we but find the mule, it would prove…"

"It would prove nothing, Martha," Daniel interrupted. "Maxim could be left to wander anywhere. Believe me, I would bring Watkins before justice without delay, but there is no proof, none that I can see."

"How…plant without…mule?" Ezekiel asked faintly. "God's wounds, this head…do ache."

"Be still, man. Do not talk now," Martha ordered. "Sleep 'til ye be well and do not fret." Catherine saw tears in her eyes. Tough, practical Martha, who seemed to meet misfortune with calm sureness, was crying over Ezekiel.

Chapter Ten

It was past midsummer. The tobacco stalks were five feet high, thriving in the sun's inferno. This was the time to pluck the buds from the plants, to reserve strength for the leaves. All household members, even Ezekiel now, were moving along the rows plucking buds as quickly as they could.

Daniel was certain as everyone shifted to begin new rows that Catherine had maneuvered to keep her distance from him. During the days since the marriage announcement, days in which he and Ezekiel had recovered from their injuries, she had scarcely spoken to him. This was in marked contrast to the growing trust their earlier conversations had seemed to bring about. Granted, the healthy adults had been busier than ever, but they were not so busy as to be without speech.

He frowned as he worked and puzzled once again over his own reactions. He was angry that Catherine was so obviously judging him. It did not help that he was ashamed in the face of her innocence, that she was justified. Mixed with the anger was hurt, a feeling of being abandoned by a friend and doomed to Mary's vacuous company, which still left him feverish for the bodily pleasures he could not have since he had promised himself not to make a husband's claim on her again until the union was blessed by the sacrament. He suspected that his attitude about Catherine was womanish, an affront to his manhood, but the simple fact was that he missed her companionship.

Thus it was when the shift made at the end of the next row placed her unexpectedly beside him, he found that he did not know what to say. Her face averted, she worked in silence; he did the same. Words he might have said came to mind…*I am sorry, Catherine, for what I did to your sister….I have missed you, Catherine….Can we not be friends, Catherine…?Your silence is somewhat insulting, Catherine….You cannot avoid me forever, Catherine.* But one after one, he rejected each overture as his confusion deepened. By the end of the row, all that remained was the anger at himself for the position he had put himself in and at her for judging.

Catherine could not have spoken to Daniel if she had wanted to, and she had told herself firmly that she most certainly did not. She had been avoiding him, had used every tactic she could to keep clear of him and to cope with the pain that finally seemed to be subsiding somewhat. Now, however, when she found herself next to him, she wanted nothing so terribly as a few kind, friendly words. She felt his presence as something almost physical and his silence as a weight on her shoulders. Stubbornly, she kept her eyes fixed on the plants though Daniel hovered on the edges of her vision and invaded her consciousness with renewed hurt. How long was her indenture? Four and one half more years to be thus embedded in ice. She shivered as they reached the end of the row, and she worked now beside Mary, the twins on Mary's other side, and Daniel three rows away.

A sudden movement by Jonathan caught Catherine's attention. He had grabbed the stick he wore fastened at his waist, calling it his sword, and was sweeping it into the air. Curled over it was a snake which sailed toward Mary, struck her on the shoulder, and dropped to the ground. Catherine ran toward her as she shrieked with terror and kept on shrieking, pointing to the snake slithering down the row. Daniel reached Mary's side just before it disappeared between the plants.

Catherine watched him take her into his arms, murmuring into her ear, stroking her head, trying to still the unearthly screams that still rent the air. Gradually, her screaming subsided, turning into great sobs. Between those sobs, Catherine could hear Daniel reassuring her. "It was not venomous, not dangerous. Try to stop crying. You are safe."

By this time the others had joined Catherine in silent witness to Mary's distress. But it was not Mary's terror that tortured Catherine. Mary was safe after all. What tortured her was the sight of Daniel's arms around Mary, the kindness with which he reassured her. Jealousy raged through Catherine until she found herself on the edge of tears herself. "*Oh, God,*" she prayed silently, "*do not let me hate her. She is like to my own child. Take away this wrath at my sister.*"

As Mary quieted and Daniel could look around at his household, his eyes sought Jonathan, who was nowhere to be seen. He breathed deeply, shook his head as though in disbelief and addressed Martha.

"Should Jonathan return to the house tonight, give him no supper. I will deal with him as soon as he can be found. Now, if you will all go back to work, I will take Mary to a cool spot where she can recover."

He then led her into the edge of the wood where a split log provided a seat. Sitting and drawing her down beside him, he tried to decide how to cope with the tears that continued to fall.

"Mary, please try to stop crying. It was an ugly prank, but no harm is done..."

"They hate me," she wailed. "See how they hate me..."

"You must try a little to win them over, show some kind..."

"They hate me. I cannot win them over. I can do naught but work, in a field of useless weed one cannot even eat, these cursed plants harboring snakes, plants that need constant care...row after row after endless row...and in such heat as should be reserved for hell!"

At these words, tears began again to stream in greater numbers down her cheeks, and she blotted them on her sleeve. "And what is there to show for it? We do not have even a cow for fresh milk...and we are to be wed, yet I have no clothing save that fit only for a beggar."

Daniel realized for the first time that the clothing she wore, indeed had arrived in, had been too fine to withstand the demands being made on it. He hadn't even wondered at the time where it came from. The captain probably.

She had paused, and Daniel was about to answer her, but her voice rose almost to a note of hysteria as she spoke again.

"And I must be wed in the papist fashion when all of my life I have been taught to hate it."

As Daniel listened to Mary's complaints, the depression that had been lightened by a return to activity descended on him again. To wed Mary would be the disaster of his first marriage repeated, and he had only himself to blame.

He put his hand beneath Mary's chin, turning her face toward his, but when he dropped his hand, she looked away again.

"I am sorry you are so opposed to the ceremony, Mary, for it is one thing I insist upon." *God's blood*, he thought, *to marry me was her choice. She knew of my faith, though I no longer know what to call it*. He put his irritation aside, chiding himself that it did no good now.

"The lack of a cow is one of the many reasons we work so hard at the tobacco, so we can purchase a cow. Everything that comes to us must be worked for."

Mary closed her eyes as though what she wanted to close were her ears. She did not want excuses, he knew, but excuses were all he had to offer.

"As for the dress, you must know we have had damaging losses. Cloth all of us need so badly is out of the question. He pointed to the knees of his breeches. "If there were not mending threads in these, there would be no threads at all. Come, Mary, please understand that I will provide for you better as soon as I can."

Then he remembered something and looked at her quizzically. Should he suggest it? Why not? "I have several skirts and bodices that belonged to my first wife," he said tentatively.

Mary made a sound that expressed her contempt for such an offer, but he continued. "They are faded and would be a poor fit, but they could be dyed and perhaps made to do with a little cutting and stitching."

She made no answer, only sat in an angry silence.

"I must get back to the field now," he told her, "but you may rest and try to comfort yourself for your many sorrows. Walk to the stream perhaps. Dip your feet in and splash your face to cool and refresh it."

He moved away to return to work. Anger would have helped, but there was no anger in him now, just a great sadness for himself, for Mary, for his children, for all of his household.

Catherine dumped the last bucket of water into the dye pot as Martha pushed another slab of wood into the fire beneath it. Mary would have a new outfit, and Catherine wished that she might have one as well, but a diligent search had yielded but a single skirt and bodice.

Mary sat nearby pulling the last stitches from her predecessor's skirt, complaining loudly.

"They are horrible. They will never fit. I shall look like a jester."

"But you will be the only one in this house with freshened clothing. I dare not dye the other things lest they fall apart in the pot," Martha snapped, wincing as she rose from tending the fire.

"The woman had no bosom," Mary continued to whine. "She was fifteen hands tall and skinny as a pole."

"Mary, wait and see what we can do," Catherine admonished. "You may be surprised."

"If it is fit to wear, yes I will be surprised," she said.

"There be things we can do to surprise you," Martha informed Mary. "What we cut from the bottom, we can use to make the bodice larger, and do we use more indigo than alum and goldenrod in the dye, then we get the color of the sea in sunshine." She picked up a piece of the cloth and ran her roughened fingers over it. "This be good strong stuff, Mary. It will take the dye and last you a long time." She took the dried indigo and the alum gathered weeks ago in the woods and the fresh goldenrod from the roadside and plunged it all into the water.

"That will do it. Now, we let it boil before we pluck the plants from it."

Mary's face had brightened a little and brightened still further as Jonathan, who had been scampering in and out of the house with Judith, walked by and actually smiled at her.

This did not brighten Catherine's mood, however. As far as she could see, Jonathan, who had gotten a beating for the snake, had not grown in his liking for Mary; the opposite was more likely. Why was he smiling? She promised herself she would investigate.

Martha claimed her attention. "Come and see the lovely color," she said happily. "It is a pleasure to see it happen."

The rest of the day was spent in steeping the cloth, hanging it out, and then doing the laundry as the fabric dried to a beautiful blue green. Catherine forgot that she had meant to find out what the twins were planning. She remembered it again when Mary had just gone up to bed, and there came from the loft a series of horrified shrieks.

Daniel was the first up the steep stairway, Catherine just behind him. Mary stood in the middle of the floor screaming in anger and frustration as a number of frogs, many still located on her sleeping pallet leaped about in the dying light from the window.

Daniel could not believe that Jonathan had done such a thing after the thrashing he had received for the last prank, though it occurred to him briefly that Jonathan was so full of hatred he no longer cared whether he got a thrashing.

"Catch those creatures and get them out of here," he yelled at Jonathan, whereupon the two children began to run about making a game of their task.

"There will be little to smile about when you know your punishment for this," he shouted at them.

Mary was dressed only in her shift, so he handed her the skirt and bodice which lay over a trunk nearby and waited for her to put them on. This became difficult as a frog emerged from the bodice when Mary picked it up, and her screams began anew, but finally she quieted enough that she could dress, and he could lead her down the steps and out into the summer twilight. She was crying tears of anger this time, and he did not blame her.

"You do not punish them hard enough," she accused.

"Mary, ! have punished them as much as I know how. They have had food denied them, been confined to the loft, been whipped, even my little girl, as far as I dare go without doing real harm, yet still they persist. And of course, I will punish them again."

He took Mary's arm and drew her to the fence by the garden, lifting her up onto the rail. "But listen to me, and do not get angry," he said. "You, yourself must do something to change their feelings."

"It is impossible! What could I do?" Mary sniffed disdainfully.

"Offer to help them with something they must do," Daniel told her. "Teach them a new game, a new song. Make them something. Do anything to offer peace…even sneak them honey cakes after I have confined them to the loft. Do whatever you can think of."

"And if I do not?" she asked.

"Then they will continue to taunt you, and I will continue to punish them, and we will go in a great circle of taunt, punish, taunt punish. Oh, it will not be easy, I know, but you must try." Mary's rigid form gave Daniel the feeling he was throwing these comments into a void.

"Then they might do whatever they wish, and I must be good to them. That is most unjust."

"Just. Unjust. These have nothing to do with it". He raised his voice in frustration. "They are but children. You are a woman grown. At least you should be."

Mary began to cry again. "You do not love me, Daniel."

Daniel's surprise at such words almost unseated him. He grabbed the fence post to steady himself. When had he ever talked about love?

"Tell me, Mary, who do you love?" he asked.

She hesitated as though such a question had never occurred to her. "Why you…and Catherine, of course."

"And how do you show your love for me?" Daniel thought that if she said she had given him her body, he would push her off the fence.

"Why…I…," she began, then was silent.

"Demand things you know I cannot give you? Refuse to do what would benefit the household? Refuse the rituals of my faith that are of deepest meaning to me?"

"Other people here marry without the church's blessing all the time. Why must we have it?" Mary asked angrily.

Daniel could feel his indignation rising. "Because it is required by God," he snapped and watched as she struggled to appear coquettish.

"Am I not beautiful for you?" she asked.

"Oh, you are quite beautiful, but more is needed, much more. If I were rich, I would laud you as an ornament of my wealth, but I am poor, Mary, as poor in worldly goods as you are in loving spirit."

"But you desire me…"

"And wish I did not."

Mary gave a moan of dismay. "You see, you do not put value on me. How can I love you enough? …but I love Catherine."

"And how have you shown that?" Daniel asked sharply.

"By…" Mary hesitated again.

"Eating her food and allowing her to starve on the voyage," Daniel supplied.

"That is unfair. She was sick from the ship's motion…"

"She was near death when you got here," Daniel interrupted. "Had you not noticed? And still you let her labor for you as you do now."

"But I am mistress…"

"Of a poor man's house where all must be of use."

"And I am useless." Mary's voice rose like that of the fishmonger at the docks of Bristol.

"You need not be…"

"But I am useless!" Her words were shrill and ugly.

"Yes, useless," Daniel snapped, wanting to turn her over his knee. And this time, desire had nothing to do with it.

Chapter Eleven

The sky was an unbroken expanse of blue, the day unusually cool. Catherine and Mary were to visit Eleanor and Hammet this day on the property of Josiah Hook. Catherine believed that a feeling of freedom should have lent wings to her feet, but it did not.

The walk was long; it would take nearly two hours, almost all across land belonging to Hook, who owned huge tracts he had not yet even been able to cultivate. His dwelling was at the far side of the property.

Catherine thought about Daniel, who faced a journey, too, this morning, hauling last year's tobacco to the wharf for appraisal and storage. (Shipment and therefore payment would come much later.) He, Edwin, and Ezekiel would have to pull the barrels called hogsheads themselves because they no longer had a mule. Daniel had said he feared the price would be too low. He hoped it would not drop under seven cents a pound, but he was not optimistic.

The thought of tobacco problems began to tug at Catherine, to slow her steps, until she vowed to push such worry away for the day. But to look at Mary reminded her of another, more immediate dilemma. The dress Mary had so disdained had become, with Martha's help, a perfectly fitting garment of a vibrant blue green. It set off Mary's eyes and accented the perfection of her figure. This new dress and the day's outing had made her cheeks glow, and smiles had replaced her perpetual frown.

How Catherine wished that she, too, might have a finely dyed garment, one that enhanced her body and her coloring. How she longed to be the one whose hands Daniel would take as he told her she was beautiful. It was a sin, this coveting of that which was Mary's, but Catherine could not seem to escape it. She hoped that Mary did no complaining today because if she did, Catherine knew her own tongue would turn vicious.

They approached Hammet's house, which was not as large as Daniel's, and Eleanor ran out to meet them. She threw her arms around Catherine and then around Mary, exclaiming how wonderful both of them looked. Catherine accepted the compliments. Mary looked exquisite, she herself healthy. And Eleanor? Eleanor looked to be with child.

"There is a baby coming?" Catherine asked.

"Yes, in the winter," Eleanor answered. "Me, a mother! It is hard to believe."

Catherine thought about the hopes she had once had to bear children for Daniel and felt sadness pull at her again, but she pushed the feeling aside, an exercise at which she considered herself an expert. She enthused with Eleanor about the arrangements to be made for a safe birth and the baby's care.

Mary listened silently.

Eleanor noticed. "Mary, hev ye no joy fer me?" she asked.

"Are you not afraid?" Mary asked in return.

"A little, but ye cannot live yer life abrim with fear, so I think only of what is good…and I hev a surprise for ye. Housekeeper Hannah, the nasty witch, is gone to the wharf, so we be free to visit our old friend Phoebe, and ye can see Hook's house. It is a wondrous fine place. We will hev some peachy to drink, and then we will go."

Catherine had heard of peachy, a sweet beverage of fermented peaches with a decided bite that could set you drunk if you took too much. She was thirsty from the walk and curious to try it.

"It is delicious," Mary said, gulping down a fair quantity. Eleanor refilled her cup, and she drained it again.

"Be careful, Mary," Catherine warned. "You must be able to walk home again." She sipped her own, which was indeed delicious, but when Mary began to giggle, she knew she must prevent another cupful, so she quickly drained her own portion, rose, and suggested that the three walk to the main house to see Phoebe.

The path led past stables with a feature unusual in Mary's Land, fenced pastures, in which Catherine counted five horses, eight cows, and three mules. How happy Daniel would be to have such a wealth of livestock. And there must be more because Hook and Hammet had surely ridden horses to town and hitched mules to the many tobacco hogsheads. Catherine also saw a man with black skin leading a mule across the enclosure and remembered that Hook kept slaves, though not all of the black men in Mary's Land were slaves.

The women walked past apple and peach trees and buzzing beehives to the kitchen gardens, which were lush with vegetables, herbs, and flowers.

What a joy this garden was! Catherine had a vision of herself as mistress of such a spread and allowed the happy dream to expand until it included Daniel as her husband. When she saw Phoebe coming toward them from the house, the bright bubble of her imagination became the joy of reunion.

"Catherine, I would never hev thought to see ye still alive this day, much less so abloom. I was full certain when I left ye at the wharf ye would soon breathe yer last."

"Happily, no one told me I was to die," Catherine replied, "and Martha took such good care of me that I recovered."

"She hev a good name in St. Mary's, that Martha," Phoebe commented. She turned to Mary and put her hands on Mary's shoulders. "And Mary, always a beauty, more beauteous than ever. It is a pleasure to look upon ye."

"Thank you," Mary said demurely. "It is good to see you again, Phoebe...and I have news. Daniel and I are to be wed."

Phoebe looked puzzled for a moment, and then said, "I hope it will be good fortune for ye."

Eleanor said nothing at all.

Mary looked disappointed that her news caused so little reaction, and Catherine wondered at the lack of enthusiasm. Phoebe's reply seemed odd, as though she suspected good fortune to be unlikely. It occurred to Catherine that the people of St. Mary's might see Daniel as dangerous or untrustworthy after his attack on Watkins.

"Come, Phoebe, let us show them the house," Eleanor urged.

"Yes," Phoebe replied. "We will look about, and then I must hurry to the tasks Hannah hev set for me, or there will be hell to pay."

On entering the scullery, Catherine was impressed by the size of the fireplace and the numbers of tables full of utensils, many of which she did not even recognize. In the center of the room sat a trestle table much like Daniel's.

"Do all eat here, the master and servants?" she asked, thinking Hook not so far above Daniel in finery.

Phoebe and Eleanor laughed. "Never," Phoebe said. "This table is only for servants." She led the way into the adjoining great room, and Catherine gasped.

It was so large. Sunlight shone in through the diamond patterns of the leaded glass windows. An intricately carved clothes press sat against one wall, its wood shiny and smooth as was the wood of the floor. Chairs with leather seats and backs were grouped about the fireplace, and there were small tables with hinged extensions that could be raised should they be needed.

A large table sat firmly in the center of the room, its legs resting on knobs carved to resemble claws. Phoebe said the heavy covering that lay on part of the gleaming table top was a Turkey carpet, and Catherine remembered that Daniel had dreamed of Turkey carpets for himself.

She watched Mary, whose eyes became wider and wider. "It is a wonder," she was murmuring. "Can you imagine living in a place like this?"

"But come. There be more," Phoebe said, leading them into a second, smaller room. One of its walls was filled with shelves of books, and it was Catherine's turn to murmur. Books were so rare and so costly, and here there were so many. How she longed to take one home, use it to teach the children, and read from it herself. She ran her fingers gently down the spine along the printing done in gold. "What wealth," she said. "What incredible wealth."

"Let me show you one more room," Phoebe whispered, and Catherine surmised that this one was somehow more forbidden, as indeed it was. It was the bedchamber of Josiah Hook. The four women entered and peered quietly around. Perhaps this was the best room of all for a great bed sat at its center, a bed, which had a canopy and was surrounded by curtains. Those and the fabric that covered the bed itself were embroidered intricately with dragons and waterfalls, designs that had to have taken years to make.

There was another clothes press, and there were more shiny tables and chairs with carved backs and embroidered cushions. Pitchers and basins of a beautiful blue and white pattern sat about as though Hook needed more water for washing than an ordinary man.

"He has no wife?" Mary was confirming what Catherine was sure she already knew.

"No," Phoebe answered. "Women with rank the likes of his do not much like it in Mary's Land."

"Is he papist?" Mary inquired innocently as she fingered a gold ring that lay upon the table.

"He be of the king's church," Phoebe told her. She was starting to fidget. "Let us get back to the scullery…" she began, but a deep voice interrupted her.

"What is happening here?" it demanded to know.

Catherine whirled around and looked upon a man scowling at the assemblage of women who did not belong in the bedchamber.

"Well? Phoebe? Eleanor? What have you to say?"

Phoebe pointed to Catherine and said in a surprisingly bold voice. "This be Catherine, who is Daniel Falconer's servant, and this be her sister Mary, who will marry Daniel."

The man, obviously Josiah Hook, let his eyes travel to Mary, and a silence followed, one that gave Catherine an opportunity to look at him more closely. Of Daniel's height and and dark-haired like Daniel, he squinted a little as he stared at Mary.

Finally, he spoke again, his angry tone now reduced to a more dignified utterance in keeping with his fine ruffled linens and velvet breeches and gold buckled shoes.

"Phoebe, it was not seemly to offer my private quarters as a curiosity," he said quietly. "I will expect better of you in future."

"Yes, sir," Phoebe answered quietly, respectfully.

"But I will show these ladies, my neighbors, around the estate," he continued. "You may return to your duties." He turned and held out his upturned palm in the direction of the door, and when they had heeded his gesture, followed his visitors from the room.

The estate tour for the 'ladies' was, in fact, for Mary alone. Catherine followed along behind or well to the far side of Mary, who was feigning interest in explanations that had to have been boring her nearly to dust. This did not keep her from the flirtatious behavior she had shown with Captain Hudgins and with Daniel. She batted her eyes during provocative sidewise glances, showed her ankles, bent down unnecessarily, the better to show off her bosom, and blushed becomingly, all the time exclaiming over Hook's cleverness in running his great estate so well.

Catherine was so disgusted she thought she might scream. Instead, she clamped her teeth together until her jaw ached and waited until they had said farewell and arrived home via the cart supplied by Hook, who had explained he would have sent them on horses had they been accustomed to riding.

As the driver turned the cart about and drove away, the two climbed to the loft so Mary could change into working clothes. Catherine was already wearing hers since working clothes were all she owned. She was ready to vent her spleen as Mary dressed.

"How dare you behave so with Hook?" she hissed. "You, who are to be Daniel's bride. You behaved like a wanton. I was so ashamed, Mary, and you should be, too."

"He is a handsome man, is he not…and so wealthy."

Mary had obviously not even heard Catherine, or perhaps she was so used to Catherine's criticism she no longer paid it heed. Whatever the cause, Catherine became so enraged that she slapped Mary across the face with the back of her hand.

Mary's eyes widened in shock, then narrowed ominously. "When I am mistress, you will be gone from this place," she said, "and I will no longer have to listen to your ugly disapproval." She fastened the last hook on her bodice. "And you will never touch me again," she called back as she disappeared down the stair.

"It is madness to roast a goose in this heat," Mary complained as she sat outside the kitchen door turning the spit over the coals and reaching out with the spoon when Martha reminded her to baste the bird that was to be part of the celebration when the men returned from the appraisal of the tobacco.

Catherine was inside removing the coals from the oven, now hot enough for Martha's peach tarts. She was ready to fuss with Mary for her complaints when she heard the creak of the cart and went instead to the door. The twins joined her there as Daniel approached the house, leaving Edwin and Ezekiel to take the empty cart to the shed.

"Well, Father," Jonathan said, "did you get a good price?"

Daniel did not answer. He did not have to. The despair on his face was answer enough. Silently, the waiting group stood aside to let him enter so that he could go straight to the table and sink down on the bench.

"Bring me apple brandy," he said to no one in particular.

"The price, Daniel," Martha said. "What was the price?"

"One penny a pound," he muttered. "One paltry penny a pound. No small freehold will survive. We would have done as well to accept Virginia's plan. I cannot now pay any of my debt at all." He put up his head and looked directly at Jonathan. "The brandy, son. Get me the brandy." Jonathan hurried away.

"Did all sell?" Martha asked.

"No. Some of them held back once they knew. I suspect their leaf will go somewhere other than an English port, but I have no contacts. I would not know what to do. I, poor fool, considered selling elsewhere, but remained loyal to the king. I abided by his laws."

Catherine felt like her heart had turned to stone as she watched Jonathan bring a mug of brandy to his father, enough brandy to render him unconscious, should he drink it all. She wanted to take the drink from his hands and offer her bosom for greater comfort. She wanted to hold his head against her breast and run her hands through his hair and whisper to him that all would be well. Instead, she stood impotently as Mary sat down beside him and reached out tentatively to put an arm around him.

As though she cared, Catherine thought to herself. She has just discovered and attempted to bewitch a rich man. She would leave Daniel in a flash if Hook would have her. How dare she play the loving bride-to-be.

Daniel did not respond to Mary's brand of comfort, and soon she looked disgusted that he had not noticed her overtures and rose from the table, bumping against it as she moved. There was a clink as a metal object fell to the floor. Catherine saw what it was just before Mary extended her foot to cover it. It was the gold ring with the great red stone that had lain on the table in Hook's bedchamber.

Speechless, Catherine stared at Mary. She could not believe Mary had stolen the ring. Catherine understood that her sister was a thief of hearts, but to commit a criminal act such as this? How could Mary be capable even of considering such a thing? And why…why would she keep the object on her person?

Martha had returned to her tasks and not seen the incident, but Judith had.

"What is that?" she asked Mary.

"What is what?" Mary responded with studied innocence.

"That object you just put your foot on," Judith pressed.

'There is no object," Mary lied.

"But there is; I saw it," Judith insisted.

By now, Daniel's head was up; he was paying attention. "Move your foot, Mary," he said.

Mary sat, not moving.

"Mary," Daniel repeated, "move your foot."

Still, she sat quite motionless.

Suddenly, Daniel was up from the bench, bending over, grabbing Mary's ankle, lifting her foot, and exposing the ring. He reached down to pick it up.

"Where did you get this?" His voice was frighteningly quiet.

Mary's face reddened. "I found it in Josiah Hook's garden," she lied again.

Catherine took a deep breath and told herself to remain quiet.

"Why did you not return it?" Daniel asked.

"I…meant to…but I forgot."

"As you forgot that your foot was upon it just now I suppose." His voice was rising. "Do you suppose you would remember more clearly if Hook had you put in the stocks?"

"Surely you would not tell him," Mary gulped.

"Do you think he would be too stupid to suspect the cause of its disappearance?"

Daniel's head began to ache as he waited for Mary to answer. Her response was to burst into noisy tears. Daniel expected her to shout that he did not love her, but she merely ran from the house, nearly colliding with Hook's man Wilken in her headlong rush across the path toward the empty tobacco barn.

Before God, the man has discovered his loss already, Daniel thought as Wilken bowed with a formality that seemed absurd and handed him a folded piece of paper. Daniel's hands shook so badly he had trouble breaking the seal.

"To Daniel Falconer, esq.," it said.

You and your affianced bride are invited to dine
with me on Sunday next at noon. I will send my cart for
you if you will be so kind as to tender an affirmative reply
this night to my man.
Faithfully yours,
Josiah Hook

What kind of a game is the man playing? And what will happen should I decline? Daniel asked himself. Just when you think life could not become more difficult, you are proved wrong.

The messenger stood impassively as Daniel struggled to maintain his composure and to decide what he must do. If Hook did not yet know of his loss, it would be foolish to turn down the invitation. He might have other matters of importance to discuss, the purchase of Daniel's land, for instance. And if he did know of the theft, it would be even more foolish to turn him down. At any rate, to refuse what was probably a summons was the worst possible course.

He looked up and tried to smile at the waiting man. "Tell your master we would be most happy to join him," Daniel said.

The man gave something of an abbreviated bow and turned away.

Catherine approached Daniel. "Does Hook know already?" she asked.

"I cannot tell from this note," he said.

He would have liked comforting words from Catherine, but remembering she had already turned her back on him, the need for succor turned to something sour that escaped with his next words.

"The little left to me was a reputation as an honest man, but now Mary has put that in doubt. And will you judge her as you have judged me?" he asked.

"I have not judged you…" she began, all the while recalling that perhaps she had done a little, though she had not told him so.

"Do not lie, Catherine. It ill becomes you."

Never before had he leveled harsh words at her, and she did not deserve them now. Hurt became anger.

"I do not lie," she said. "Mary has done the thieving, and you have reserved your censure for me!"

"Indeed. Perhaps I was just following an old pattern, one you described to me. Mary commits the crime, and you take the consequences. It is why she cannot be responsible now. You have never let her suffer for her wrongdoing. Is that not so, Catherine?" he asked cruelly. "So while you are judging, reserve some of that judgment for yourself."

Catherine had been astonished by Mary's behavior, but she was struck dumb now. She could tell that something was happening to her face, whether turning red or deathly pale, she was not sure, but she felt herself sway a little and reached out for the table to steady herself. How she hated this inconvenient tendency to faint.

"And if you think fainting will help you, you are mistaken." Daniel said. "You may lie there until doomsday, and I will not pick you up." At this, Daniel stormed from the house.

All Catherine could do was stand staring at the floor in confusion. How had she merited such an attack? She felt an arm around her shoulders and looked into Martha's sympathetic face.

"He does not mean it, sweeting. He is sore troubled, and the ring was the last blow."

Catherine could feel the tears coming now, and knew she could not will them away even though she suspected they might never stop.

"But I want ye to keep one thing in mind," Martha continued. "Ye have kept yer distance from him, and it hev bothered him. It is a fair guess that he cares what ye think of him. Take comfort in it."

Daniel stalked along the path to the river in a haze of self-loathing. Why did he seem always to take the course he most hated, allowing himself to be seduced by a female who was the devil incarnate and then subjecting a blameless woman, who was of such value to him, to cruelty? He was a wretch of the lowest sort.

He did not understand why he had attacked Catherine, but of course he was going to lose her, anyway, as well as Martha, and the two men. All he would have left was a thieving, lazy little wench of a wife and his poor children whom she hated. He began to entertain the rogue thought that he could hire himself out to Watkins and be done with it. Perhaps Mary would then seduce Watkins, and Daniel's attempt to save her from him at the auction, the impulse that had caused all his problems, would then have been completely in vain.

And the damnable ring! What was he to do about the ring?

He pulled it from his breeches and looked at it as though it would give him an answer.

Should he wait to see if Hook knew? Should he put the ring in a prominent place on Hook's property so it would be found? Should he return it and claim that he had come by it in an odd way? If so, what way?

He sat trying to decide what he must do, but no sooner did one course of action seem the most logical than another would appear to be more so.

He was still not close to a decision as the sun sank behind the trees throwing their shadows across the river. Reluctantly, he stood and retraced his steps to the house even though he had not the heart to face Catherine.

Chapter Twelve

Mary sat as far as possible from Daniel in the cart as they bounced their way over the rutted path to the estate of Josiah Hook. Despite the heat of the sun, she looked radiant, which Daniel found puzzling.

He was not merely puzzled, however. He was also ashamed to be taking his ragged self with his patched clothing and tattered hat to a place of wealth. He was to visit a heretofore elusive neighbor who must want only to accuse Mary or Catherine of theft or to bargain for land Daniel did not wish to give up, though circumstances promised to force his hand.

Daniel noticed in an absent-minded way that Hook's livestock, even cows and sheep, were fenced in. It made good sense if you had servants enough to keep the animals fed, which was certainly why he and most planters, he suspected, allowed their animals to run loose, fencing crops instead. A mule trotted to the fence, and Daniel was taken by its resemblance to his own poor old creature, Maxim. As the cart drew closer, he saw that it was indeed Maxim.

"Wilken, stop here," he commanded abruptly.

Wilken's reluctance and lagging obedience spoke a lack of respect that rankled, but Daniel forgot about it as he climbed down from the cart and walked over to examine the animal more closely. There was no doubt; it was indeed his mule, and the creature, though he looked healthy enough, seemed glad to see him.

"His ear is notched with my mark," Daniel commented to Wilken as he climbed back on the cart. "Why has no one returned him or told me of his whereabouts?"

"Don't know," Wilken muttered. "It isn't none o' my affair."

"When did you find him?" Daniel persisted.

"Do not know."

"Was he hurt?"

"Do not know."

"Where was he found?"

"Do not know."

Daniel was tempted to ask Wilken if he had all of his toes or if he could see from both eyes, just to find out if the man would still *not know*. Instead, he set himself to mulling about which was more important, a gold ring or an aging mule, and even whether Hook was behind the damage done to his land and his servant. But since he could not imagine why, he dismissed the thought as absurd.

They drove up to the wide oaken front door of a large brick house set among carefully tended flower gardens and clipped boxwood, now pungent in the sun.

A woman in formal servant's garb opened the door as Daniel helped Mary, who seemed near bursting with excitement, down from the cart. Led by the servant into the great room, Daniel was able to look with appreciation on its appointments as Josiah Hook rose from his chair, nodded briefly to Daniel, and bent to kiss Mary's hand.

"We meet again, lovely lady," he said. "Come sit with me by the window where there is a breeze."

He turned to Daniel. "It is a beauty you have here, Daniel Falconer," he said. "No doubt she makes the flowers pale in comparison." He pointed to an enormous bouquet in a Chinese vase that graced the center table.

"Oh! Daniel," Mary said. "Give Goodman Hook the ring we found in the cart, Catherine and I, when last we visited."

Daniel gasped at her audacity.

"Josiah," Hook corrected her. "Call me Josiah."

"Give *Josiah* the ring," Mary repeated with the hint of a shy smile. "I do hope you have not been concerned about it." Had she been a cat, Mary would have been purring.

"Concerned?" he repeated. "I had not known it was gone. I cannot imagine why it was in the cart. I never ride in the cart. I must see to my servants, I will wager." He rose to pour amber wine into sparkling glasses. With a careless motion that spilled the liquid onto Daniel's breeches, he handed him a glass and then presented the wine to Mary as though he were handing her the queen's jewels or wished he were.

Mary, for her part, used every flirtatious device available to woman as she and Hook chatted about the weather, the crops, the danger of shipping on the high seas, the trade in sugar and rum that sea captains engaged in when there were no tobacco cargoes.

Daniel watched her pretense at avid interest as he sat virtually ignored, becoming increasingly enraged with a wrath he did not feel free to express.

He did, however, manage to inquire about his mule.

Hook looked at him as though surprised at his continued presence. "Your mule? In my pasture? Why, I cannot imagine how Hammet could have permitted such a thing. You will certainly have to take it back with you this afternoon. I will have Wilken secure it to the cart as you return."

He placed his attention on Mary again. "You must learn to ride a horse, Mary. The cart is too slow and undignified and uncomfortable for someone like you."

Mary smiled her most beneficent smile. "But we have no horse," she told him.

"A pity," Hook answered, looking at Daniel. "Indeed, a pity." His look conveyed that Daniel was pitiful in having failed to provide something so basic. After that, he continued to behave as though Daniel did not exist.

Watching Hook, Daniel had a fleeting feeling that there was something familiar about the man, that he had somehow had a contact with him in the past. It was common knowledge that Hook was of the king's faith, but Daniel searched his memory of the Puritans in England who had so destroyed his family. Had Hook been among their number, firmly attached to the side that was in power for the moment? Daniel could recall nothing specific and soon gave up the task because stifling his rage with Hook was becoming more difficult with each moment.

Why could he not make himself simply rise, order Mary to leave, and treat Hook to the sound thrashing he so richly deserved. It would be better to be thought a boor than a milksop, a bumbler. But an instinct told him violence was what Hook desired, a confrontation that would put Daniel at a disadvantage, perhaps even incite him to a duel.

The sight of Mary behaving with such wanton abandon sickened him so that he sat at the endless meal of crab and quail and pies of every description, unable to eat more than a mouthful or two. There would, of course, be no wedding. As a matter of fact, he would turn Mary off the property while it was still his. On reconsideration, he decided that this would be foolish. She would only run to Hook, who would then be rewarded for today's rudeness. But take her to wife? Beating her would be the more appropriate course by far.

As the two climbed into the cart to leave, Hook did not even bother to address Daniel in farewell. He merely hovered over Mary as solicitous as an old nursemaid about her comfort.

The cart rumbled roughly along on its return journey, slower now because Daniel's mule was tied to it.

"Was Josiah not a gracious host?" Mary asked him.

He glowered at her. "Why did you see fit to play the bitch?" he growled, whereupon she turned her back to him and spoke not another word.

He had not wed Mary, Daniel told himself upon the return from Hook's, yet already he was as well as cuckolded. Had he a mirror, he would look for horns to be sprouting from his forehead, the sign that his woman had taken another man. Were this a comedy on the London stage, the audience would be howling with laughter at the beauty and the bumpkin.

Even the journey home with his future "bride" had been laughable because the mule so obstinately preferred another direction.

And there was another absurdity. How could Hammet have claimed the mule for Hook, and not noted Daniel's mark on its ear when all of St. Mary's knew that the mule had been lost? This added to Daniel's feeling that he was little more than an object of derision wherever he went.

As evening fell, Catherine found him working by candlelight, vigorously honing the blades for harvesting the tobacco crop as though he were going to do the task tomorrow rather than many weeks from now.

Daniel looked up at her suspiciously, and she almost lost her courage. She had intensified her efforts to avoid him, for should he berate her again, she feared she would crumble and embarrass herself with tears. But she had to know.

"The ring, Daniel," she said. "What happened? Was Hook angry?"

Daniel rolled his eyes, and his voice trembled with an emotion she could not yet name. "He did not know the ring was gone. It was clear the reason for the invitation was Mary, who lied so skillfully about the ring I almost believed it myself. The man scarce knew I was present. He had words only for Mary and she for him. In fact, she treated him to every seductive wile known to woman. Your 'sweet' little sister continues to humiliate me."

Dear God! Catherine had hoped he would see Mary's behavior with Hook and therefore reject her, but it had not occurred to her that Daniel would feel humiliated.

"It was much the same when she and I met him…" Catherine began.

"The same!?" Daniel's shout was like a musket fired. "And you did not see fit to warn me!" Daniel's eyes were now wide with wrath. Catherine had never seen him so angry. When he rose and stared at her, a terrifyingly short distance away, she feared he would strike her.

"It was the ultimate attack on my manhood!" he shouted, "and a word from you would have prevented it. I have enemies on all sides, and perhaps you have been the worst. I have been led to attack a man in public, and I have paid a huge price. In a moment of weakness, I have been seduced like a mere stripling by a self-seeking little hussy who seems to want nothing further to do with me though I am pledged to marry her. And now my promised bride assaults my pride by…by…frankly offering herself to another man right before my eyes."

Daniel's voice became low and threatening. "And you could have stopped it. You needed only to tell me, and I would have used another method to return the ring…a few words, and I would not have been so debased. Am I so despicable to you that you would allow me all unknowing to put myself in such a position?"

He sat back down. "Go away, Catherine. Leave me alone. It will be painful to look upon you, little Mistress Innocence, the viper I thought to be a friend."

He watched her as she hung her head and stumbled along the path to the house. As suddenly as it had come, his anger melted away. Why had he attacked her so? It was as though he had put all that troubled him in one barrel and poured it over her head. He began to have a longing for the simpler days when he had felt free to confide his dreams to her, to sweep her into celebration for the few small victories that had been his since her arrival, to find contentment in her presence. And now that she bloomed with sparkling eyes and a woman's true figure, now that his sick hunger for Mary had fled, he had turned Catherine against him…irreversibly it was certain.

But, he reminded himself in self-defense, *she had been the first to turn from him. She had judged him. She had allowed him to experience humiliation which she could have stopped.* The anger crept back, and he let it come. It was better than the darkness that threatened to engulf him.

Catherine was not sure whether she crawled or walked away from Daniel, all the while asking herself just how much blame was hers. He had told her once she had been too young to understand what was happening with Mary, and now he blamed her that she had failed to curb Mary's waywardness. Had she had more foresight, she could have saved him from a painful experience, but she was not to blame for all the other crimes he had leveled at her. What, for example, had she to do with his attack on Giles Watkins. That could be laid in a strange way at Mary's feet, certainly not at her own.

She found herself at once too angry to cry and too hurt for cleansing anger. It was clear that Daniel hated her now that she knew almost for a certainty that he would not wed Mary.

She thought of the beauty of his singing, his love for the children, and his hard work. But there was no place for her in his world. All she had from him now was disdain, and the thought of living with such contempt was more than she could bear.

She would run away; that was what she would do. She wondered at first if he would trouble himself to bring her back, but then recalled that his need for her work was genuine, that he could even display his scorn by having her placed in the stocks or beaten for such a flight.

And the children. She could not desert the children or Martha, nor allow them to witness any such punishment. No, she must stay. She tried to calm herself by walking into the fragrant kitchen garden and counting her blessings. There was good food and the love and respect of all but Daniel. Not Mary, of course. Mary had respect for no one.

Mary! From whom all the trouble came, the beautiful child who had become so distorted inside that she had even begun to appear outwardly ugly to Catherine. Anger flared again, this time at Mary so that she lashed out when Mary approached her in the garden.

"How could you?" Catherine hissed at her. "For a lifetime I have tried to teach you right from wrong, and you have not understood."

"Oh, I have understood full well what I was taught," Mary replied very slowly, each word sharply defined and hurled at Catherine like an arrow. "You were not my only teacher, Catherine. I had an older, more knowing one, and she was the one who was correct as it turns out."

For a moment, Catherine could only stare open-mouthed at her sister. "What are you talking about?" she said finally.

"Goody Menton taught me what will be of most use as you will soon see."

"Goody Menton!?"

"Yes, Catherine, Goody Menton, who warned again and again that the only person on earth I need take care of was myself." Mary paused, a look of bitterness creeping across her face. "Of course, I did not realize because she so often rewarded me that she was looking out only for herself, that I was a mere tool for her gains…"

"What rewards, Mary? For what?"

Mary smiled, remembering. "Oh, sweetcakes and pretty ribbons and hot water for soaking in the big tub by the scullery fire."

Catherine leaned weakly against the gate. "Where was I during these soaks? Why did I not see the ribbons?"

"It was when you were abed because you began your work so early in the morning. She said I should tell no one what we talked about, not even you, that my business was mine alone, that the way to get what one wants is to go about it quietly."

Catherine hung her head and ran her fingers back and forth over her forehead as though thereby to brush away the evil of what she had just heard. Then she remembered to repeat her question.

"For what were you rewarded?"

"Oh, she showed me how to attract men when I served patrons at the inn. She said it would get me a wealthy husband." Mary laughed in a self-deprecating manner that was unusual for her. "She did not tell me it would bring *her* wealth when she sold me to become mistress. But I have learned her lesson well. It will be of use. You will see."

Catherine could see, all right. She could see that she herself had not been the one protecting Mary. It was Goody Menton all along who had been preserving Mary from starvation, from blemish, from physical harm, from discontent...so that Mary could be sold to the highest bidder. The woman had obviously even taken care to preserve Mary's maidenhead. All the while, Catherine had believed her own work in the scullery so efficient that she had been too valuable to wait on patrons and Mary so unskilled that the waiting was all she could do. Now she saw that she had been kept safely away from the lessons in seduction. And if Daniel with his stern faith could be so enticed, what had kept the carousing louts at the inn from doing Mary harm?

"What did she do about drunken men?" Catherine asked. "How kept you from rape?"

"As soon as they approached unruly states, she hid me away and made certain that other women were available."

Catherine could scarce fathom the life Mary had led, all unbeknownst to her. A cold cynicism took hold of her and brought another thought.

"Did you...did you...steal?" she asked.

"Yes." Mary's voice dropped. "It was to receive sweetcakes. It was easy, done very carefully and only after Goody chose the object and set the stage." Mary's tone became somewhat regretful. "It was like an old habit returned when I took Hook's ring. It was so easy."

"What did you hope to gain?"

"I tell you, Catherine, it was just habit, and I rued the impulse that drove me to it."

"I should hope so." Catherine's mind was awhirl. *Goodwoman Menton*, she thought. *Goodwoman! How absurd. Evilwoman would not have begun to be title enough.*

Catherine began to feel relieved because she could now stop blaming herself for what Mary had done, and she could even show Daniel the error of his accusations. But understanding the source of Mary's wrongdoing did not prevent a new surge of anger for all the anguish Mary had brought.

Mary's expression was one of challenge. She was waiting for Catherine to argue with her, but Catherine felt suddenly too tired and too powerless to respond. She merely closed her eyes and shook her head and then took herself up to the loft to try to sleep.

This, of course, was impossible. Every part of her body was stiff with indignation. Frustration seemed to travel from her toes to the top of her head, and this worsened when Mary came and lay down unspeaking beside her.

Catherine knew what would happen. Mary would fall asleep immediately as she always did, even when the remainder of the household was wrestling with the strife she had brought. She somehow managed to achieve the rest of the innocent when there was no innocence in her.

But tonight Catherine was wrong. Mary tossed restlessly beside her while exhaustion finally pulled Catherine into fitful slumber that was filled at first with images of Mary's willfulness. Then another kind of picture drifted into her dream, a vision of Mary as the affectionate child she had been.

Catherine was suddenly wide awake as other memories followed: the smiling tot saving her marzipan for her big sister, the dimpled little girl hugging a chambermaid and feeling troubled because the maid looked so sad, the sunny little moppet crying because her big sister had burned herself and was in pain.

Mary, her child, whom she loved more than life. A beautiful, innocent girl trained by Goody Menton to play handmaiden to the devil. Given a canker that would destroy her. Mary's mortal soul was in danger. She was doomed to hell, and all Catherine had been able to see recently was that which affected herself.

What could she do to exorcise the terrible evil? Perhaps only God could reach Mary now. Perhaps all that Catherine could do was pray. Would someone else's prayers be enough to save Mary from the fires of hell? She must ask Martha and Daniel to pray, too. Then, she remembered she could ask nothing of Daniel, a thought which brought tears.

Suddenly, Mary was sitting up. "What is wrong, Catherine? Why are you crying?" she was asking.

Mary would not understand, of course. She had no idea how hideous her revelation had been. Catherine was tempted to begin the work of transformation with a scolding, but knew, almost as soon as it occurred to her, that such a thing was useless. Perhaps there was only one way to begin, reminding Mary she was loved. Catherine had just realized herself that she did indeed still love Mary. Terribly.

She threw her arms around her sister and held her close and cried. That it had been so long since she had given Mary even the smallest sign of love strengthened her grasp.

"I love you, Mary," she choked out. "What Goody Menton has taught you is wrong, all wrong, but I love you. I will always love you."

"Truly, Catherine? I did not believe you did any longer." Mary did not return the embrace, but neither did she move away.

"I did not know it myself. I have been too angry, but I'm not angry any more."

"I love you, too, " Catherine thought she heard, but the words came so softly, she wasn't quite sure.

Mary drew away from Catherine and used her sleeve to blot Catherine's tears. The two became quiet, holding hands.

If she truly loves me, that is at least a start, Catherine thought, so she pulled the unused blanket over their heads as she had done on the ship so they could talk and not be heard.

"What about Daniel?" Catherine whispered. "You cannot think to wed Daniel now." She listened for the children to stir, but they did not.

"No!" Mary said emphatically, then continued more softly. "In Daniel I saw the passion Goody Menton had taught me to inflame, and oh Catherine! It was so unpleasant. It is a hateful thought to submit to him, to his touch. I am afraid of it. Oh God! I am afraid of it."

I am a madwoman, Catherine thought, *and this is the madhouse.* Mary did not want Daniel for a husband. She disdained his touch, that same touch for which Catherine so yearned. It was all absurd. Mary's outrageous conduct had won her the right to Daniel's body, and she did not want it.

"Besides," Mary added, "I thought that to marry Daniel was to free myself from this wretched business in the fields, but I know now that in such a household I cannot escape it. It is a living death. I have even thought that ugly old Ephraim Tanner at home in England would be better."

"So now you will attempt to win Hook?"

There was a long pause. "Daniel hates me," Mary replied. "I must do something."

"Daniel hates everyone just now," Catherine said sadly. "He hates me as well as you."

"Surely not," Mary countered. "You have been his friend."

"He says I am to blame for your behavior, and clearly he hates me for it."

"But you are not…"

"Tell that to Daniel…even though he will not listen." Suddenly, Catherine wanted to lie upon her pallet, close her eyes, and never open them again. "Oh, let us just sleep now," she said.

But when she and Mary had quieted besides the sleeping twins and a softly snoring Martha, she found that she could scarce keep her eyes shut, and Mary, uncharacteristically, was tossing about again.

Catherine must have dozed a little because once she became aware that Mary was gone and did not remember when she had left. Later, she awoke at first light to find Mary crawling onto her pallet.

"Did your stomach trouble you?" she asked as she sat up and shook her head to clear it of the cobwebs.

"Yes," Mary murmured, turning away from Catherine and lying still.

Chapter Thirteen

The next night Catherine was aware again that Mary had left her pallet and wondered if she had a sickness that called her from her bed. Presently, Catherine heard horses' hooves and tried unsuccessfully as she fell asleep to puzzle out who might be abroad so late.

In the morning Mary was gone.

When Catherine arose, Mary's pallet was empty, but Catherine supposed her to be up and about somewhere near, fetching water perhaps or visiting the necessary because she was unwell.

By the time household members were finishing their breakfast ale, Catherine was worrying in earnest. She did not want to ask the others if anyone had seen Mary because she feared their answers would be unpleasant, so the question did not arise until Ezekiel spoke it aloud as he left the table.

"Where is Mary?" Simple enough.

"Yes, where?" Martha echoed, looking at Catherine.

"I do not know," Catherine answered, her voice soft because the answer was so reluctant.

Daniel looked at Catherine pointedly in silent accusation and continued to direct his gaze at her until she repeated, "I tell you truly, Daniel. I do not know."

"Perhaps I do," he said finally as he left the table, Edwin just behind him.

Catherine hung her head. She remembered Mary's night exodus and the hoof beats she had heard, and suddenly she did know. Mary had gone to Josiah Hook. Despite all she could do, tears welled up, those damnable tears that betrayed her again and again. Judith moved next to her and put both arms around her waist, but this only intensified the crying.

"She hev run to Hook," Martha said.

Catherine nodded and was just able to say, "Yes, I think so."

"Will ye feed the hens the way I showed ye?" Martha said to Judith, and when the child had scampered off, she brought Catherine a bowl of water.

"Here, love. Wash yer face. There is little enough we can do now. Just stay busy to keep the shakes away."

"Martha, could you…could you…pray for her immortal soul?" Catherine forced out.

"I can do that, though only God knows if my prayers hev any weight in heaven."

"She did not even say goodbye," Catherine complained.

"She did not want to be stopped," Martha reminded her.

"I heard the horse," Catherine whispered because that was all her throat was capable of. "I heard her get up. I was too dull witted to put the two together. I was near asleep."

Suddenly, Daniel, his face dark with fury, burst into the room waving a piece of paper.

"The mystery is solved," he shouted. "Just as we thought. She is with Hook. And he has had the effrontery to inform me of the fact. Was that not kind?" he said with harsh sarcasm. "Do you know what the man wants?" he asked Catherine. "A wanton in his bed and a challenge to fight from me, the right to kill me, perhaps. Why else would he dangle such a thing so brazenly before my face? I do not know precisely what game the man is playing, but I will not engage in it. Mary is not worth it."

He swept a mug off the table. It crashed against the wall, the pieces clattering to the floor.

"And she has obliged him in his plans with a sweet compliance." He smiled a false, ugly smile and then came and looked into Catherine's eyes.

"With assistance from her sister?" he questioned in a shrill falsetto.

"No, not with assistance," Catherine answered angrily. Another unwarranted attack from Daniel had led wrath to override sorrow.

Scant days ago, Catherine would have been contrite, fearing she had indeed had a hand in Mary's sins. Now, however, she knew with certainty that she was not the villain, that Daniel's censure was outrageous, and outrage gave her the will to fight back. She had to force herself to be civil as she said, "I will go and talk with her, perhaps bring her back."

"Bring her back?" Daniel roared, taking Catherine by the upper arms, gripping with such strength that it was quite painful. "She will never again enter a doorway of mine," he shouted, glittering eyes boring into Catherine's.

"I have just learned why Mary behaves as she does…" Catherine said with a steadiness she did not feel.

He dropped her arms in surprise, narrowed his eyes and lowered his voice. "What is there to learn? She has been forgiven her faults so long she thinks they are virtues. No one from this household will have any traffic with that of Hook."

"But are you not relieved…?" Catherine began, her voice harsh, her nerves steeled for battle.

"Her crimes are an affront not to be born," Daniel overrode her words.

"An affront to your pride. I will not let your pride keep me from my sister."

"You are my servant," he erupted loudly again. "You will do what I say." Suddenly, he stopped short and closed his eyes as though the accusation of pride had just reached his ears. "Yes," he said, "my pride suffers, but that is not fatal. What she has done is an offense to decency. She leads all who must deal with her into error: me, you, the children, perhaps even Hook, though I think he is capable of error without assistance. She is just too dangerous."

Catherine stood her ground. "And what would you do if told you could no longer see your brother, though he be but several hours away?"

"It is not the same. He is an honorable man. Mary's ways are the very devil's tools. She puts our immortal souls in danger."

Catherine hated this new sanctimonious Daniel. He might be merely irritating were it not Mary's soul that was so endangered, were he not hinting that Catherine was too weak to escape the net of wickedness. And after all, he was the one who had been snared. Who did he think he was to play the Lord Almighty? He was not going to batter her down again, not without a fight.

"Did God anoint you guardian of all our souls?" she asked. "Are you so pure you can now be my mentor and tell me what I must do to get to heaven?" A part of her looked on at herself in shock that she, who had always been subservient, could take such a tone. But that did not stop her.

"You may take me before the council. You may have me put in the stocks." Her eyes narrowed. "You may even beat me, but as long as I have two legs that move, I will visit my sister. She needs me."

"I repeat. You are my servant and will do what I say…if I have to lock you in the shed to force you."

Catherine heard Martha gasp.

"You do not even treat your animals thus," Catherine retorted. "Or maybe I am not as valuable as the pig."

"Do not even hint that you are treated like an animal." Daniel's voice was rising again.

"No, you do not rail unfairly at the animals nor blame them for your troubles as you do me."

"Stop that foolish talk, woman!" Daniel barked. "Such nonsense will be the death of me!"

Catherine stalked from the house, so furious she could no longer answer him.

Well, I would not want to be the death of him, she thought. *I will not stay to be the death of him. I will go to see Mary, and then I will flee.* She began to run to the path that led along the river, then through the woods to the seat of Hook's estate. Periodically, she would slow to a walk to get her breath, and then she would run again, driven by the thought that she had done nothing, absolutely nothing, save work for the good of Daniel and his household. She had given him her allegiance and her heart. To have hurt piled upon hurt, to see the depth of his hatred for her, to experience the vicious attacks…It was unbearable!

Once she had to stop walking altogether. Loss and pity for herself began to break into her protective anger, and she did not want it there. Try as she might to prevent it, though, the rage crumpled with vivid memories such as Daniel's elation, his impromptu dance holding her when the tobacco thrived.

"Great God," she spoke aloud. "Help me to let go of false dreams. Help me see clearly what is true now, what I must do. And, oh God, show Mary the evil she has fallen into. Show me how to help her."

For a time, she felt too weak to walk any farther and sat on a fallen tree to focus her mind and her strength on what to do, to open her mind to what God was telling her.

Presently, she felt stronger. Though she knew nothing of what must come after, she was at least certain she must continue on her way to talk to Mary.

She saw neither Hammet nor Eleanor when she passed their house, but Phoebe came out to meet her as she entered Hook's kitchen garden and embraced her with a reassuring strength.

"It is a bad day that has brought the girl here," she said.

Phoebe's sympathy made it difficult for Catherine to talk, but she managed to say, "I must speak to her, Phoebe. Could you fetch her so that we might talk?"

"The seamstress be with her now. She be rewarded already for what she has done with all manner of frippery. But Catherine, I dare not let anyone know ye are here, though I was full sure you would come. I must hide you 'til Mary is alone and I can bring her." Phoebe looked around, first to the kitchen, obviously to see if anyone was watching, and then to the wooden outbuildings that lined the path from the kitchen garden to the barns.

"The smoke house," she said finally. "There be no use for the smoke house just now." She pointed the way. "Hide yerself there 'til Mary comes, or I come, should she not be able. I will bring ye ale and food while ye wait."

Catherine could feel herself swaying a little, and Phoebe grabbed her arm.

"Hold fast, girl. Hold fast. Ye may yet be able to save her."

When she entered the semi-darkness of the smoke house, its stench made Catherine sick at her stomach. Phoebe brought the promised ale and bread, but they were of little help. There was a bench within that she tried to wipe clear of greasy soot with her bare hands, but the attempt was ineffectual, and she had to sit upon it anyway, sit and stare and weep as the shed heated under the afternoon sun and then cooled slightly when darkness fell.

Mary was not coming. Phoebe had twice brought fruit and fresh water and more food, and told her to be patient, but there was no sign of Mary. Catherine began to plan how she would simply rush into the house, shouting and demanding to see her sister.

Once, she heard the voices of Hook and another man as they approached, and she began to tremble with fear that Hook would open the door and find her there. As the two passed, and she was letting out her breath in relief, she heard the other man say, "Do not fret. It was an excellent report, Josiah. Remember how pleased you were. I myself would have been persuaded of its truth, of all possible measures taken, had I not been the one to direct the writing."

It was no surprise, Catherine thought, that Hook was guilty of some dishonesty. She wondered what he had been untruthful about.

Full dark arrived, and Catherine found herself grateful that the place was not now so hot. Her bodice was thoroughly wet with perspiration, her skirt only slightly less so. She thought perhaps she should leave and get away from the pervasive, sickening smell of rancid fat and ash. Probably, Mary did not intend to come, and Phoebe was too busy with the evening entertainment to bring that message.

Where would she go? She still had no idea. Seeing Mary had been the first consideration; all else had seemed unimportant.

She began to hear late night sounds, the hoot of an owl, the bark of a fox, the low growl of another animal, and she felt certain that Mary would not appear now, that she might as well lie on the bench and succumb to the weariness that pulled at her.

She had just arranged herself in a curled position that seemed least likely to lead to a fall when the door opened softly, a sweet perfume wafted in, and the moonlight outlined the figure of Mary.

"I know what you intend to say, Catherine," Mary said, "and I tell you now it will do no good."

Catherine stood up and took her hand, but Mary withdrew it immediately as though fearful of contamination.

"Mary, why did you do this?" Catherine asked.

"Why?" Mary asked, astonishment in her voice. "Why, indeed. It should be so obvious, Catherine." She placed fabric, probably that of her sleeve lightly in Catherine's dirty hand. "Feel that. It is silk. I have been here only one night and one day, and already I wear silk, and the seamstress prepares more for me. I will never have to work in the fields, nor grind corn, nor fetch water, nor turn the spit…"

"But. Mary," Catherine interrupted, "why, when you would not be mistress to Ephraim Tanner back in Bristol, nor wife to Daniel, would you now be mistress to Hook?"

Mary chuckled. "Had I known what was in store in Mary's Land, I might have accepted Tanner. But I will not be mistress for long. Soon I will be wife. You will see."

Catherine drew in her breath. "You are dreaming. Hook will not marry a nobody who is neither a lady nor a virgin. Why would he trust a girl who has run from her promised bridegroom to the arms of another man? All you will have is the town's scorn. People will be horrified at your behavior."

Catherine heard Mary sigh in exasperation. "You do not know what Josiah will do, and what care have I for the town, for their gossip?" She took Catherine's hand, willingly this time. "I now live here. I tell the servants what to do, and they do it. They treat me with courtesy. They had better."

Catherine squelched the desire to shout in order to penetrate such wrong thinking. "You were afraid to submit to Daniel's body. Why would it be any better with Hook?"

"It *is* better," Mary confirmed Catherine's fears that she was already too late. "I do not love it, but I pretend to. He is gentle, less…threatening. And Daniel did not even like me. Josiah…makes me laugh."

"Suppose you get a child?" Catherine asked. "What then?"

"Josiah has told me to drink each morning a brew made from the lacey white flower that grows by the roadside, so there will be no child."

Catherine knew nothing of such things, but there was much else to pursue. She found herself shaking her head in the darkness. "He will tire of you, and what will happen then?"

"Catherine, you are silly. I will see that he does not…"

"But, Mary, do you not understand? It is a sin, what you do." Catherine could hear the desperation in her own voice. "The fires of hell await you."

Mary laughed. "Sweet Catherine," she said. "How worried you are, but you are wrong. Goody Menton assured me again and again, there was no such place as hell. It was an invention made so men could control each other. So you see, you must not fret yourself on my account."

These were the most frightening words of all. They punched Catherine in the stomach, and she started to argue, but the sound of voices came from the house, causing Mary to look up in alarm. "I must go now. I will persuade Josiah that you cannot change my mind, and then you can visit without hiding away."

She gave Catherine a quick kiss on the cheek and ran from the shed before Catherine could do or say anything to stop her.

What would stopping her matter? Catherine asked herself. Mary firmly believed in her own power to control Hook. She would do just as she pleased. The angels in heaven could not stop her.

Catherine sank down on the bench with her elbows on her knees and her head in her hands. Sorrow and frustration set her mind to whirling. She had failed with Mary, but must try again, perhaps after the glow of newness had faded. Mary was so sure of herself, so blindly unaware of the heinous door she was opening.

For a long time, Catherine sat still, Mary's stubbornness and Daniel's cruelty roiling alternately through her head. Then, there came more immediate questions. Where could she go? What could she do? What was there left?

Finally, crushed with fatigue, she lay back down upon the bench for a fitful sleep and awoke at first light with the memory of a dream fresh in her mind. Father Thaddeus, that kindly priest from St. Stephens, had been talking to her and telling her that God's ways are mysterious.

Father Thaddeus. The mission at St. Stephens. That was where she could go. She thought about Daniel's faith before the rage overtook him, a faith that had wiped away any prejudice she had been given in England of the Roman church. Now, out of her need and her confusion, she would seek shelter and counsel from Father Thaddeus. She opened the door of the smokehouse and found that there was just enough light to see the path, so she walked quickly down the road.

Chapter Fourteen

It was late in the day when Catherine approached what seemed to be a chapel at St. Stephens. The heat had battered her almost to insensibility, and she felt weak from hunger. It was a little cooler at this time, and she had rested once in a Piscataway hut in the forest and begged a ride across a wide creek in a canoe. Still, she could barely drag one foot behind the other as she entered the tiny chapel, which was empty now. She lay gratefully on one of its crude benches.

The next thing she knew, someone was pushing her shoulder, an insistent voice saying, "Awake, child. Awake. Are you ill? Come, speak to me."

She opened her eyes to the glow of a candle, shut them against the small light, then looked beyond the glow to the face of Father Thaddeus, a welcome sight.

"Are you well?" he asked.

"Well enough," she answered as she struggled to push herself up.

"Where do you come from?" He did not recognize her.

"I am Catherine, servant to Daniel Falconer," she told him. "I have run away." She paused, expecting him to berate her for such behavior, but hoping he would listen with sympathy. Listen to what? She had come all this way without deciding what she must say. Could she tell him she had run away because Daniel was cruel? Would he think harsh words constituted cruelty? Suddenly, she was afraid they would not.

"That puzzles me," Father Thaddeus was saying. "I would have expected Daniel to be a kindly master."

He was not berating her. Thank God for that. He was merely silent, waiting for her to go on, but she found herself unable to begin an explanation.

"Perhaps you would like something to eat and drink," he suggested.

He was not even going to demand that she respond to him. He was willing instead to tend to her physical needs.

"I am thirsty," she managed to say without a sign of a quiver in her voice, and when he went to fetch wine, she wiped rogue tears from her eyes.

After she had sipped a little, she felt able to tell him something of her story, except now she must recount something of Mary's sins because it was unfair to lay all villainy at Daniel's feet. She found she did not want to do that either, but there was little choice.

"My sister was to wed Daniel," she began.

Father Thaddeus nodded. "Yes, I knew," he said.

"But she has run away to Josiah Hook." Her voice threatened to betray her, and she stopped.

Father Thaddeus was shaking his head sadly. "I am sorry to hear that," he said.

"And Daniel forbade my seeing her."

"Understandable," the priest commented. "He must have been very angry."

Catherine pondered a question. Since Daniel had obviously told Father Thaddeus of the marriage promise, had he also confided its reason?

"And did you go to see her despite his wishes?"

Catherine nodded her head and answered weakly. "Yes."

"Why did you not wait until his anger died a little? I cannot imagine that Daniel would keep you from your sister forever."

"But..." Catherine began, then stopped.

"But?" he asked.

"But he had threatened to lock me in the shed, and I wanted to try to bring her back before...before...it was too late."

"And Daniel did not want her back?"

"Daniel did not want her back," she repeated lamely.

"And were you in time?" His questioning was insistent, but there was no blame in it, only a kind of softness.

"No," Catherine whispered.

"Do you not think that now you can return to the freehold, that Daniel's anger will be less, that he might even be concerned for your safety?"

"Oh, I cannot return. He hates me." *Oh dear*, she had not meant to say that.

"Why do you think so?"

"He says that I am to blame for Mary's sins and that I have been judging him."

"Ah. I begin to see a little better," he said. "Come, Catherine, to the house with me so we can get you something to eat. If you will be so kind, I would like to hear more."

In the small, neat wooden house that rather resembled Daniel's, a woman Catherine took to be a Piscataway moved silently about in her soft moccasins to bring bread and cheese from the larder and two succulent peaches. Then she bade Father Thaddeus a courteous good night, nodded to Catherine, and left the house.

Catherine had not realized how hungry she was until the food was set before her. After several bites she felt a little more willing to respond to this small, wise man, whose eyes were fastened on her, indicating that the questions were to resume.

He settled on the bench across the table. "Now, tell me," he said, "why are you to blame for Mary's sins?"

"Because all her life I have done her work and taken her punishment and given her my food, and Daniel says she has gotten away with her sins so long she thinks they are virtues." Catherine's words now seemed to be rushing out.

"Have you done these things?"

"Yes, but Father, she is like my child, and I the only mother she has ever known. I did not know I was doing wrong." She paused to take another sip of her wine because her voice was breaking down again.

Father Thaddeus took her hand. "Listen to me, Catherine," he said. "You cannot blame yourself. Neither can Daniel blame you. If you but give love and kindness, most people will give it back, but I am convinced there are those locked within themselves who can see naught but their own desires. They will take and take and ask for more, but find no meaning in giving. Neither the best of mothers nor the worst have powers of their own to change them..."

"No, no, Father!" The tears came now, and Catherine didn't care. "You are saying she is doomed to do evil, but that is not so. That is not so!" she repeated herself on a sob. "The woman entrusted with our care was training her to steal and to seduce men and to care only for herself, and I did not know..."

"You did not let me finish," he said quietly. "I was going to say only God and our continued love can change them."

"Yes, and I pray, oh! how I have been praying ... "

"And I will pray as well. All is not lost. Now try to be calm, child, and tell me but a little more. Did you tell Daniel about the woman who corrupted Mary?"

"He would not let me speak, Father."

He leaned his elbow on the table and placed his hand over his chin and frowned. "I do not believe your so-called failure with your sister was the source of his anger. Tell me. You mentioned he believed you were judging him. For what?"

"For…for…" It was Daniel's business. Catherine was not free to speak of it.

"For bedding Mary?" he asked.

He did know of it! She nodded.

"And *were* you judging him?" Father Thaddeus' pursuit of truth had become relentless. It began to feel like prying.

"A little, but it was nothing I spoke of."

He raised his brows. "Then what made him think so?"

"I no longer talked to him." The words were no sooner out than she wished she could take them back.

"One would certainly feel judged under such circumstances, would one not?"

"Yes."

"Was your judgment not the reason for your silence?"

"No."

"What was the reason?"

Catherine began to feel defiant. She had nothing further to confess save her own very private feeling of love, a love which was now shattered, and lingering pain all that remained of it.

"Father, I do not believe I can answer any more…"

"And I have been pressing too hard. I am sorry, my dear. It is a way with a priest when one of God's children brings him her troubles." He paused and looked at her as though trying to make a decision. That decision apparently made, he continued to speak. "You need not answer me to confirm or deny, but I have supped with you and Daniel and the rest of the household, and I am an observant creature. I would venture to suppose, based on my observation there, what you have just said, and what you have felt unable to say, that your silence was born of pain because of your care for Daniel."

Catherine took a deep breath preparing to deny his supposition, but knowing that, in truth, she could not.

"And I would say that if your silence was troubling to him, that there is an answering caring in him," the father continued.

Catherine shook her head vigorously. "Martha said the same thing, but you are both wrong. You were not there. You did not hear the insults and accusations he hurled at me. The Daniel I thought I…" She had done it again. She had said too much. This man could bore into your very soul.

"Loved?" he supplied.

"Yes." She hung her head. "That Daniel never existed, or if he did, he does no longer."

"You will pardon me if I say he is a good man in a sea of very bad troubles."

"You may say it, Sir, but that will not make it true."

Father Thaddeus gave a half smile and rose from the table. "I think I have not earned the privilege of making a suggestion, but I will do so nonetheless. I will escort you to the humble dwelling of the native woman you saw earlier and several other women. They will make you welcome and provide you with a place to sleep as they have other weary travelers. And in exchange, you and I will pray for God to reveal the truth to us and to lead us where we should go. Can we agree on that?"

"As long as God reveals as much to me as he does to you."

Father Thaddeus laughed. "That is quite a bargain, Catherine, quite a bargain," he said.

Chapter Fifteen

Daniel did not search for Catherine. Instead, he tended his rage as one might tend a barricade, maintaining it with hard labor. His only words were peremptory orders barked at the members of his household, his only activity attending to the crop from first light to last, as though whatever price it sold for next summer was actually going to be his. Moreover, his outrage deepened when a court representative visited briefly.

"You must vacate the freehold by Christ's Mass," the man said, stuttering in what seemed to be embarrassment as he sat across the table.

"God's blood, why?" Daniel felt his stomach turn.

"Elijah Mason has sold the debt you owe him to another party, who has called in the debt."

"With no word to me!?" Daniel jumped to his feet and leaned over the table. "Who?" he mouthed, though he could not get sound past his lips.

"I cannot tell you more. I do not know. I think you must petition the court to find the answer."

Now, Daniel was speechless.

The visitor hastened to finish. "You are advised to harvest and hang your tobacco in order to reduce the debt still further. Then, it would be best to look for someone to hire you and someone to buy the indentures of your servants."

He stood and walked toward the door. "I am full sorry that I had to be the bearer of bad tidings," he said.

Still, Daniel said nothing, but as he watched the man walk down the path, the full import of what had been said hammered on him until his head ached, and his stomach turned to water. He felt at the moment helpless to do anything. He was certain Watkins was the culprit; the man obviously wanted land as well as revenge, but Daniel did not even have the will to accuse Watkins and see what the reaction would be.

Soon, he found himself stumbling aimlessly along the path to the river. He sat under a tree and watched the water flow calmly toward the sea. Its gentle movement suggested a peace he might never know again.

I will harvest my crop for Watkins' profit when hell freezes, Daniel told himself.

So why had he been working away so intensely on the tobacco? The answer crashed in upon him, an answer that should have been obvious. He had been thereby fencing out truths he had not wanted to see. He had been blinding himself deliberately.

And what were those truths, other than the loss of his property, in itself ugly enough?

First, there was the behavior of his family. They had not spoken to him since Catherine ran away. Judith only glared at him and cried to Martha that she wanted Catherine. Jonathan avoided looking at him altogether, and so did Martha. They did his bidding with a grudging silence.

The men were a little more responsive, but seemed to be spending much time carving toys for the children as though to comfort them for the loss of Catherine.

Daniel looked at the sparkling water and wondered what it would be like to weight himself down and sink to a cool oblivion. But responsibility called, and suicide was a sin. He had already committed sins enough.

What other truths had he refused to see? His fierce pride. His violence. His unholy desire. His attack on Catherine.

Catherine! There was the worst pain of all. Where was she now? Wherever it was, in whatever plight she found herself, he was the cause. She was an innocent he had driven away. He had made her a mirror and imagined seeing reflected there all that he hated in himself. And he had smashed the mirror.

He pictured her sparkling hazel eyes dulled with pain, her body that had grown lovely in the past months now injured or endangered. A spark of desire at the thought of that body surprised him. Desire had seemed to die in him, had been one thing he had willingly let go.

Had Catherine gone to work for Hook? Had she found work elsewhere, a simple matter in a Mary's Land so devoted to tobacco, so in need of labor? Wherever she was, she would be in danger, of course, in danger of rape or of offering herself in wedlock to an unworthy man.

Catherine wed! It was an extraordinary thought that drew his muscles taut and sent a shiver of fear through him. Ministering with those gentle hands to the nicks and bruises of some ill-suited husband. Laughing merrily with an inappropriate mate and listening with sympathy to his poor dreams, bedding with a clumsy lout, bearing his children. Oh God! What had he done, Daniel asked himself. What had he done?

On an impulse he lurched to his feet and ran back to the house.

"Where is Catherine?" he asked Martha as he stood panting for breath. "Do you know where she is?"

"How would I know that?" she snapped. "Did ye think I had her hidden away? Why would ye bother to ask now when it is too late?"

Daniel had expected her anger, her rudeness, and now paid it little heed. "Do not hide the truth from me," he said. "I will not try to bring her back if she does not wish it. I only want to know whether she is safe." *Not fully truthful*, he admonished himself.

"Did I know where she was and if she was safe, I would still not tell ye where to find her, but God's truth, I do not know." Her eyes filled with tears. "Damn ye, Daniel Falconer, I do not know. Edwin went to Hook to inquire, but she was not there, and the servants did not know either where she was, not that it would be a good place for an honest reply."

Martha slammed her spoon into a bowl of dough and whipped it as though she wished she could be beating Daniel.

He left the house and asked the same question of all the others, though he knew it to be useless. They claimed no knowledge, and Judith did not answer her father at all, but ran away in tears.

Daniel wandered despondently back to the river, removed his boots, and waded in up to his shoulders. It was all he could think to do to cool the burning pain. He had considered himself a good man, a moral man, and now he had heaped one sin atop the other until there was a pile so high it had toppled over on him.

He stooped, submerging himself completely in the water, wishing he could thereby be cleansed of his wrongdoing.

If he but knew how to swim, he thought, he would swim away from himself and his failures. He would swim down the river and through the creek to St. Stephens and seek solace from a steadfast friend, Father Thaddeus.

St. Stephens. He could not swim, but he could walk to the mission. He could seek comfort he did not deserve. He could do penance. Perhaps he would even be able to pray. It seemed a long time since he had been able to pray.

Daniel sat down at the table with his silent household, sat but could not eat. He pushed the food about on his trencher before he finally broke the quiet.

"I am sorry for the trouble that I have brought on you and for my treatment of Catherine. I ask your forgiveness for it as I ask God's forgiveness." He stopped speaking to avoid choking on his next words before he could continue.

"The council agent told me yesterday that we must quit this freehold after Christ's Mass." He hung his head, unable to look at the expressions on the faces that surrounded him, wishing he could close his ears as well to the gasps, the sighs, and the occasional sob.

After a time, he spoke again. "I am certain that all we own will go to Watkins, so I want work on the tobacco ceased. We will not harvest it for his benefit. Henceforth, our labors will go only into providing food for now and for the winter and into the production of goods any one of us might want and be able to take away."

He closed his eyes. "Think about what that might be. At the moment, I cannot. I do not even know whether tools and household goods and animals are mine to keep or forfeit to the man who bought my debt and called it in."

There was now absolute silence. Martha's face had taken on a ghostly pallor, and Ezekiel gazed at her with obvious concern. Edwin stared stonily at his plate, and Judith clung to Jonathan, whose hands clutched her back with such force his knuckles were white.

"There will not be another freehold like this," Edwin said. "Ye hev spoilt me fer another master."

"You never know about that." Daniel was grateful for the compliment despite his guilt. "And time will pass. One day you will be your own master. Ezekiel, you have little indenture time left, and both you and Edwin will be in demand, for you are known to be honest and hard working. I will try to be sure it is a worthy place you go to. Martha, you are free, of course, to go your own way."

"It will be with the children," she declared.

This declaration almost cost Daniel the little composure he had. Struggling with himself, he was finally able to answer. "Thank you, Martha," he whispered.

No one ate or moved as silence settled back in. Daniel broke it finally. "Ezekiel will be in authority here for a few days while I go to St. Stephens…"

"To look for Catherine?" Judith broke in hopefully.

"Partly that." Daniel smiled at her as he rose to leave the table, and she gave a weak smile in return. He knew, however, that he had few hopes of finding Catherine at St. Stephens. He could not imagine why she might seek sanctuary with a priest, however rebellious that priest had been of his vows.

Ezekiel followed him from the house. "It is bad to let the crop go," he said. "Ye must pay what ye owe somehow, else they will force you to a new indenture or take all ye can earn."

Daniel knew Ezekiel was right, but had neither the will nor the energy to go back and redirect his household.

"Do what you think best," was all he said before he walked slowly toward the path that would take him to Father Thaddeus.

He was grateful no one was about when he arrived at the mission and entered the crude church in the early afternoon. He knew what he wanted, to prostrate himself before the Christ and pray to be forgiven.

But his attempts to pray, even positioned as he was, went sadly astray. His mind stubbornly insisted on wandering to the pain and danger he had inflicted, then to an image of Catherine in distress.

How did monks maintain lives of constant prayer, he wondered, when he, with all his needs, could not keep a steady focus on God for even a short time. Disappointed in himself, he rose to see Father Thaddeus standing in the doorway.

"Ah, Daniel. I prayed that you would come," Father Thaddeus greeted him.

"It was a potent prayer, then," Daniel answered, "for I stood by the river and felt its call."

"You have come in answer to its call, not with a purpose of your own?" Father Thaddeus smiled.

"Oh, I have great purpose, Father, great need of spiritual guidance, great sin to confess."

"And you wish to begin immediately? Not to eat or drink or rest first?"

Daniel laughed briefly, dispiritedly. "If I could but rest, I would, but it is a luxury that has eluded me these last days."

Father Thaddeus did not answer, but walked to a small shelf and fetched ale for the two of them. Then he sat on one of the benches and beckoned to Daniel to sit facing him.

"Now, tell me about your sins," the priest said, handing Daniel the ale.

"It is a strange brand of confession," Daniel commented as he settled on the bench.

"It is a talk between two friends with a greater friend listening," Father Thaddeus replied.

And Daniel began. He poured forth his troubles, laying blame on himself at every step. Father Thaddeus interrupted him only long enough to pry away false blame, to remind him that in some of this he had been a victim of circumstance.

When Daniel's words slowed to a trickle, Father Thaddeus began to question him.

"Why was it that Catherine's opinion troubled you so greatly?" he asked.

"She was my friend, my comfort…my…" He broke off, unable to find the appropriate word and began again. "She betrayed me far worse than Mary because…"

"Because?"

"Because I trusted her."

"Trusted her to do what?"

"To…to accept me."

The priest regarded Daniel quizzically, then spoke again. "What made you so certain she no longer accepted you?"

"She no longer spoke."

"Could there have been no other cause for her silence?"

Daniel shook his head. "No," he said tentatively. "No," he said again more strongly. "What other reason could she have had?"

"Hurt, perhaps."

"Hurt?" Daniel shook his head again. "Hurt over what? This silence occurred before I became angry with her. It was much of the reason for my anger, I think."

"Hurt that she had lost you, perhaps?"

Daniel contemplated such a thing with hope, but pushed it away again as impossible. What one might wish for had little to do with truth.

"That could not be the case," he informed Father Thaddeus.

"Tell me, what did you do to break her silence?"

Daniel hung his head and discovered on his shirt a spot, one among many, which required scraping with his fingernail. "I shouted and cursed at her and accused her," Daniel mumbled.

Father Thaddeus sighed. "It was hardly the way to gain her acceptance. When you see her again…"

"*If* I see her again," Daniel corrected.

"*If* you see her again, will you beg her forgiveness?"

"Of course!" Daniel was surprised at so obvious a question. "But it will do no good. If I were Catherine, I would not forgive Daniel."

"Perhaps she is somewhat more forgiving than you." Father Thaddeus glanced at him sidewise, waiting for an answer.

"Yes, surely, but…"

"But?"

"But I want more than that. I want her trust. I want her companionship…I want…"

"Daniel, could you not settle for one thing at a time? Could you start with gaining forgiveness and then work at regaining the rest?"

"I suppose it is all I *can* do, but this resolve is empty. I do not even know how to find her."

Father Thaddeus stood slowly, his body obviously shedding its stiffness with difficulty.

"Come with me, Daniel," he said. "I have a gift for you."

Chapter Sixteen

Catherine stood in the shade of an oak behind the hut where she had been sleeping, a shelter woven of shore reeds in the Indian fashion and strangely comfortable. Her muscles ached as she worked at the endless task of grinding corn, stone on stone, with a method used, she supposed, since time began.

As always, she was asking herself what would happen if Daniel found her. Would he demand that she resume her labors with him? Would he subject her to humiliating punishment and the cruelty of his hatred? Or would he simply reject her and refuse to have her back altogether?

She pictured a continued existence here at the mission. Father Thaddeus was kind, and she had learned already to speak a little of the native tongue, just as the women seemed to be learning a little more of hers. To remain was not an unpleasant prospect, but it was empty. She could see now that the only truly happy time in her life had been the period that included intensely hard, but satisfying work, Martha's friendship, the love of the children, and Daniel's presence. She had not known then as she did now of his treacherous ways or Mary's training in evil.

That innocence was gone, she told herself. And she was now a lawbreaker hiding away from the one who had paid for her indenture. Moreover, she was too far away from Mary, therefore more powerless than ever to help her.

Father Thaddeus had said to pray about what she must do, and she had indeed been praying, but this seemed to have left her with no clear answer, only more confusion. Father Thaddeus continued to advise patience.

She had just looked at the pitifully small pile of ground corn and resolved to work a little harder when she heard someone call her name. The voice sounded like Daniel's, but she told herself she was being foolish as she looked wearily in the direction of the sound.

It *was* Daniel! He was standing perhaps thirty paces away. And if she had thought herself adrift in confusion before, it was nothing compared to what she was experiencing now. There was first an absurd flash of joy, which turned to anger at the memory of their last meeting, and then became fear at the thought of what he could do to harm her, both her body and her heart.

Though her vision had become a blur for some reason, she could see that he was smiling. Ah, perhaps he was going to play the kind Daniel this hour, or perhaps it was only a smile of triumph.

"Are you well, Catherine?" he asked.

"Well enough," she answered stiffly. "And you?"

"Better now that I have found you."

What did that mean? Now that he could demand the return of her work for his investment? Now that he could purge his anger through punishment? Or that he was genuinely glad to see her? To hope for this last, of course, merely risked disappointment.

She wanted to back away as he walked slowly toward her, but she straightened her back and stood her ground.

"I have come to say I am glad you are safe and to ask for your forgiveness for my cruel words. You cannot know how I have suffered over the memory of what I said."

He need not have suffered, Catherine thought. She had suffered enough for both of them. God in heaven, this was the most treacherous Daniel of all. She could feel herself beginning to melt at the core under the gaze of his brown eyes and knew she could not let that happen.

He stepped even closer and reached for her hand, which she snatched away as though she had been burned.

"You do not feel inclined to forgive, do you?" he said in the face of her silence. "I cannot blame you. I can only ask you to return to my house and let me show you what my repentance means."

She was tempted to say, "until you become angry again," but she found she could not.

"I will not force you to come back," he said. "I know I do not deserve it. I only ask you to do it despite all. We miss you, all of us."

She could not bear this pretense of caring. She hung her head, wanting terribly to return, but determined not to let him see how much pull his semblance of kindness exerted on her. Instead she replied, "I have made a contract, and I owe you my labor; I will return." Stating the bald facts were the only means she had to retain her last shred of dignity.

"At first light on the morrow?" he asked.

"At first light."

"Thank you, Catherine." He stood looking at her silently for an agonizingly long time and then turned without further speech and walked slowly away.

He had wanted to say, "*I* miss you," but he had not dared, had changed the "I" to a "we". She was not going to forgive him, not yet anyway. She was only returning because her indenture demanded it. There was a knot of anxiety and yes, a little anger in his stomach that she had turned herself into a stone wall that faced him blankly, without feeling. The best he could hope for would be a very slow regaining of her trust, and by then he would be forced to sell her indenture.

Sell her indenture! She would be gone from him! The knot in his stomach began to burn.

She had just stood before him, little wisps of hair blowing about her clear hazel eyes, and he had wanted to brush them away, to touch her lips, but she had shrunk from any touch at all.

Her return was the beginning of a victory, but he did not feel much joy in it.

Catherine stood to one side of Father Thaddeus, Daniel to the other, as he held their hands and prayed for guidance and for a safe journey. She was not really a participant in his prayer because she felt betrayed. The priest had told her to seek guidance from God and then straightway sent for Daniel. He had a right to do so, but he had led her to believe she would have a say in the matter.

At the conclusion of the prayer, Father Thaddeus embraced each heartily. "God go with you," he said before they climbed into the canoe that would carry them across the creek.

"Thank you for your hospitality," Catherine said as the Indian man pushed the vessel away from the shore with his paddle. She was at least grateful for this.

"And your guidance," Daniel added before he began to assist in propelling the craft toward the far shore.

This journey was short and silent, and the silence continued as Daniel and Catherine clambered up the far creek bank and resumed their journey on foot.

Daniel was the first to speak. "It was providence that led me to St. Stephens."

Catherine glanced at him, puzzled. "Did Father Thaddeus not send for you?" she asked.

"I think God did," he told her. "I stood by the river wishing I could swim from my troubles, and the thought of swimming to St. Stephens came to me."

If that were true, she had been not nearly gracious enough to Father Thaddeus, but a spark of guilt did not prevent her next words.

"And did you swim?" She had trouble keeping the amusement from her voice. It was a little like the conversing they had once done so easily.

"Since I cannot swim, it would have been the death of me, though it occurred to me that death would not have been such a bad thing."

"You have been that troubled?" Catherine stopped walking, waiting for an answer.

Daniel faced her. "Do you not understand, Catherine? I have suffered because of my cruelty to you. I have been tormented that some calamity might have befallen you."

Do not trust him, she was repeating over and over to herself. *Do not let him break through your armor.*

"Were there not other troubles as well?" she asked innocently as she resumed her walk. She would not look at him any longer.

"A court representative told me we must leave the freehold by Christ's Mass and that I must sell the indentures as well."

So that is it, she thought. *Therein lies the true source of his despair.* He had lost his freehold, and he could scarce sell her indenture if he could not find her. She wondered if he would be able to recover the cost of Mary's indenture from Hook. She was perfectly correct, she saw, for her suspicions about his motives.

She said nothing more, but as she pondered his situation, she was saddened by the enormity of it. Where would he go? What would happen to the children? Would she ever see him again?

Damnation! she admonished herself. *Catherine, it would be best if you never saw him again. You must not be the kind of woman who wants to pick at sores.* But then she considered his dreams and the hard work he had put into achieving them, and in spite of herself, she felt a new surge of sadness.

"I am sorry, Daniel," she said finally. It felt too good to say his name aloud. She would not do it again.

They spoke no more. Daniel wanted to ask her about Mary, but he did not dare broach the subject. He would have to earn the right to ask.

Perhaps he should feel grateful for her refusal to speak further, he told himself because as he glanced her way or she went a step or two ahead of him, he found the specter of his old nemesis rising again. Desire! He observed the grace of which she was so completely unaware, the delicate beauty of her profile, the tantalizing thrust of her breasts, and again he called himself a fool. How self-defeating his impulses were. He had allowed himself to feel the physical lure of this worthiest of women only after he had destroyed the trust that had existed between them.

Her coldness toward him could be a blessing for now. He would not be able to give in to the temptation to bed her. He could see, however, that when he began to win back her friendship, that particular temptation would be his greatest peril. Then, he almost laughed aloud at his own audacity. "When" he won her back. "If" he could win her back was more to the point. One thing was certain, though. She would never prey on him for her own purposes as Mary had done.

The sun was at its highest when they approached the house. An unfamiliar man stood by the front door shading his eyes as he watched them come.

Probably more bad news, Daniel thought as he lengthened his stride to find out as soon as possible what new trouble faced him. Surprisingly, the fellow began to run toward him. And then, suddenly, Daniel could discern who he was.

His brother! William!

Chapter Seventeen

Catherine slipped quickly into the house as the men approached each other. She did not know who the newcomer was and told herself she did not care.

Martha's eyes widened, and the skillet she was holding clattered to the floor when she saw Catherine.

"Catherine! The Lord bless us. Ye are back!!" She threw her arms around Catherine. "Ye are safe and sound!"

There was much comfort in Martha's unaccustomed embrace and in the shouts of the twins as they clambered down the stairs from the loft and threw themselves at her. In their joyful laughter and enthusiasm, they pushed her off balance, dropping the three to the floor.

"Catherine do not leave us again," Judith said.

"Promise!" Jonathan finished.

Catherine could feel the smile fading from her face as she stood and pulled the children to their feet. "I cannot promise," she said. "We must wait and see."

Wait for what? she asked herself. Her indenture to be sold? Life made too unbearable by Daniel? Oh! but now was not the time to think of such things. This was a time to find contentment from moment to moment. Moment to moment. That must be all.

Tears of happiness streamed down Daniel's face as he embraced his brother. He stood back to look at William, laughed with joy, and embraced him again.

"Where have you been? How did you find me?" he asked as he ran his sleeve across his eyes.

"You found me, brother," William answered. "A fellow Virginian returned from Mary's Land and looked into the court record of indentures. It seems that you sent him."

"Yes, yes, I did, but I had long given up hope there would be results." Daniel remembered Catherine, turned to introduce her, and saw that she had disappeared.

"The young woman went into the house," William said. "Your wife?"

"Someday, perhaps," Daniel said wistfully.

William chuckled. "I suspect therein lies a tale. Daniel, you look healthy, but your breeches and shirt are naught but rags. Is there a tale in this, also?"

"Too many to count." Daniel shook his head. "They seem very small at the moment. God's blessings, William, you are a grown man. It is a wonder to look upon you. And your breeches speak of greater prosperity than mine. But come. Let us get ale and food and take ourselves to that log yonder so we can talk." He closed his eyes and sighed. "I cannot believe it. I feared I would never see you again this side of the grave."

In the house Martha and the twins smiled at Daniel for the first time in days.

"Our uncle is a fine man, is he not father?" Jonathan said.

"Very fine," Daniel answered a little absently as he saw Catherine slip from the room.

Daniel and William carried their mugs and cornbread to the shade on the edge of the woods and settled down for a long session. William complimented Daniel on the freehold and the quality of his servants and then began to question the causes of his troubles. In fact, Daniel felt he was being pelted with questions, but the relief of talking to his brother once again, of receiving a sympathetic hearing, overrode all else.

He confided everything, the sabotage on his farm, the attack on Watkins and its outcome, the loss of his freehold, his lust for Mary, the consequent betrothal, the betrayal by both Mary and Hook. His words faltered as he described his unforgivable treatment of Catherine, and William began to pull words from him to learn what his true feelings were.

When he was finished, William shook his head sadly. "Ah, it is too bad, Daniel. It is a great shame that these things have befallen you. A terrible shame." He studied the ground at his feet for a moment and then spoke again.

"I would ask you to join me in Virginia, but despite my appearance, I am in much the same quandary. Perhaps you and I and our households could go off together to an altogether new place."

"The same quandary? Why, William?"

William rubbed his forehead in a gesture Daniel remembered well and shifted on the log. "I, too, have land I am like to lose," he said. "When the price of tobacco dropped, I prided myself that I had had the foresight to plant flax as well so that we Virginians could sell linen to you foolish men of Mary's Land, who depended on tobacco alone."

His eyes twinkled with humor, but for a moment Daniel felt only an old irk. His brother had bested him. Then he smiled at his own absurdity. "Yes, we fools," he said.

"Flax grows wild in Virginia, and it grows even better when you cultivate it, so while I was sorry to get so poor a price for the tobacco, I was reassured by my other crop until…

"Until?"

"Until a plague of grasshoppers descended on me and devoured it all."

"God in heaven!" Daniel exclaimed. "Were all the planters so plagued?"

"Satan in hell is more appropriate," William responded. "No, not all were so afflicted." Then he added wryly, "I was just one of the lucky ones. Both crops gone and debts piled to the sky. The only good that came of it was that with no crops to tend, I could come sooner to this land and find you."

"And did you leave a wife and children?"

"Dead of the fever, both of them." William's voice broke a little.

"When?" Daniel asked.

"A year ago."

"I am so sorry, William. Can you bear to talk to me about them?"

"Yes." William smiled a sad smile. "Jonathan was but two. Yes, he was Jonathan also, and he died within days of my wife Elizabeth. She was a good woman, Daniel, and fair, but not as lovely as your Catherine."

"Would that she were my Catherine," Daniel commented, remembering how unlovely she had been when he first saw her. "What malady took them?"

"It was the fever that takes so many. I have always suspected that the bite of the mosquito is the cause of that terrible yellow illness, but there are many theories as you know. No one is sure." William was quiet, swallowing several times before continuing.

"As for my holdings, I have been often too discouraged to care what becomes of them, but perhaps we could work together, you and I, in Mary's Land or Virginia. I could sell what is left to me to pay at least some of your debts, or you could return with your household to Virginia to work land there and hope for a better year."

Daniel rubbed his temples with the thumb and fingers of one hand. "You are as generous as ever, though I ask myself when either of us will be able to be generous with something other than our poverty. Let us think about what is to be done for a day or two, shall we?"

He put his hand on William's shoulder. "One thing is certain, whatever we decide, to be doing it together is better by far than to be doing it alone."

That evening, as the household prepared to sup, Catherine was introduced to William and truly looked at him for the first time. For a moment she was overwhelmed by his likeness to Daniel. This made her smile broadly until it occurred to her that such a display of enthusiasm was unwise.

She resolved to keep a sober face, but the resolution was soon broken as William teased the group about the shortcomings of the colony in Mary's Land and poked fun at those of Virginia. Catherine would find herself laughing merrily until she glanced at Daniel, only to see him watching her. Then, her merriment would fade briefly until William's good humor brought it forth again.

Daniel sat at the table fighting a stab of jealousy. He had seen Catherine's quick smile at his handsome brother. It had pierced him like the point of a knife and seemed to be working its way into his gut now as she laughed at William's joking. How quickly his joy at William's presence had taken on a layer of discomfort. But he must not let this unworthy feeling mar their reunion. Instead, he would redouble his efforts to win Catherine back. And if he lost her…? No, he would not even consider its likelihood.

Helping with the work and attempting to be cheerful, William remained with him for more than a few days. Catherine avoided Daniel with considerable skill, and when he did manage a word or two, her responses were so stiff and formal he found himself stumbling through the minimal conversation like a confused schoolboy.

On occasion, he became angry enough to wonder why he was allowing himself to be so tormented. Then, he would observe her quiet efficiency, hear her gentle voice, or glimpse the curves of her body as she went about her tasks, and the answer would be clear. All unknowing, she was going to continue to torment him thus, and he was going to be doomed to feel its sting.

On the Sabbath, Catherine approached Daniel as he sat talking to William. She hoped William's presence would encourage Daniel to grant the request she was afraid to make.

"I would like to visit Mary, today," she said.

His answer was immediate. "Yes, of course, as long as someone accompanies you."

"And who would that someone be?" she asked, regretting immediately her lack of civility. Was not the fact that he had said yes enough for her?

"It could be I or Edwin or Ezekiel," Daniel told her.

"I am not a prospect?" William asked politely.

"No," Daniel answered as though slamming a door shut.

Catherine looked at him with surprise and thought that William had as well. "Why must I take someone, Daniel? You all deserve a chance to rest on the Sabbath, and I have walked there alone before. I have walked all the way to St. Stephens alone.

"That you have done it before does not make it safe."

"I will ask Edwin," she said, giving in.

Catherine and Edwin trudged to Hook's estate. Approaching Hammet's house, she saw Eleanor in the doorway facing the road. Eleanor was bound to have seen the visitors, but when Catherine waved, there was no answering gesture. Instead, Eleanor went inside and closed the door.

"Her thoughts must have been elsewhere," Catherine commented to Edwin. "I will just knock to say good morning. I would not want her to think I have overlooked her."

She glanced at Edwin who was frowning and shaking his head. This confirmed a fear she was trying to overcome that her visit would be only trouble.

There was no response to her tap on the door, nor to her call, or to a firmer knocking.

"Have I offended her? Why will she not answer?" Catherine asked Edwin.

"It is more that ye will be offended, were I to judge," Edwin told her. "She will not want to face ye"

"Me offended?"

"No questions yet," Edwin suggested, "not 'til ye hev been to the big house."

"Yes, of course. I will wait and see," she answered absently. She guessed it would not take long to discover what was troubling Eleanor.

Discovery was swift as it turned out. They approached the back of the house through the kitchen garden, but instead of Phoebe, Josiah Hook himself appeared.

"What do you want?" he asked, both his manner and his voice abrupt, unwelcoming.

Catherine summoned her courage and tried to speak as though her request were perfectly ordinary. "I want to visit my sister."

"Well, you cannot," he answered. "She does not want to see you."

Catherine's hopes fell. "May I request that you inform her of my presence in case she would like to change her mind?"

"No, you may not. It will not be necessary," he almost snapped. "I bid you good day."

Catherine began to take deep breaths to hold back her dismay. Hook was pointing to the road over which they had come, and though she wanted to run past him toward the house and shout Mary's name, she could not quite muster the courage to do it. The best she could manage was a choked "What have either of you to fear from me?" before turning back toward Edwin, who had stood a short distance behind her.

"Now ye know," he said sympathetically as Hook strode back into the house.

"Yes, now I know." Catherine was shaking.

Edwin spoke no further. It was almost as though he knew words were useless to her now. Instead, as they approached the river, he led her to its edge and suggested she splash cool water on herself and then for a time sit in the shade of the trees that hovered over the bank.

"I must get to her somehow," she told Edwin. "I cannot walk away and do nothing. She was not angry with me when last I saw her. I do not believe she wishes to avoid me now."

"It is not likely," he agreed.

"Will you come with me again late enough that I can approach the house in darkness?"

"If Daniel say so," he answered.

Daniel would not allow her to visit again. She would ask, but he would not agree. She was as sure of that as she was that the sun would shine. She would have to go alone, sneaking away, leaving near dusk and returning at first light. And then she would just have to face Daniel's fury.

Chapter Eighteen

"No!" Daniel said firmly as he glared across the table over his breakfast ale. "You may not go. I will wager from all that has happened and from what Edwin has already told me that there is more evil afoot there than we know. You will endanger yourself. You must not do it."

Catherine knew Daniel's resistance came in part from his belief that Mary was beyond redemption, that whatever befell was richly deserved, but she persisted in her request. "That Hook would not allow me even to see her could mean she has come to harm. It frightens me…"

"As should another journey to the place."

Catherine felt choked with frustration. Daniel had been so kind these last few days, had made dangerous inroads into the shell she had built around her heart, but now his stubborn refusal to understand the anxiety that tormented her restored that shell quite adequately.

He could offer to go with her; he could take Edwin, Ezekiel, and William along as well and demand that Hook produce Mary. He could do for her what he might have done had his brother been in difficulty. But he did none of these things. He merely stood firm as a stone wall, an obstacle so overwhelming all else paled.

"She has brought this trouble on herself," Daniel added.

Catherine rose and began to remove the trenchers from the table. She did not care that it was in part Mary's doing. She knew what Daniel had refused to hear, that this was not entirely Mary's fault, that it came from the roots of evil forcibly planted in her, roots that must be weeded out like thistle from a garden.

Watching her move about the table, Daniel thought he had never seen her so forlorn. Losing Mary was so difficult for her to accept, but allowing her to place herself in peril was something he could not accept.

When he and William had left the table and walked out into the intense summer sunshine, William began to question him.

"Why should you not go with her, aside, of course, from the consideration that she does not want you?"

"You do not understand, William. I have described it all to you, but one would have to observe Mary's behavior to know that she is evil incarnate."

"Daniel! That is an exaggeration. You should be ashamed. You wish her to be evil. That excuses you to some degree from your wrongdoing." William's expression was stormy.

"I make no excuses, William. I am not ashamed to say it. It is no exaggeration." Daniel paused, envisioning Catherine's obvious love of her sister. "By the virgin, I want to hold Catherine and persuade her it is a cause lost and comfort her for her loss, but she cannot comprehend that Mary lacks completely the ability to love."

"I think she must see Mary again if she is to be satisfied it is in vain."

"A thought on which you and I will have to disagree," Daniel answered.

Chores from the evening meal were finished. Catherine made no excuses, told no lies. She just left the house through the shed and walked along the edge of the woods where she was not likely to be seen. As soon as she was out of sight of the freehold, she began to run and continued to do so until her breath came in gasps, and she had to stop. When her breathing returned almost to normal, she began to walk at a pace that was not quite a run.

She was exceedingly frightened, but there were three things she hoped for: that tonight's half moon would soon appear, that Hook would be in attendance at the meeting for the colony's major landholders, and that there would be no dogs about. She was not sure why the thought of dogs plagued her. She had seen none on her two previous visits, though she had heard them.

Occasionally, she was almost certain she heard someone on the path behind her, but when she stopped and turned, no one was there.

See, you are creating phantoms out of your fear. Hold true. Trust God, she whispered to herself as she came closer to the estate and concentrated on walking as softly as she could.

As she entered the kitchen garden, she heard only the bark of a dog in the distance. There was a dim light. Through an open window she could see Phoebe, and when she tapped on the window, Phoebe looked up and saw her, which brought an unreadable expression to her face. Opening the door, Phoebe came out and gestured to Catherine to follow her to the smokehouse again.

"Is she well, Phoebe?" Catherine asked in a whisper, once the two had gone into the acrid darkness and closed the door.

"If she ate, she would be better," Phoebe said. "She is full stricken that things are not as she hoped. I am glad ye hev come, but ye must not be found. The master is not above blows should she irk him."

Catherine sucked in her breath. "He beats her?"

"Not so much any more. She hev learned to mend her ways. It did not take long."

Catherine moaned softly as Phoebe opened the door. "I will hev her here soon as I can."

"Thank you, Phoebe. You risk a beating to help us, do you not?"

Phoebe chuckled softly. "It would not be the first of my life."

Her footfalls faded, and silence fell except for the sound of crickets and the occasional squawk of a chicken nearby. Catherine sat on the bench in the gloom feeling that she was revisiting a nightmare. Would Mary come back home with her? Would she have seen her error? Would she be battered? The time crawled by, and Catherine became increasingly agitated. She thought once she heard someone moving around outside, but then heard nothing further.

Finally, there were slow, soft footsteps along the path, the door opened, and Mary came in. Catherine moved to embrace her, but she pushed Catherine away as she gently closed the door and then leaned against it.

"Shh…" she cautioned unnecessarily.

"Mary, are you well treated?" Catherine whispered, already knowing the answer.

"If I do what I am told and make no error and submit to all that Josiah asks, I am well treated," Mary whispered back.

"Submit to what?"

"Things of the bedchamber," Mary whimpered. "You do not want to know about them." She laughed, a peculiar little laugh that had the sound of desperation. "And I was afraid of the marriage bed with Daniel. Oh, Catherine, you cannot imagine…"

"Mary, come away with me tonight," Catherine pleaded. "You do not have to stay."

"I tried to run away once, and he beat me. Oh, how he beat me, and he said if I did it again, he would shave my head and break both my legs." Mary's voice was rising so that Catherine needed to shush her.

"Oh, Catherine, why did I not listen? All that work, the heat of the fields, the miserable pallets to sleep on, as bad as it was, it was so much better than this."

"Mary, come. We will hide you. Daniel's brother William is here. He can take you to Virginia."

"No. I am afraid. He will catch me. I must go. She started to open the door, and then stopped and whispered. "One thing, though, something I heard. I want you to know. He told his agent that Daniel's brother was here, then said something strange. He said, 'Now there are two of them, both brothers together.' What difference could that make to Josiah?"

Mary then threw her arms around Catherine. "I love you, Catherine," she said. "I wish I had listened to you because you were right, but I love you." Then she was out the door, her footsteps fading away.

For a time Catherine felt too weak to move. She stood numbly, waiting to recover, if only a little, from the agony of what she had just heard. Then she opened the door, but just as she stepped out, she heard horses and barking, barking that became hair-raising growls. Confusion followed. Should she run for the woods to escape Hook or should she duck back into the smokehouse where the dogs could not get to her, but Hook could? Terror drove her to opt for tearing open the door and running. Almost immediately, something pushed her on the upper back, knocking her down. It happened so fast and so hard that her forehead hit the earth before she could get her hands out to break the fall, and as she scrambled to get up, the biggest dog she had ever seen lunged for her throat. She screamed and threw up her arm to protect herself, and its jaws sank into her arm.

Daniel wondered where William had gone as twilight forced him to leave the making of shingles. His brother's coming had given him enough new hope that he could not now make himself leave off the care for the freehold.

The twins came clamoring as he approached the house. "Hear our prayers tonight, Father," Jonathan requested.

"Well, yes, of course," he said, surprised that Catherine had not already done so. "Is Catherine too busy?"

"No, Father," Judith answered. "We do not know where she is."

Anxiety immediately began to gnaw at Daniel's stomach.

"Where is Catherine?" he asked Martha, but her answer was the same.

He gently disengaged Judith's hand from his own. "Wait, little elf. I will be back for your prayers in a little while."

Judith and Jonathan settled happily at the table to wait, and Daniel went to ask Edwin and Ezekiel, who had seen neither William nor Catherine for quite some time.

Daniel circled the buildings calling their names, and when there was no answer, anxiety became mixed with anger. He knew where they were. They were on their way to Hook's despite his wishes. He understood Catherine's need even though for her own safety he would never have honored it, but that William would take matters into his own hands and endanger both of them in such a manner was inexcusable.

He fetched a tinderbox and a chunk of wood, one end of which had been dipped in grease, to light the way when the moon disappeared, and then he tore off along the path in the direction of Hook's.

Chapter Nineteen

"Cerberus, down!" a stern voice commanded, and the dog let go, growling still, as though to let Catherine know he continued to be in command here.

There was suddenly the sound of additional footsteps as someone else brought a torch, and Catherine saw Hook and Wilken looming over her and then another man. William! She tried to overcome a wave of terrible weakness as she wondered what William was doing here. Was he in league with Hook?

He bent over to help her up, and then Mary was there crying her name.

"Catherine, oh my God! Catherine. The beast has bitten you!" She ran to Catherine and lifted her arm to examine it. When Catherine cried out with the pain, she saw Mary wince, her face distorted with anguish.

"It is the fate of a trespasser!" Hook didn't speak the words. He spat them. "What made you think you could come skulking around my home at night? Your sister is here of her own free will. You will have the courtesy to remember that."

He turned to William. "And you would be William Falconer, would you not? I ask the same courtesy of you."

"The lass would not have skulked had you the decency to allow a visit with her sister," he snapped. "Now, in the name of that decency, let us clean and bandage this bite, and it would not be too much for you to provide a cart that I might take her home."

Catherine felt herself swaying dizzily as the interchange continued.

"She will go the way she came," Hook snarled.

Mary went to him and put her hand on his shoulder. "Josiah, please," she begged.

"Please be damned!" He pushed aside her hand with vehemence and addressed William again. "You may take her to the kitchen to treat the bite and be quick about it. Then begone or I will set the dog on you both." He grasped Mary's wrist, though she tried to twist away, and dragged her fighting form behind him as he strode off.

"Let me stay to attend my sister!" The words bit into Catherine as the torchlight disappeared around a building. She could not make out Hook's reply, but she could hear the cruelty of the tone.

Phoebe was outlined by the light behind her at the kitchen door. Catherine could have walked unaided to that door, but she was grateful for William's support because the dizziness had not left her, and the pain in her arm had just intensified. He guided her into the room where Phoebe exclaimed over the depth of the bites as she cut the torn sleeve away, mopped blood, and washed the wounds.

"It is good that it bleeds, fer the blood will be cleansing," she said as she applied a greasy salve that looked terrible and smelled worse and then covered it all with strips of cloth. Catherine had meant to ask her what the salve was, but after she had looked closely at the cuts on her arm, she could no longer remember what the question was.

As Catherine accepted a tea that Phoebe said would help the pain, she could see that the woman looked distracted. "Ye cannot walk home tonight. Yer face be fish-belly white," Phoebe said. "Ye need to rest."

"Phoebe, I must," Catherine said. "William will help me." She glanced at William, who looked none too sure of the wisdom of a journey. Neither was she, come to that. Mary's suffering, the terror, the pain of the bite, her aching head from the fall, her helplessness; all had combined to wipe away her strength.

"She is right," William said. "We cannot stay here. We will get back if I must carry her."

"But ye must let her rest," Phoebe insisted. "If only fer a small time."

"Yes," William agreed. "Catherine I want you to lie on the table until your color returns."

Catherine let herself be grateful that she could do so. William lifted her until she sat on the edge of the table, and she swung her feet around and lay back on its scrubbed surface, a mound of fabric Phoebe had provided under her head. She closed her eyes, but the nightmare of what had happened kept intruding on the rest she might have gotten. She found herself moving about restlessly. Once, she even caught herself muttering aloud.

She was aware of William's pacing and of a bell that seemed at intervals to summon Phoebe away from the scullery. Presently, William's footsteps came to a stop beside the table.

"You are not rosy, Catherine, but you are less pale than you were. We must go now."

Catherine pushed herself up gingerly and stepped down from the table. William steadied her until she could feel herself walking normally, and Phoebe hovered anxiously over her, fastening a sling and explaining that there would be less pain that way.

Catherine was filled with gratitude. "Thank you Phoebe, for such kindness," she said. "I will help Mary. Right now I do not quite know how, but I will help her."

Phoebe kissed her lightly on the cheek. "The Lord go with ye," she said. "I do what I can fer Mary, but it isn't much as things are now."

Catherine had to put those last words from her mind so that she could begin the journey before her will deserted her. It was good that William held her right arm and that her left was in the sling as they walked too slowly by far.

Catherine saw with dismay that the moon was sinking fast toward the horizon and then found her thoughts careening from one fear to another. Her throbbing arm made her worry that if the dog was mad, she would die.

"Cerberus," she said aloud. "What a strange name."

"It was the three-headed dog the old Greeks said guarded the gates of hell," William reminded her.

"How fitting," Catherine commented. "It is like Hook has deliberately created hell right here in Mary's Land."

"Daniel seems to know that," William said. "He has tried to keep you safely away from it."

"Did he send you after me?"

"Send me!" He laughed. "More like he will wring my neck that I did not stop you. You see, Catherine, I followed you to try to protect you."

"To stop me would have been the only possible protection in Daniel's eyes." Catherine winced as she stepped into a depression in the path, and the jarring of her body sent a bolt of pain through both her arm and her head. William steadied her again.

"So, why did you not merely prevent my leaving?" she persisted.

"Were I in such a situation as yours, Catherine, I would move heaven and earth to help my brother. I would simply wait until I could slip away." He stopped talking as they came to a fork in the path, and Catherine pointed the way. Then he resumed. "It was a thing I knew you must do, that the best I could offer was to try to keep you safe, though I have certainly not been successful."

"I think I heard you several times. You frightened me."

As he was apologizing, Catherine realized her footsteps were slowing, her strength waning, and she wondered what would happen if she could not make it back. William had a knife at his waist, but what protection would that be against man or beast in the full dark. The dank odor of decay in the woods suddenly spoke to her of further evil.

William slipped his arm about her waist, and there was strength in it.

"Was your visit of benefit to either of you?" he asked.

"No, none. He beats her, William." She could hear the note of desperation in her own voice, a desperation made worse for stating the awful fact aloud.

"I am not surprised. He is obviously a cruel man."

"She is afraid to come away because he has threatened her," Catherine said weakly. After those words, her legs refused to support her any longer. She pitched forward and would have fallen had William not caught her.

The question about what would occur if her strength drained completely away was answered because he picked her up and carried her along the shadowy path while the moon hovered briefly just above the horizon, then sank below it. Complete darkness was almost upon them.

He spoke no more. Catherine knew he was putting all his strength into carrying her. It was too bad she was not the walking pile of bones she had been when she first arrived in Mary's Land.

Presently, he asked if she thought she could walk a little, and on receiving a mumbled "yes", put her down.

The arm throbbed whether she walked or was carried, and she began to be tormented by the thought that Daniel would be angry with his brother. William had come to her rescue, but there would be the devil to pay. And now that she knew the worst about Mary, she was powerless to change it.

Do not fret so, she told herself. *Throw all that you have into getting home. Worry then, though it will do no good.*

She stumbled again, and again William swept her up. "Someone is coming," he said.

Catherine looked down the path and saw a torch moving closer.

"Who comes?" William called.

"It is a man who will no longer claim you for brother, you damnable sneak. What gall to disregard my wishes so blatantly, so…"

Torchlight shone in Catherine's eyes.

"God's blood, what happened?" Daniel's question ended on a croak.

"Hook's dog bit her, she hit her head, and she is quite weak." William eased her down for the second time, but her knees buckled. She was aware of the light falling away as Daniel caught her and laid her gently on the ground.

"Foolish woman! What have you done to yourself?" Strangely, there was no anger in his voice. Instead, he knelt in the light of the torch William was now holding, and pushed her hair away from her eyes as she tried to speak.

"I had to see Mary. Hook beats her."

Daniel closed his eyes as though the thought pained him, but his concern did not seem to be for Mary.

"And now that you know, you will suffer a thousand agonies," he said. "And you accompanied her on this mad errand," he accused William.

"I followed to assure her safety."

"May you never be responsible for *my* safety," Daniel snapped.

"Brother, we will speak more of these things later," William said calmly. "It is God's mercy that you have come with light. Allow me to carry the torch while you carry Catherine, and we will exchange tasks when it is necessary."

"Yes," Daniel agreed as he slipped an arm behind her back to lift her to her feet. Ignoring the desire to crush her against his chest and to hold her thus, he lifted her into his arms. He had not held her in this way since her arrival, he reflected. Now the circumstances were chilling.

The rest of the journey was silent. Daniel knew that to talk to William would have been to argue, to disturb Catherine, and to sap his strength. It was good that William carried the torch just a few steps ahead. It left Daniel free to test Catherine for fever by kissing her forehead and then, since that was so satisfactory, to kiss a closed eye, which opened immediately in response, and then a smooth cheek. He was about to get to her lips when she murmured, "No, Daniel," and turned her face into his chest so that he had to be content with an ear.

William stopped walking. "You are slowing, Daniel. Shall I take her?"

But she was a precious bundle he was not going to relinquish. "I am fine," he answered.

Carrying Catherine seemed to lend him the strength he needed to get home where he found Martha, as he might have expected, sitting by a tiny glow of coals in the fireplace, waiting. A guarded cry that would not wake the children was her only sound on seeing Catherine.

"I will be fine, Martha," Catherine assured her. "I am just a little weak for now."

"Hook's dog bit her," Daniel explained as he laid her down on his bed, suppressing an absurd desire to lie beside her and thus to continue to hold her.

161

"What can I do?" Martha asked.

"Let her sleep, I think." Daniel answered.

"A kind woman at Hook's attended the bite," William said.

"That would be Phoebe." Martha ran the back of her hand along Catherine's cheek. "Will the arm be of use again?"

"It was an ugly wound, but she had no trouble moving her arm," William said. "There is only the danger of..." He stopped. The term "mad dog" was a silent specter in the room.

"Go to bed, Martha. I will stay with her tonight," Daniel said, "and William and I will have a talk."

When Catherine had fallen asleep, William followed Daniel to the wood stumps just outside the door where they would be able to hear Catherine if she called. Daniel felt his anger to be softened somewhat, but it was still there.

As he settled himself on the stump, he said, "Well brother, explain yourself. Why did you ignore my wishes in the matter?"

"Tell me, Daniel. If I were in trouble, and you were told you could not go to my aid, what would you do?"

"Go anyway, but you damnable fool, I am a man..."

William interrupted him. "And if you were stopped in your attempt, what would you do?"

"That is beside the point."

"That is very much the point. You would try again and yet again, would you not unless perhaps you were chained to a tree?"

"Do not..."

"Of course, when I saw her steal away, I could have stopped her, it is true."

"And should have because..."

"I did not stop her because she had to go, and I did not fetch you because you would not have allowed it."

"You are very right about that. And now you have seen why I would not."

By now, both men were facing full front, neither looking at the other. Daniel was hunched forward, his hands across the back of his neck. He could almost feel William lounging comfortably and smugly beside him. There was in his speaking the tone of one who held the high moral ground. It was infuriating.

"I swear, William, if she dies of the bite, I will kill you."

William ignored those last words. "And I have seen things you were wrong about," he continued.

Daniel jumped up and faced the dark seated figure that was his brother. "Damn you, William," he hissed. "You have been here but a few days and already you know everything. You were ever thus. It is not enough that Catherine looks on you with great favor while she has nothing but disdain for me." He realized he was raising his voice and strove to lower it again and to rid himself of the jealousy that had just led him to such petty speech. "Now you have interfered with affairs you know nothing about."

"Listen to me, brother." William was leaning forward now, the calm reasonableness gone from his speech. "I saw that girl fleetingly in torchlight, but still long enough to know she is enchantingly beautiful. I now fully understand why you were so affected."

"That is a pointless observation!" Daniel snapped.

"But I tell you something you have not seen. She was distraught about Catherine. Despite what you say, I know she is capable of caring for at least one other. That was most clear tonight."

"She is such an actress she could take a London stage by storm. I tell you again, you have not seen what the girl is capable of. Trouble follows her like a hound behind a bitch in heat."

"An interesting comparison. I cannot argue further on that score, Daniel." William stood and stretched. "But I can tell you this. The man Hook is a monster. You have got to get the girl back, if not for her sake, then for Catherine's. Catherine will have no peace while her sister is so abused, and she will never trust you unless you help her to help Mary.

He then astounded Daniel by chuckling and saying, "Besides, I would like to feast my eyes on her again. I am going to sleep now, and I want you to think about this. Mary is, after all, your servant. You bought her indenture. If you want Catherine to accept what she must and to renew her friendship with you, go to whoever enforces the laws in this colony and demand that your servant Mary be returned to you. Good night, Daniel."

Daniel could not find any words to answer his brother, who was walking toward the quarters he would share tonight with Ezekiel and Edwin. Daniel went back into the house and gazed with longing on Catherine, then lay upon a pallet Martha had placed on the table. For a long time he stared at the faint coals in the fireplace.

Catherine awoke with the memory of Daniel's kisses, but when she moved, pain shot through her arm. Her head throbbed, and she remembered the dog,

Hook's cruelty, and Mary's hopeless resignation.

She closed her eyes, wanting to shut it all out, but neither agony of mind nor of body would go away.

Martha brought her a tea brewed of lemon balm to help with the pain, and Catherine sipped it gratefully as she looked for the first time at the sun and shadow through the window.

"Oh, it is late in the morning," she said with dismay. I lie abed and cause extra work for you when I should be helping.

"Ye will help soon enough. Rest 'til yer body tells ye it is time to be movin' about."

Catherine laughed ruefully. "It tells me at this moment it will be never."

"Well, then, do I know ye, Catherine, as I think I do, soon yer mind and yer body will hev a fight. Yer mind will win, and ye will be at yer tasks full hard." Martha squinted and peered out the window. "Daniel and William hev gone to town, but I see no sign of them yet. I hev water fer yer washin' if ye want it."

The luxury of a bath was the signal to Catherine's body to move. Gingerly, she sat up and watched while Martha scooped the water from the bucket and then unwrapped her arm. Scabs had formed around the bites, but no telltale red streaks warned of danger. Not for now, at any rate. The mad dog danger still lurked, but whether she had escaped such a horror would not be known for some time yet.

Water soothed her face and her skin and brought for an instant a feeling that life was good until she looked at the bites on her arm and was reminded again of Mary's peril, as though she could forget it for very long.

In a short time, bandaged and clothed, feeling freshened, she pulled her skirt above her knees and bent over to buckle her shoes. This, however, caused a sharp pain to pierce her head, and she sat up a little too quickly, which made it worse. Putting her hands to her temples, she sat perfectly still, waiting for it to pass.

The door darkened, and she saw Daniel standing there with an odd expression on his face.

"Your head still pains you," he observed.

"A little. It was sharp just now," Catherine told him, "but it will be better shortly."

Daniel glanced down at her legs, which she realized were exposed, so she quickly pushed her skirt down.

He knelt before her and pushed the skirt back up a little. Startled, she straightened and tried to move back, but he sucked in his breath as he took hold of her ankle and ran a finger along one of the long scars on her leg.

"Who did this?" he asked.

"It was Goody Menton's punishment for stealing food for Mary," she answered as she attempted to pull her ankle away.

He tightened his hold. "We have both paid a heavy price for the luxury of eating," he muttered, "you with scars and I with prison."

Catherine tugged again.

"Wait, Catherine," he said. " I am only going to fasten your shoe, or what is left of it after your many walks."

Briefly, all else paled as those simple touches, his fingers on her scar, his hand on her ankle, sent warmth coursing through her, but she fought for a return of her good sense and struggled once more to move away from him. He only intensified the warmth with a firm hand on her other ankle as he buckled that shoe also and grumbled, "I hope the hottest spot in hell is reserved for the woman who made these scars.

"Thank you for securing my shoes," Catherine said weakly, trying unsuccessfully not to smile.

Daniel's face took on a still more serious expression. "Catherine, I have disappointing news," he said.

She wondered how things could be more disappointing than they were now.

"I have been to town to demand the return of my servant, Mary."

Catherine's hand flew to her chest. She knew she was gaping at Daniel in surprise. He would allow Mary to come back, had indeed attempted to secure her? The realization brought tears to her eyes, but she couldn't speak. What was the disappointing news, she wondered.

"Hook has paid the court her indenture price to be placed in reduction of my debt. The good burgher did not see fit to ask my permission. It is a fact accomplished, and I have been reminded that I have no claim on her now. If I wish to dispute the decision, I must wait until the full court meets, and that will not be for weeks yet.

It had not occurred to Catherine that securing Mary's return as an indentured servant was even possible, so why now did the failure of the attempt cut so deeply? She struggled with that question until she saw that Daniel stood expectantly before her.

"I am most grateful that you tried," she said.

William spoke for the first time. "The problem now is that should we try to get her away, Daniel will be breaking the law again."

Daniel laughed with that brief chortle Catherine had come to recognize as a sign he felt trapped by something absurd. "Why should that matter?" he said. "What more can they take from me?"

"Your freedom," William suggested.

"Yes," Daniel said. "I could be made an example of someone who does constant harm to others because of my monstrous ill will." He shook his head, Catherine thought perhaps to clear it of self-pity.

"Catherine," he said, his tone gentle now. "It has just occurred to me that you and your shoes are ready to move about, to complete your chores, I would wager. Please, do not do that yet. You still look pale, and I can see that you have quite a bit of pain. Do not do anything more strenuous than lessons with the children, not today. Will you promise me that?"

"I promise," she said, knowing full well she would not have been able to do much more anyway and wondering if it would be safe to trust this new Daniel, who seemed so concerned for her welfare.

Be cautious, a little disturbance deep within warned her as she watched him leave the room. *Already you thirst for more of the sweet nectar of his touch and his attention. He will only disappoint you.*

She remembered Martha's presence and glanced around. A whisper of a smile played about Martha's lips.

William was chuckling as he accompanied Daniel back to the barn. "Yes," he said, as if in answer to what Daniel was thinking. "She does indeed have handsome legs despite the scars. You will see them all afternoon as you work."

"You know me too well," Daniel answered. "I will see her smile, too, only a hint, but still a smile."

Chapter Twenty

As the days went by, and she was no longer troubled with headaches, Catherine watched the wounds on her arm diminish. There would probably always be scars, but they would be small, insignificant, really, compared to the scars of Mary's folly and her own mistrust of Daniel. Oh, he was trying, she told herself. He was kindness itself, and she was so tempted to succumb to it, but the memory of his terrible harshness held her back. And when she felt driven to explain the truth about Mary's wanton ways, that same memory locked the words within her throat.

Today, she stood in the doorway watching the wind bend the plants in the fields almost double and whip the branches in the tops of the trees. Dark clouds scudded across the sky. She had never seen weather appear so threatening.

In the distance she could make out a horse-drawn cart approaching. So fast was it moving that its driver seemed to leave the seat with every bump. As it came closer, she could see that the driver was Phoebe, and was astonished that the woman should be here in what had to be Hook's cart. Moreover, Phoebe's inexperience with the horse was becoming painfully obvious.

"Stop, you son of Satan," she was shouting as she jerked back on the reins so hard that the animal whinnied and tried to bolt against the unaccustomed assault on his mouth. He came to a stop just past the house, and Catherine ran to help as Phoebe half jumped, half fell from the cart.

"What are you about?" Catherine asked as Phoebe stood holding her stomach and panting.

"It is Mary," Phoebe answered. "He hev broke her leg, maybe both, and she is sore battered..."

"Dear God, take me back with you," Catherine wailed, her worst fears realized.

"I can't. Hook will make me dog meat do I not return afore he does. Phoebe doubled over for a minute, then straightened with a grimace and continued. "She is not at Hook's. That devil was going to leave her to lie in the dirt, but Eleanor and me, we hitched the horse and lifted her into the cart. She would not come here, said Daniel would ne'er allow it."

Catherine found herself shaking. "But, Phoebe, why did you not bring her here just the same?"

Phoebe closed her eyes and shook her head. "She was full piteous when she begged me to take her to the Indian hut in the woods and then fetch you, and oh Catherine! I hev to get back fast. There be beatings, and then there be worse." She heaved herself back into the cart, and slapped the reins over the horse's back to set him moving.

Catherine's gorge rose, and she had to pause to relieve herself of breakfast, another of her infernal weaknesses, before she could run calling for Daniel or William. When no one responded, she told Martha where she was going and why and asked to have Daniel follow with mule and cart, though she was not a bit certain he would do so.

She was too full of fear for Mary to listen to Martha's pleas to wait, so Martha quickly gave her clean cloths, a cup, and a bag of cornbread. Catherine filled a hempen bag with water, slung it on a rope over her shoulder, and half ran, half walked to the path along the river and into the woods, a route she had traveled twice before and so was certain of the way.

If only the sky were not darkening like an evil spirit. The wind was howling in the treetops, and once Catherine heard an enormous crack, followed by a thud, and she knew a big tree had fallen. She found herself moving faster and faster, and when she entered the Indian hut, she almost dropped to the ground, spent and helpless.

But Mary was a whimpering heap, and despite the dimness of the dwelling, Catherine could see gashes about her face and streaks of blood. Both eyes were swollen and black, her nose crooked, and her lips so cut and bruised, she could scarce open them. Catherine also saw that one foot was turned awkwardly to the side, a result, no doubt, of the broken leg that Hook had promised should she run away.

"Oh God! Mary, what has he done?" Catherine cried as she knelt beside her sister, horror, fear, and rage at Hook battling for supremacy in her head.

"Catherine," Mary was croaking. "You have come." The words were spoken past closed lips. It was obviously painful for Mary to speak through a mouth so damaged. Catherine wondered if she had lost teeth from that beautiful mouth. Then she chided herself. To worry about teeth! What foolishness! It was Mary's life that was the worry.

"You have come," Mary said again. "Now I know there is a God." She closed her eyes as Catherine looked down on her. "There is a God," she repeated.

Where to start? Reassuring her? Bathing her face? Straightening her leg? Creating a mound for a pillow? Catherine wished she had brought her cloak, for Mary was shivering.

"Water," Mary moaned, and Catherine reached for the bag, poured water into the cup, and held it to Mary's lips. Most of the water ran down her chin, but she got a little. Then Catherine set about gently stroking the gashes on her face with a wet cloth.

"No," Mary objected hoarsely. "It hurts."

"Mary, I must," Catherine insisted, wishing she had Martha's healing plants. "To keep the fester away. That could kill you."

"I am already dying," Mary said, though those swollen lips barely moved. "Let me be."

Catherine paused, so shaken by such words that she was momentarily unable to move. Mary began talking again, and Catherine took her hand and leaned forward to hear her.

"Do you think hell will be as hot as the tobacco fields?" she asked.

"Mary, do not talk so," Catherine began.

"I will burn there, Catherine. I am an adulteress and not even a very good one. Josiah said I learned to seduce, but not what came after. Had I known, I would have seduced no one." A tear ran from beneath the distorted eyelid. "A small square of earth will be my own private Mary's Land."

Mary doomed to die? Catherine's terror was as intense as the damnable wind. She squeezed Mary's hand until Mary winced and pulled it away. *What is she dying of,* Catherine asked herself finally, as her own body recovered somewhat from the shock of the words.

She began to poke gently about Mary's ribs and stomach, asking with each prod, "Does that hurt?"

"No," Mary would answer each time. Finally, she said, "Stop, Catherine. It is my head and my face and my leg that hurt. Oh! it is my leg that is killing me."

"Then you are not going to die any time soon, and you can change your ways so that you are not doomed to hell when you do," Catherine told her, relief tinged with surprising irritation at the unnecessary fright. "Now be still and let me wash your face."

Catherine decided she would look to the injured leg next, but feared she had not enough skill to do what should be done. Moreover, she was beginning to be very aware of the wind, which was surely getting worse if that were possible. She heard the crack of another tree, but no resulting thud, and worried about what that might mean.

Daniel and William came in from the tobacco fields panting from their exertion.

"God's wounds, I have never known such winds," William groaned.

"It will flatten the tobacco! Ruin it! It will blow the roof from the house and uproot the trees!" Daniel threw himself upon the bench and clutched his head in both hands. "It is the final straw. No crop at all. We will go to Virginia and hope for better there."

"The crop may yet be spared," William encouraged. "We must wait and see."

The wind slammed the door behind Martha as she came in with a basket of eggs, her face gray and drawn.

It occurred to Daniel that in such a tempest, there was more than the crop to concern him. Where was Catherine? Where were the children?

"The twins be holding each other in the loft. They be that frighted. It is where I will go now, but Daniel," and here her voice broke. "Catherine hev gone to be with Mary at the Indian hut."

"What!?" Daniel jumped from the bench and advanced on Martha as though he meant harm. "In God's name, why?"

Martha backed away. "Hook hev beat her bad, and Phoebe took her there and came for Catherine."

"Why not here?" Daniel realized he was shouting at Martha in his consternation. "Why, Martha?" he said more quietly.

"Mary be frighted to come here."

Daniel stood briefly, running his hand through his hair, trying to get his breath back and to deal with the thought that Mary had finally gotten what she deserved, but that she had put Catherine in danger again.

"I must go for them," he said. "I must take the cart. Martha, get the children and their pallets downstairs while this wind lasts and bring down a pallet and other bedding for the cart. William, get brandy and meal and fruit. I will hitch Maxim." He could feel his hands shaking as though affected by the gust of wind that had just torn by.

As Ezekiel placed an axe in the wagon, he advised Daniel to wait until the storm was over, but Daniel paid no heed. William met him at the door of the house with the required items and several others he had thought of such as the tinderbox and a torch. Martha and the children loaded the bedding into the cart along with two small bags of dried herbs.

"This dark bag be for pain, this light one to clean open skin," she said. "Boil the water."

Hoping he would remember which was which, Daniel secured it and threw a hempen cover atop the cart, lashing it down. Then, he took the reins and walked on one side of the mule while William walked on the other, trying to keep the animal moving.

"William, you do not have to come," Daniel said. "Stay and look after the children."

"Ezekiel and Edwin are here," William answered. "You need me more." William failed to mention his desire to help Mary.

They traveled as fast as they could, but at many spots, small trees lay across the road so that they had to lift and chop their way through. Branches flew through the air, sometimes slapping into them, and larger ones seemed to fall all around them.

"A tree will fall on the hut," Daniel moaned. "Catherine will be killed. You see?" he shouted to William over the din. "Wherever Mary is, there is naught but trouble."

But William did not answer. He had lowered his head against the flying matter and was plunging silently ahead.

Catherine listened as rain began to fall. She hoped the thatch would not leak too badly. It was not thick like English thatch, and now was the time to tackle Mary's leg, a task harrowing enough without attempting it while being soaked by rain.

Gingerly, she pulled up Mary's skirt and gently ran her hand up and down the leg. She remembered that sometimes a jagged bone thrusts out through the skin and was reassured to find that here none did. She could see, however, that halfway down, Mary's lower leg veered oddly off to the side. This was the break, and you should pull the leg straight and tie it to something flat so that it healed straight. The thought of putting Mary through such pain was daunting, but she would have to do it.

First, she put off the evil moment by tearing strips from the cloth Martha had given her. Then, she approached the door to decide in which direction she would find the most likely piece of wood. Before exiting, however, she turned around because Mary had begun to moan loudly.

In that instant she collided with someone and had opened her mouth to cry out in fear when she saw that the someone was Daniel. Before she knew it, he had pulled her back away from the door into the hut and thrown his arms around her muttering, "Thank God. You are safe."

Briefly, her world shifted. She felt an enormous relief and a sense of well being that had nothing to do with the predicament in which all three now found themselves. No. All four. William was there too.

Daniel looked down at her and brushed wisps of hair from her forehead. "You were leaving the hut. Where on earth were you going in this storm?" he asked.

"To find something flat for Mary's broken leg," she told him.

"No!" she heard Mary's voice, shrill with fear. "It is Daniel! He will beat me!"

"Mary, I have come to help you," Daniel said, and Catherine saw William look sidewise at him as though it were not quite true. *It was me he came to help*, she told herself with a small thrust of joy that was ridiculously inappropriate just now.

William began to carry things through the door, and Catherine realized that they two had brought the cart.

Daniel approached Mary, who seemed to be trying not to moan so uncontrollably now that the men were present. "Let me look at the leg," he said, "and I will get what is needed." He looked down on her face and then knelt beside her. "Dear God," he said.

Tears slid down her face again.

He reached down and ran his fingers along her nose, though she tried to turn her head away. Then he grasped her by the chin, and Catherine was astonished to see him push on her nose. Her scream would have waked the dead.

"I am sorry," he said as the noise died. Had I not done that, you would have been as crook-nosed as I."

She shrieked anew as he pried open her mouth. "Some teeth loose, but all there," he announced, rather lightly, Catherine thought.

He held a hand over one eye and pried the other open. "Can you see me?" he asked.

"Yes."

"That eye good. He covered it. Let us test the other." "See me still?"

"Yes."

"That eye good, too. Now let us see to the leg."

"No, do not touch it!"

Daniel did not touch it; he just looked. It was already uncovered.

"Good leg," he said. "It will be good again." Then the airy tone he had been using disappeared, and he said kindly, "But we must fix it first, Mary. We can make it right, but you must let us."

"No! No!" she cried.

"Catherine, give her some brandy while William finds suitable wood and splits it. I see you have cloth strips torn already."

Catherine did not know when she had felt as relieved as she was now to have Daniel with her and seemingly so knowledgeable about what to do. She wondered how he had learned so much.

The brandy obviously burned Mary's torn mouth, but she drank it as carefully as she could, trying not to lose any of it. She understood, Catherine thought, that it would ease the pain when Daniel attempted to straighten the leg.

"We will lift her forward a little," he said. "So that William can sit behind her and grasp her."

"No, you cannot," Mary hissed between those terrible lips.

"We can. We must," Daniel said. "We cannot leave here in the storm, and we do not know how long it will last. I have never seen its like. Your leg cannot wait. Besides, it will pain you less if it has been decently tended when we take you home."

"I have no home," she whispered bitterly.

"Of course you have," he said. "With me and with Catherine."

Catherine was beginning to fear that she must be dreaming. He had been so hideously angry, and now he was taking care of Mary and would have her back.

William returned with a slab of wood. He was dripping rainwater, his clothes plastered to his body in sodden swaths. "I will split this here just inside the doorway," he announced. "I cannot even see to work in that rain. Turn your heads away and protect Mary from flying wood chips."

His request obeyed, he soon produced a slab with two flat surfaces.

"Excellent," Daniel said. "Just what is required. Now, William, that was the easy part. As soon as the brandy has had time to do its work, I want you to help me lift Mary forward while Catherine places the pallet beneath her. Then, sit behind her with her head between your legs, put your arms beneath

173

hers, and hold her secure so she cannot move. Catherine, you will hold her other leg and attempt thereby to keep her in place."

A little later, when Daniel's instructions had been followed, William and Catherine sat holding Mary as tightly as they could while Daniel pulled on the leg, then pressed along the bone with his fingers to ensure that its ends were realigned.

Catherine almost sobbed aloud at Mary's pain because she was shrieking heart-rendingly. She was also cursing with vile language as bad as any Catherine had heard on the ship.

Gradually, the shouts quieted, and Daniel's hands were still, the task accomplished.

"Good girl," Daniel said to Mary, and Catherine choked. "Good girl," he had said even after the filth that had spewed from her mouth.

"What she said..." Catherine began.

"She sounds like she heard it in the taverns of Bristol," William finished for her.

Catherine pictured Mary in Goody Menton's tavern at the inn, waiting night after night on rough men as well as gentlemen, and knew that William had been uncannily accurate.

"Do not worry about those words," William continued. "It means merely that she has been exposed to them and calls on them in her pain. They do not make her a bad person." He chuckled. "As long as she does not speak them day after day. I have known..."

But his words were interrupted by a blast of wind that ripped the thatching from the roof and sent a torrent of water pouring over them.

"It is like a waterfall," William shouted over the din of wind and water.

Daniel grabbed the hempen cloth Catherine had seen him use many times to cover the cart. Silently, as though with one mind, she and William took edges of the sturdy fabric and pulled it over the little group, who huddled beneath it, making a circle of sorts around Mary and sitting on its edges to anchor it because nothing else would work to keep the wind from whipping it away. Most of the rain, though not all, ran down their improvised covering until the water they were sitting in was as deep as a hand.

Catherine envisioned the hut filling with water and drowning them all, but quickly saw that as absurd. What was truly possible was that trees would come crashing down on them or that the remaining thatch and framework of the hut would be blown away. She shivered, realizing how cold she had become.

She looked at Mary, and saw that though water lapped at the pallet, her head lay above it on William's leg. She was asleep after all that brandy and pain and fear. Catherine knew Mary was not yet finished with pain and wished she had at the very least something dry with which to cover her and keep her warm, but everything was soaked, the pallet and bedding Daniel had had the foresight to bring, and all their clothing.

Daniel reached across Mary's leg and took Catherine's hand in his, and it warmed her so much her shivering subsided somewhat, so she let it stay.

How like her, Daniel thought. *She braved the storm to get to her sister, assisted with fortitude in working on the leg, and now she shakes with the cold, yet never a word of complaint.* Her hand in his was like a talisman promising that they would return safely, and that she would yet be his.

Chapter Twenty-one

The storm raged on and on. Night came and deepened, and still the wind howled; the rain fell.

Daniel was aware that Mary was the only one not cramped. The others had to remain sitting because that was all there was room to do if they were to keep Mary covered and prevent the cloth from flapping about wildly, admitting the relentless rain.

He heard the cracking of trees and felt that his back was about to crack as well. He was certain Catherine and William suffered the same agony.

Catherine began to speak. "Where did you learn to care so well for the injured?" she whispered.

"I had to care for my mother," he told her. "That was one way to learn, but I also found myself caring for injuries in Mary's Land. You see, I do not know the healing plants as does Martha, but once every full moon the master who bought my indenture would declare himself a brandy holiday and drink until his brain was sodden. Then, he would fight everything that moved, myself included, until he dropped, dead drunk. You can break large numbers of bones in four years. In fact, it is why my own nose is misplaced."

"He must have been a very poor farmer," Catherine commented.

"He was a very rich farmer, much like Hook in that regard. Others did the work."

Catherine laughed. "And would you like to be so rich some day that others do your work?"

"Do you not know me better than that?" he teased. "Without work I would become a malcontent, as I suspect you would yourself."

Catherine chuckled. "It is true. I would. And I do not think you could give over control of the work to another."

"I would say you know Daniel only too well, Catherine," William commented wryly.

The group fell into a silent tension. Daniel imagined all were trying to ignore their discomfort. He became aware that Mary had begun to stir, to moan and fuss, and he remembered the herbs Martha had given him, but had no idea where they were now. Nor could anyone have used them; there was no way to boil water.

Presently, Mary began to talk without sense. Once she said, "Ah Catherine, I am so sorry. You are here in hell with me." Another time: "Goody Menton, look, I have it. I have the ring. Was I not good?" The trouble came when she sat up suddenly and gasped, "No, Daniel. Do not make me. 'Tis terrible…terrible."

Catherine, who had just reached for Daniel's hand again, withdrew it, to Daniel's great dismay. He had never made Mary do anything but work. What did William and Catherine think now? The suggestion of ill treatment or worse lingered over the huddled group, and he did not know what to say that would make them believe otherwise. Later, William might listen, but Catherine would not, and these words had to come just when she was softening to him. He found himself wishing he could vent his frustration with the language Mary had used.

A feeling of helplessness grew as he began to think again about the great measure of ill will from Hook, evil that had almost brought this household to a standstill. Daniel considered again the missing mule that had appeared in Hook's pasture, the obvious incitement to a duel over Mary, the injury first to Catherine and then to Mary, a second incitement to duel. Hook's seduction of Mary might have been blamed on passion. Daniel could certainly understand that, though not the way the seduction had been carried out. But the latest crimes far exceeded mere response to passion. They were the acts of a sick, cruel man.

Had he been blaming the wrong person all along for the earlier property destruction, Daniel asked himself. Was Watkins innocent of wrongdoing? Daniel could not imagine why Hook might be the single villain, but he allowed his suspicion that this was so to form. And if it were Hook behind it all, how pleased he must have been about the attack on Watkins. Daniel pressed his eyes shut, reviewing in his mind every contact with Hook and with Hammet. He recalled that Hammet had paid him no attention whatsoever and then suddenly become friendly, wanting to see the progress of the freehold. It had seemed odd at the time, and now it seemed even more so.

What had they talked about? His damaged fencing, Daniel remembered…and…God's wounds, he had told the man the deed had been done far from the place where Watkins' land met his…and the next attack had come at the place where Watkins' land indeed adjoined his own.

It is nonsense, Daniel told himself. *It is but chance, and I try to make a tale of it.* But the suspicion lingered and tormented him until gray dawn arrived along with slowing rain and dying wind.

Carefully, Catherine pushed the canvas up. Daniel could see she was trying to make the water lying on it slide away from Mary. The attempt was at least partially successful.

Daniel stood and stretched to ease the stiffness and cramp of his body, then went to the door to look about.

"Damnation," he muttered to himself. It was a world gone awry. The forest floor was littered with leaves and branches. Tall weeds wrenched from the soil had been swept up against trees that still stood. Everywhere, trunks, large and small, lay upon the ground. Panic for the safety of his children assailed him, and there was no doubt the tobacco had perished, though that scarcely seemed to matter now.

Then William was behind him. "God's wounds," William said softly. "There has not been such destruction since Noah. Daniel, how will we get that girl home?"

"Home! Is it even still there?" Daniel asked him. "And how did this flimsy structure stand up under it all?"

He and William walked away from the hut and looked back on it.

"The trees," William said.

"Yes, the trees," Daniel repeated. He could see that sturdy oaks, their branches now sparsely dotted with leaves, anchored the hut, perhaps broke the wind a little. "Indian ways are not to be taken lightly," he said.

"Daniel, how will we get Mary home?" William asked again. "The cart is still here, but where is the mule?"

"I let him go. I could not bring him into the hut, and I hoped some basic animal sense would lead him somewhere safe. I did not want to tie him. Now, it seems a nonsensical decision." Daniel called Maxim's name a number of times, but was not surprised when there was only silence in response.

Finally, he answered his brother's original question. "We will pull the cart ourselves. Ezekiel, Edwin, and I had to pull our tobacco to the ship that way. You and I can do this."

"Another story therein, no doubt, one I have not yet heard," William said, "but Daniel, look at the path."

Daniel focused his attention where once a path had been. What remained was impassible. As far as he could see, trees lay scattered across it. The small ones could be lifted or cut away, but the two men would have to make their way around the large ones, whose vast roots lay by the gaping holes they had left, whose branches spilled out for great distances over the land. And where there were no trees, the path had been transformed to a deep gully full of rushing water.

"We must make a new path," William observed.

"Or leave the cart here and carry Mary in a litter," Daniel amended.

"Either way, I think we must travel the route and prepare the way as best we can before we take her over it," William mused.

"Yes," Daniel agreed. "Yes. We will walk to the house first, see if my children are safe, and return with the tools we need for working our way back."

"You will leave Catherine here?" William asked.

"Did you think she would leave Mary alone? I have no choice," Daniel reminded him.

"No, I suppose not," William said.

Daniel deeply regretted the look of dismay on Catherine's face as he explained what they must do.

"Mary is so cold," Catherine said, and Daniel could see that she spoke through teeth firmly clamped so they would not chatter and give her own chill away.

"Hang some of the bedding from branches to dry," he suggested.

"You will be that long?"

"I do not know how long we will be. Look for yourself, Catherine." He could feel his voice soften as he said her name.

She left Mary's side to pass through the door and to stare wide-eyed at the destruction.

"Things should dry quickly," Daniel said. "See how fresh and clear the air is."

"It is uncommon odd," William said.

"Martha has sent medicine," said Daniel, "and we have brought food, but it is ruined. I am sorry to leave you here, but we have to make preparations to carry Mary." He smiled down at Catherine, wanting to embrace her for her sake as much as for his own.

"Take heart," William was saying to Mary. "We will be as fast as we can."

The two set off. Catherine watched them struggle for a brief time as, carrying the axe, they climbed over trees and scrambled through gullies. When she turned back to Mary, she saw that her sister's face was wet with tears again.

"I wish I had Martha's brew for your pain," Catherine said.

"Why does Daniel help me?" Mary gulped. "I do not deserve it. He should hate me!"

"He is a good man," Catherine answered, and suddenly, she believed it. "I think he has forgiven you."

"Is that what being good is? Forgiving? You see, Catherine, I can never be good. I could not forgive Josiah."

"Not now. Someday perhaps," Catherine reassured her.

"Never!" Mary declared, fresh tears brimming.

"I cannot think that makes you bad," Catherine hastened to say. "Besides, that you could not do what Hook demanded shows that you are not evil, only misled. To be good you must care for the needs of those around you as well as you care for your own."

"As you have done." A wave of greater pain must have swept through Mary because suddenly she shut her eyes tightly and drew her mouth into a tight downward grimace.

When the worst seemed to have passed, she spoke again. "I have twice been the victim of Goody Menton's belief that myself is all that matters. I did not learn the first time, but I have learned now, and there is so much to make up for. I must not let others do my work, especially you. I must make friends with the children. I could make Judith a doll and teach them both songs."

"Not tavern songs."

"No, not those. Also, I must not complain about what cannot be helped. I must…" Her voice broke on a sob. "Oh God! Catherine. I have been so dreadful, and yet you care for me."

"Each day is new, Mary. To put the past behind, there are many things you can do, but now you must rest." Catherine took Mary's hand in hers. "I love you, Mary, and see, the sun rises and warms us like God's love perhaps."

It was the tobacco fields Daniel saw first. The crop was flat, sodden, and useless. Wherever he looked, it was the same, but he found he was not mourning his loss. Perhaps he had already given up on the freehold and not fully realized it. Moreover, the crop was not nearly as important as the safety of his children.

He could see the rooftree of the house as they neared. It had survived the onslaught, but most of the shingles had not. First worried and then terrified about the fate of the twins, Daniel ran the rest of the way home.

They were outside, all of them, Judith, Jonathan, Martha, Ezekiel, and Edwin. They were draping bedding over every available rope and branch. Judith saw Daniel first.

"Father!" she shouted before racing to him and throwing her arms about his legs. Jonathan was close behind.

"What did you do to the roof?" he teased them, but Judith burst into tears.

"It was the wind," she wailed. "It was so awful. Oh, Father, I was so afraid!"

"As was I, sweeting."

"Where is Catherine?" Jonathan's voice was carefully controlled, probably, Daniel thought, to hide the fear in it.

"She is with Mary, who is sore injured. William and I must go back for them."

"All because of Mary," Jonathan muttered.

"Now, now," William admonished. "Mary is in much pain. We must all be good to her."

"I will not be bad to her," Jonathan answered. "But…"

"We will all be good to her for Catherine's sake," Daniel remembered to add. They would do it for Catherine. They would do anything for Catherine.

"But what about the house?" Daniel questioned as he looked once again at the skeletal roof. He walked toward the door, and everyone followed.

"The floor of the loft protected us," Martha explained.

"But it rained right through the floor, though not like outside, and water came down the stair!" Judith explained breathlessly.

"Ezekiel and Edwin shoveled this ditch right out the door so the water would run away…" Jonathan began.

"We sat on the table to keep our feet dry," Judith interrupted.

"I was telling it," Jonathan complained.

"You did very well, all of you," Daniel praised them. It occurred to him that his shaving of shingles during so many times of stress would not have been in vain.

"Tobacco's gone. Ruined. All of it," Ezekiel commented.

"I saw," Daniel said. "It is much labor lost, but what does it truly matter?" Daniel shook his head and sighed. "What does it matter?" He looked around at his gathered household. "Now we must leave you again, the twins, Martha, and Ezekiel." He turned to Edwin. "William and I need your help. We need to clear a way to bring Mary home, by litter, I fear, though we will try to use the cart." He looked up at the sky as though to beg for help. "Maxim is gone again."

He could hear Martha muttering to herself. "…naught but trouble…" he could make out.

And she was right. He was bringing trouble home again, or perhaps continuing with the same trouble was more accurate.

The day dragged on. Since high sun Catherine had hoped to hear the sound of Daniel's voice, though she knew some of the difficulties the men would meet. But there was no reassuring voice, only the fuss of the birds and the rustling of a soft, cool breeze as though the heavens sought to apologize for their harshness.

Catherine was torn between the desire to hover constantly over Mary whenever she moaned and the need to dry the bedding in order to keep her warm and to use the tinderbox Daniel had brought to coax wet fuel into a small fire so that she might cook the wet corn meal on hot rocks as the Indian women had done.

She would hold a cup of water to Mary's lips, sympathize heartily about the pain, and then run to accomplish some small task to increase their comfort should the men take too long to return.

She tried to put aside fears that she and Mary would be alone come darkness in a forest filled with roving animals whose habits had been as disrupted as their own. As the sun sank lower in the sky, she was grateful that the bedding was now dry, but became more desperate to get a fire started as protection against the animals.

Hunger gnawed at her stomach, and Mary complained of it several times, but Catherine could see that, true to her resolution, Mary was trying not to bemoan that which could not be helped.

Finally! Just outside the roofless hut, she was able to coax a small smoky flame from a pile of twigs and to keep it going somehow with much blowing and constant tending, adding small, damp boughs until the fire glowed hot enough to dry larger pieces of wood.

She was ready to push a rock from the fire, thus to cook the meal, when she heard the sound of voices. Daniel was back and with him Edwin and William.

Edwin remained behind as William greeted Catherine and went straight to Mary's side while Daniel tried to take Catherine's hand. She moved away though she longed to be soothed by his touch, settling instead for his compliment that she had done well to create what comfort there was.

"We chopped our way to the freehold and shoveled our way back here," Daniel said. "The path along the river is now *in* the river."

"You must be fit only to sleep for two days," Catherine commented.

"Would that I could," Daniel answered. "Would that I could."

Catherine could hear William telling Mary that her face was less swollen, and she wondered if that was so. She had been too preoccupied to notice. She also saw that William held Mary's hand and was patting it gently, reassuringly. She even detected a hint of a smile on Mary's part.

"We will use this excellent fire to brew sleeping tea for Mary," Daniel declared. He held up a small pot and one of Martha's herb bags. "Then, we will sleep." He poured water and dried herbs into the pot, shoveled coals away from the flame, and placed the pot on them. After that, he pulled dried apples, smoked venison, and corn bread from his pouch, and all satisfied their hunger.

Later, when Mary had drunk the tea, her pained restlessness had ceased, and her face had relaxed into slumber, Catherine rolled up in one of the blankets and lay beside her. She was both happy and dismayed when Daniel settled himself to sleep on her other side. The other two lay beyond Daniel, all of them crammed together within the small enclosure. Just outside the door, the fire, carefully banked, glowed throughout the night because Edwin occasionally rose to shift it and add a little fuel.

Catherine had been exhausted, sure she would sleep, but Daniel's nearness brought her to full wakefulness. Her body became so tense, it was almost morning before she finally dozed off.

Daniel awoke to gray light and the cooing of doves in the distance. There was not a bone in his body that did not ache from yesterday's exertions, but his pains were forgotten when he propped his chin on his elbow and watched Catherine as she slept. Here she lay, only inches away, but the privilege of enfolding her was still a distant dream.

As the morning brightened, Daniel left the hut and returned to find William feeding the fire. Mary moaned softly, and William's hands began to move more swiftly as he put the pot with Martha's brew into the fire and blew on the stubborn coals until a small flame licked the tinder.

"You have become quite a nursemaid in your old age," Daniel commented.

William chuckled softly. "Have I?" He looked up at Daniel and whispered. "I think the girl is brave, and I am so sorry for her."

"I doubt you will be for long," Daniel whispered back, "though I wish it were not so." He fell silent for a moment, then added, "She has brought us much grief. Still, I do not wish to see any person suffer."

The pot now satisfactorily settled on the fire, William stood with his hands on his waist and moved his body about to stretch muscles. "You will tell me I have not seen enough to truly know, but I do not think she is as wayward as you believe."

"Perhaps you are a victim of her outward beauty."

"Perhaps," William replied with honesty. "Only time will tell which of us is right."

Then Edwin rose, and Mary asked for something to drink. Catherine, waking because of Mary's voice, arose and stood rather shakily for a moment, ready to oblige her, but William spoke before she could do anything.

"Soon, Mistress Mary. I'm preparing the pain brew. It will be ready shortly. Wait and drink it."

"It will be bitter," Mary complained.

"But it will help, will it not?"

"Yes." Mary sighed. "Yes, it will, and I thank you for it."

She thanked him again when he had put his arm behind her back to raise her up and place the cup to her lips, and still again after she had struggled to get it all down.

Then, William went outside to assist Daniel in loading the cart and preparing it to be as soft a bed as they could manage. "I would not wish to hammer on a sore subject, but the girl has to have changed," Catherine heard William say. "There is a good person emerging. You will see that one day soon."

"Yes, William, and one day men will fly," Daniel told him.

"William is right," Catherine snapped at Daniel and then was ashamed. He needed to see more of Mary's model behavior and to hear her story. Surely he would not be so full of criticism after that.

When all had eaten the meal of bread and fruit, they turned to the problem of getting Mary to the cart with the least pain.

"You carry her, William," Daniel assigned, "and I will hold the leg steady."

Catherine could see that William was a most willing participant in this maneuver and that Daniel handled the leg so gently, Mary scarcely winced.

When she had been made as comfortable as possible, Daniel and Edwin picked up the shaft that should have been hitched to Maxim and pulled gently while William walked beside Mary, trying to assure her they were doing the best they could and that it would not be too long.

Given the pace at which they were traveling, Catherine considered William's promise most inaccurate. It took too much time to ease the cart over gullies, to maneuver it through narrow openings and around fallen trees using the path the men had forged as best they could.

The Daniel she walked with today was the kind Daniel, the Daniel who made her forget her misgivings. To keep from succumbing again to his charm, she placed her attention as fully as she could on Mary, who was biting her lips to keep from crying out. And it was astounding, but she saw that William carried a wet cloth with which he wiped her face when she seemed most distressed.

"A warning," Daniel told the exhausted group as they reached the edge of the swollen river. "Mary must not wander far from the house, and no one will be told she is with us. Should Hook's people make inquiries, answer by asking why they have lost her."

Though the journey seemed endless, they finally came in sight of the roofless house. Catherine shuddered when she saw the empty rafters, looming like a dark skeleton against the sky. "God's wounds, why?" she asked.

But there was no time to ponder the answer because the twins were shouting joyously that the little party had returned. They dashed across the field to embrace Catherine, and as she stopped to press them to her, a sense of love and belonging surged through her. If only she could trust Daniel, her joy would be complete. She glanced up at him and saw that he was watching their reunion with a countenance that seemed full of longing.

Chapter Twenty-two

For three days the men worked to secure new shingles to the rafters. Daniel had to force himself not to look at his useless tobacco fields or to think about losing the house so soon after repairing it. After all, the shelter was needed now. The future was in God's hands.

When the task was completed, the household gathered over the last of the brandy and a meal of fried fish, squash, and corn. Daniel watched Mary hobble across the floor on the crutch William had improvised. She had struggled to assist with the meal as well as with anything else she had the power to do, and Daniel wondered if she was fearful that she would be sent away as soon as she was healed.

He considered calming her fears, but as quickly decided the household was better off with such commendable behavior. The problem was, of course, that she had taken William in completely. As the swelling on her face subsided, and her beauty returned, William seemed to be unable to wrest his gaze away.

When Daniel asked himself whether Mary's sterling behavior was for William's benefit, he remembered that her behavior with himself had been less than sterling. Her only tools then had been the taunting of her body to inflame his need.

Mary was aware of William's interest; that was certain. Daniel had seen some of her seductive behavior several times in the last few days. Once, Catherine had chided her for it, and she had apologized. "It is such a habit I forget," she had explained. Daniel had to grant there was probably truth in those words.

Her face briefly twisted in pain, Mary settled on the end of the bench, her splinted leg outstretched. She fished in her pockets and pulled out two objects, a tiny female doll made of straw and fabric, which she gave to Judith, and a cleverly constructed mule or horse, which she gave to Jonathan.

Judith was immediately grateful. "Thank you," she said, smiling.

Jonathan was obviously wary of the giver's motives, but he glanced at his father, and seeming to read there what he must say, muttered something resembling those words.

Daniel suspected there was a small chance that he was wrong and William was right about Mary, and this led him to review again another lingering suspicion about which he might have been wrong, that Watkins was responsible for the damage to his property and for Ezekiel's injury. There seemed to be a greater conspiracy than anyone had imagined, not on the part of Watkins, but on the part of Hook and Hammet. If he spoke of his suspicions, could anyone else in his household enlighten him further? He decided to bring the matter before them.

They listened in complete silence as he discussed what was known of Hook's behavior and what he had begun to believe. All eyes except Mary's were fastened on him. She hung her head in what appeared to be shame.

"It is what I hev thought all along," Ezekiel was first to comment.

Daniel was usually quite glad for Ezekiel's silent strength, but he found himself wishing Ezekiel had been a little less silent on this matter.

Martha was frowning. "I told Hammet that Ezekiel had gone for seedlings," she recalled. "And that he went afoot. Then, Ezekiel was set upon."

This information resembled a blow to the stomach. "Hammet had told me to go and get the seedlings and where they were!" Daniel almost choked on the words. "And, of course, later Hook had my mule."

"The evidence grows," William said. "But why? Were you a threat to Hook or to Hammet for that matter?"

"I cannot think why." Daniel ran thumb and forefinger over his brow, "unless it is his practice to persecute Catholics."

"I overheard something unusual when I first went to bring Mary back," Catherine said. "So much was happening, I had forgotten all about it, but Hook was talking to another man and said something about a false report that Hook would be pleased with." She paused. "And Mary, you overheard something strange. What was it again?"

"Yes," Mary answered. "Yes, that is so. I heard Hook tell his agent that the brother was here, that now there were two of them. Was that not odd?"

"So now we know that Hook is dishonest, as though it was not known already, and that the two of us are somehow important to him," William summarized.

"And, of course, it is obvious now that it was Hook who bought my debt and called it in," Daniel added. "How else could he have bought Mary's indenture with nary a word to me?"

He fell silent, the others with him. *What else*? Daniel asked himself. Perhaps that strange feeling he'd had when Hook stood over him after his injury. "William, does Hook look at all familiar to you?" he asked. "I have turned myself more daft than usual to recall where I have seen him before."

William pondered, sipped his brandy, and pondered more. "I only saw the man briefly in torchlight, and I felt even then that something was familiar, but I certainly can recall no contact with such a man."

"Would that I could dig the circumstances from the pit of my memory." Daniel shook his head. "But I cannot." He stood and threw first one leg, then the other over the bench. "I think that early on the morrow, I will pay Watkins a visit."

"It is perilous," Ezekiel cautioned.

"Peril is the daily stuff of our lives these days," Daniel answered. "Perhaps if I am courteous and apologetic, I will learn the truth."

"If he do not take a musket to ye," Ezekiel said.

But it was the servant's knife Daniel was leery of.

By morning, the days of crystal weather following the storm had given way to a gloomy overcast. As he walked toward Watkins' freehold, Daniel tried to convince himself he had not been unjust in his attack on the man, but his conscience would not allow it. He saw that Watkins' field was as flattened as his own and knew that he and Watkins together were victims of fate.

As he came closer, he realized, too, that the man's house had fared no better in the wind than his own, but that repairs were scarcely begun.

Suddenly, a harsh voice called from a shed that leaned sadly to one side. "If ye hev come to ask fer yer fine wiped away, ye had best go back now 'less ye want a knife in yer gullet." The speaker burst from the structure, his knife bared and ready. This was Amos, servant to Watkins, the man who had stabbed Daniel.

Daniel tensed to be ready to protect himself, but stood his ground. "Nay," he said. "It is a clear conscience I want back. I ask only for the truth."

"It is you that needs hev truth fer me, ye scum of Satan."

"Then I will start with an apology." Daniel hoped thus to placate the bandy legged little man whose stance remained belligerent, his knife thrust forward. "I think I have blamed Watkins wrongly for damage to my crop."

"It is late to ask yerself who is to blame, is it not?" Amos accused, though his knife was now lowered a little.

"I have recently realized who the culprit might be." Daniel strove to keep his voice steady and attempted to approach the fellow more closely so as to be able to lower his voice.

The knife rose threateningly again.

"You see," Daniel explained, "Watkins threatened me the day I bought my indentured servants, and when the harm to my freehold was done shortly after, I assumed it was he."

"Well, ye 'sumed wrong," Amos growled. "It is sickening the way you high and mighty judge a man afore ye know ought of him. Watkins, poor old sod, they laugh at him in town and tell stories that, 'cause he talks rough sometimes, hev but a whisper of truth." Amos' voice lost some of its bitterness as he continued. "Ye see, by sunset that day, he did not remember bidding for that fair girl, nor did he remember what ye did to his nose the day after it was done. His head do not hold any thought fer long. He be harm to no one, so when ye went fer him, I was full 'raged. I am still."

Daniel closed his eyes and shook his head. "I had not meant to 'go for him', but when he offered sympathy for my plight, I thought him gloating and lost my temper. I would like to make it up. My men and I could help repair the house. It would ease my conscience if you would agree."

In silence, Amos regarded Daniel angrily for a long time. Then, seeming to come to a decision, he sighed and slowly nodded his head. "It would be a blessing," he said. "Be ye talking true, it would be a blessing."

There was a pause and then a chuckle. "Ye cannot know how glad I was ye won the bid fer that chippie," he confided, "though it was daft to pay so high."

Daniel was surprised at Amos' change of tone, but not at the information. He remembered the argument during the auction twixt servant and master.

"There was another matter I had thought was Watkins' doing, the purchase of my debt," Daniel added.

Amos merely laughed. "With tobacco at one cent a pound, he can scarce buy breeches to cover his bum." He leaned forward as though to impart a secret. "By the by, I hev a tale to tell ye about the sunny haired servant ye won that day." Amos' face became animated.

Daniel's raised his brows questioningly.

"I saw her once in Bristol. If it was not her, it is a wonder, her semblance to a tavern wench there," Amos claimed. "It was said she could drive men mad. They flocked to the inn just to see her."

Daniel tried to hide his surprise, but then concluded it could not possibly have been Mary. No tavern wench in such circumstances could be virgin for long, and Mary had undoubtedly been virgin.

"I will not argue the point," he said, "but I do not believe Mary to be the same girl."

"I will not argue neither," Amos said amiably

"Might I talk to Watkins?" Daniel asked.

"Watkins is in town, so ye cannot 'pologize today. Will I look fer ye on the morrow?"

"Later today, tools in hand and men in tow. Will that be satisfactory?" .

"We would be obliged. Yes indeed, we would be obliged. I think it will pleasure Watkins to see ye then," Amos answered. "It will pleasure me, fer that matter, especially the repairs." He nodded his head in farewell and turned away toward the damaged shed. Daniel decided that shed repair would be a part of his penance to Watkins.

As Daniel trod slowly back to the house, he felt again the sting of shame. Because of his quick temper and even quicker assumptions, he had attacked an innocent man. Oh yes, and he had believed Amos a charlatan, yet come to see him as a man with concern for his master, not just greed for the master's holdings.

Oh that temper, that readiness to strike out before there was understanding! It was what he had done to Catherine. That tendency was tearing his life to shreds.

He found Catherine in the garden pulling up bean plants and relieving them of their dried, yellow, bursting pods. She smiled as he approached, her brightness lighting an answering flame that warmed him even while it intensified his shame.

"What did you learn?" she asked.

"I am convinced it was not Watkins. On a false assumption I have attacked an innocent man just as I attacked my sweet, innocent Catherine. Will there ever be an end to my erring ways?"

Catherine blushed and seemed for a moment to be at a loss for words. "I think we err until we die, all of us," she said finally, gently, "but do we not thereby grow wiser and better?"

"So that we are all saints, come death?" Daniel questioned. "Of a certainty, not I."

Catherine laughed. "Nor I." Then her face became serious. "While we talk of false assumptions, may I lay another matter before you?"

Daniel frowned. His first thought was that her concern would be a matter of his religion. "Yes," he said, but with hesitation. "I could scarce confess, as I have just done, to failure in understanding and not listen to you now. What is it?"

"It is Mary. "

Daniel felt as though he had been slapped, and his reaction must have been apparent because Catherine stopped talking. She was too full of love for Mary to see the truth, but he would have to hear her out. "Go on," he said.

"Mary is not the evil woman you believe her to be. Can you not see how she has changed?" Catherine's eyes pleaded for understanding, poor deluded woman.

"Her outward behavior has changed because now she has fear for what will become of her," Daniel said. "Hook's monstrous treatment gave her that fear. What will happen when it is gone? You will find her old behavior returned. I can see that you have sacrificed yourself that she might thrive, though she was never worth that sacrifice. She would sell our souls to the devil should it suit her."

Catherine's face darkened, and she threw her basket to the ground so that the beans spilled out.

"You judge!" she hissed. "You judge again. You will not listen, and you are wrong! Wrong!"

This was an issue that would always come between them. And had he not just found his judgment to be lacking, Daniel asked himself. When would he learn to seek understanding first?

"I am sorry, Catherine," he said contritely. "Please continue."

She sighed. "Goody Menton, who owned the inn and tavern, in whose care my father placed us (I've mentioned her before) was preaching to Mary to think only of herself, that all else was foolishness, that there was no God at all. She bade Mary say nothing to me, who was set early to work in the scullery and sent early to bed so I would not know Mary was trained not only to serve customers, but to steal and seduce."

"God in heaven!" Daniel gasped. So it was altogether possible Mary *was* the tavern wench Amos had described.

"She was rewarded for this behavior with fancy ribbons and sweetmeats and hot baths from the time her body began to ripen," Catherine continued, wiping tears from her eyes. The telling was clearly painful. "She was told there was no such thing as God and that hell was a place men had invented to control each other." Catherine began to breathe raggedly. "And all the while, her behavior doomed her ever more surely to that dwelling place, to hell."

"Why did she leave such an astonishing mentor and come to Mary's Land?" Daniel asked.

"Why? Because Goody Menton sold her as mistress to a wealthy man, and she did not want to go. She ran away and signed indenture papers. I found her just in time to sign the papers myself, though the captain certainly did not want me. I was 'long on bone and short on flesh'."

Daniel winced. "The captain did not know you were the true jewel." He wanted to hold Catherine and comfort her for what she had suffered on Mary's behalf. Instead he found himself pursuing his argument because he was sure she would continue to suffer, if only she realized it.

"So Mary learned to get her way through seduction. How well I understand," he said. "What you have told me makes me pity her, but warns me even more strongly how difficult it would be for her to mend her ways."

Catherine placed her palms on her temples in a gesture of frustration. "Daniel, do you not understand? The mending has begun. God has opened her eyes. If you do not believe God can change her, then the God you know has no power. She saw the evil she had been taught carried to its cruel extreme, first by Goody Menton and then by Hook, and she was the object of that cruelty. She saw that you and I were willing to care for her and forgive her, despite all."

This gave Daniel pause. He was not at all sure he had forgiven the girl, but let Catherine continue as though he had.

"She prayed for help, and we helped her, so she began to believe that her prayer was answered, that there is a God, and if Goody Menton was wrong about that, she was clearly wrong about all else, about hell, for instance." Catherine stopped, breathless, then smiled, remembering. "Mary even asked me if hell would be as hot as a tobacco field because she was sure she was going there."

Catherine took Daniel's hands and clasped them in hers. "Do you not see, Daniel?" she implored. "She has chosen the good. She will stumble sometimes; old habits keep their hold on us. But she has left the darkness and walks in the light. She was once a sweet, loving child, though I spoiled her, I and Goody Menton." Catherine's voice broke, but she managed to say, "She is learning to love again."

At this point Catherine could plead no more. She was crying too hard.

Daniel took her into his arms and held her while she was wracked with sobs as though purging herself of all the worry and fear and disappointment that had plagued her. He kissed the top of her head and ran his fingers through her hair. For the first time, he saw that she could be right. It might be so.

"I believe you," he said even as he tried to push the lingering doubt away. He wanted to believe her. He had to believe her if he was to keep her. And had he not learned today how little of what he had once truly believed was so.

Chapter Twemty-three

Catherine's storm of tears subsided. Finally, Daniel had heard her out, had met her pleas with understanding, not anger. What was more, she found herself held and comforted in the arms she had so longed for. She looked up into his eyes, saw there a need that intensified her own, and found herself slipping her arms around him, allowing herself to be pulled close.

She had not long to wait before his lips met hers and sent through her an agony of sensation unlike anything she had ever experienced. It went beyond her fondest dreams and left her breathless.

He tore his mouth away long enough to murmur, "Catherine, beautiful Catherine, my sweet Catherine."

Tears stung her eyes again until he kissed them away and returned with mounting fervor to her lips. She wanted to be able to surrender to the wild impulses this brought to mind and body, but suddenly, he grasped her shoulders and held her at arm's length. Then, still holding her away with one hand, he ran the other over her cheeks, across her lips, across her forehead, pushing back unruly wisps of hair. In return, she reached out to trace the endearing curves of his slightly skewed nose with her fingertips.

"Could you not trust me, Catherine? You are my world…"

"Catherine?" Mary's voice intruded. Daniel's hands dropped away, and Catherine stepped back, fighting to restore her breathing to normal.

"Damnation!" Daniel cursed softly, and Catherine knew he was as disappointed as she that the moment was lost. But the curse Mary had brought to his lips called back the old problems, shattering the instant of trust, the sweetness of desire into shards of doubt and fear that this would again lead only to hurt.

She saw Daniel's jaw tighten as he glanced at Mary, who was rounding the corner of the house.

"We will talk later," he said and strode swiftly through the gate and past

Mary without speaking to her.

"Why is he angry?" she asked Catherine.

"It is nothing for you to worry about," Catherine told her, knowing that she had just lied.

Daniel was furious as he walked away, but at himself. Poor, miserable, hot head that he was, he had done it again. He had let slip the very word that would negate his declaration of belief in Mary and thus trample upon the magic of Catherine's surrender. To force her into his arms again might bring about that response to him that had been so clear, but it could as easily bring about deeper rejection.

Now that Watkins' roof was repaired and William had been informed of Mary's unsettling background, Daniel and William sat silently by their fish traps in the river, each man lost in his own thoughts.

Daniel's physical torment was upon him again in full measure, but this time the object of his desire was a worthy woman. Looking back, he saw that he had sought to quench the thirst of desire with a shallow draft demanded of an unwilling woman, an act best forgotten. In Catherine, however, in that brief joyful moment, he had been astonished to find a thirst that seemed equal to his own. Could he allow himself to dream that together, they would be satisfied again and again by something like an ever flowing spring?

If only he could manage to regain her trust!

"Daniel." William broke the silence. "I must return to Virginia to attend my affairs. I have left servants to do it for too long already."

"You could not bear to let go of my good company," Daniel teased.

"Of course. Why else?" William joked. "Why else, indeed?" His expression turned serious. "We grow better tobacco than you in Virginia, brother, but we do not grow better women." He plucked a blade of grass and blew across it, creating a hint of a musical note. "I fear that Mary turns my judgment to mud."

Daniel scrambled forward so that he could look his brother in the eye. "God's blood," he said. "It is what I have been telling you all along. Just be sure you do not make her your wife."

"Ah, Daniel!" William sighed. "I know you have good reason for the bitterness you hold, but could you not accept that Mary was but a child, spoiled, misled, but still a child. She is now more like clay fired in the kiln, changed by the flames of her suffering."

Daniel knew that William was probably right, that there had been a measure of change, but he was not quite ready to trust his brother's well being to the girl.

"Then, why do you not simply wed and be done with it?" he asked sharply.

William looked out at the float now bobbing above the trap with the struggle of what looked to be a large fish. "Two reasons. First, I want to be more sure I am right and you are wrong, and I fear it is my desire that shapes my own judgment. I must get away, must think, not only about Mary, but also about what you and I and those we care for must do to survive.

Another float bobbed, indicating a second quarry caught, but Daniel took note of it only as something that had little to do with him.

"It is to die a little to give up this dream, this land," he said. "But it is foolishness to think I can keep it."

"Could you not find renewed life somewhere else?" William asked.

"Start over after I have labored so hard and built so much?"

"But you and I together…"

"Together," Daniel repeated. "Aye, together. That is the key. That is all that will make it possible, make it bearable."

"And there will be Catherine," William reminded him, as though he needed such a reminder.

"Yes, Catherine if she will but follow me when her indenture is finished. At the moment whether she will do it is uncertain."

"God's wounds, Daniel. It is quite certain she will be your wife. Any fool could see that, but about the indenture…"

"It must be sold for my debts, and Hook holds Mary's indenture. Now, there is a rough spot I will wager you had not considered."

"Whatever assets I have should settle that. I will buy their indentures, theirs and Ezekiel's and Edwin's and Martha's."

Daniel smiled, touched and gratified. "Thank you, William." Then he remembered. "Martha is no longer indentured."

"And yet she stays. You must be a good master."

"She loves the children…"

"Yes, and Ezekiel, too, or I miss my guess. She will go with us, then?" William began finally to pull a trap to the surface and to release a rockfish onto the ground.

"So she says." Daniel was reminded to pull up the second trap and to deposit a second flopping fish to the earth.

William placed a foot on his catch, securing its mouth to a rope. Then he proceeded to do the same thing with Daniel's.

"Daniel, it will be a good household we will take to forge a new dream. The question yet to be answered is where. And Daniel, I do not like growing a weed that ruins the soil, takes twice the work of other crops, drops in price at every harvest, and then makes men hanker for it even while they cough and choke and wheeze. I grew it because it was what was needed to survive, but I would prefer crops that feed and clothe."

Daniel found this declaration threatening. "How would we survive without tobacco?"

"In Virginia, there is flax, and trappers have reported rich land along a river called Shenandoah."

Daniel knit his brows. "Yes, but we must be able to ship crops. Will that land not be too far? And what of the river? Is it navigable?"

"Daniel, let me go to my holding and see what I can salvage."

"It would not support both households," Daniel broke in again. "And while I know I sound petty, I would have trouble trying to become a full partner in what has been yours. We must start as equals."

"It is an amazing thing, brother," William told him, throwing one arm companionably over his shoulder, "but I knew that already."

Daniel laughed as he picked up the rope with the fish dangling from it, and he and William strolled toward the path to the house.

William had been gone several days. The other men were hunting, the women doing the laundry, all energized by the crisp, cool weather.

Catherine watched Mary struggle from the boiling wash pot to the fence in order to drape wet fabric across it. She could tell that Mary's leg still pained her and that to help with the washing only made it worse, yet Mary had not once complained. Such behavior seemed proof that her good behavior had not been merely a show for William, nor a ploy to keep Daniel from sending her away.

Behind Catherine, Martha was saying softly, "This be the same girl who never stopped whining and left us for Hook and his riches! This is surely a changeling, did we but see it."

"I fear to blink lest she be gone," Catherine agreed. "But, look. She is tired and full pained now. Mary," she called. "You have done enough."

"More than enough," Martha added. "It is time fer you to rest."

Catherine had to smile at Martha's complete change of heart.

Mary sighed with relief. "Thank you," she said. "Thank you. I do need to rest." She hobbled to the log by the door, sank down on it with a muffled groan, and sat watching as Catherine and Martha completed the tasks.

When Martha had gone into the house to see to the baking, Catherine sat beside her sister, and seeing that her face was streaked with tears, put an arm around her.

"What is wrong?" she asked. "Is there too much hurt?" Would you like some lemon balm tea?"

"It is not my body, though it does ache. It is my soul, I think." She put her hands over her face briefly, then removed them and looked at Catherine. "Though not truly that. It is William. Oh Catherine, I fear he will not come back, and he is so kind, so funny, so good to me. He makes me feel happy, like a virtuous woman because he has not seen the evil I have done." She drew in her breath. "But he *will* know if he does not already. He will know, and then in his eyes, I will be bad, and he will want nothing to do with me."

The crying grew louder as Mary painted a bleak self-portrait. "They speak ill of me in town, and well they should because I was Hook's whore, and look what harm I have brought to you and Daniel. Oh Catherine! it would have been better to die."

Catherine took Mary in her arms as Mary sobbed out her shame and her misery. "Mary," she said when her sister had stopped for a breath. "Do you not remember? We talked of forgiveness. God forgives."

"But I want people to forgive. I want William to forgive, and even if he forgave me, he would not love me. There, I have said it. I want him to love me."

"Because you love him?"

"I love him to touch me and talk to me and be with me. It hurts to think he may never do it again. Does that mean I love him?"

"It seems so to me," Catherine answered. "But then I have no great experience of this man/woman love."

Mary laughed in the middle of a sob. "But you love Daniel " she contradicted.

"Perhaps." Catherine felt her lips begin to quiver. "Perhaps, but I do not trust him." Then she was afraid she had said too much because the mistrust was centered on Daniel's view of Mary and his resulting anger.

"Not trust Daniel?" Mary's crying ceased, and her eyes grew wide. "But he is a man who has always been one to be trusted. And you do love him. I have seen how you look at him and talk to him. And before our betrothal, I felt I had to hurry and capture him before you did." Her voice broke on a moan. "Oh God, Catherine! How selfish I was. You loved him, and I wanted him as a tool to make life easier, and I tried to take him away, but he did not even like me."

Mary ran her hands across her swollen face as Catherine tried to think how to comfort her without dishonesty.

"Did you not hate me?" Mary asked.

"Yes. Sometimes. I was very angry."

"You see, even you, who loved and cared for me for so long. And if I made a tool of Daniel for my own ends, am I trying now to make a tool of William, to have someone to take care of me?"

"But do you want to take care of him?" Catherine felt more sure of herself now. It occurred to her that she must love Daniel because her own answer to such a question was a rousing "yes!"

Mary frowned. "I had not thought about it, but yes, I do. I do not want him to come to harm. I want him to remain proud and safe." She ran her fingers over her healing nose. "It would hurt me if he were hurt. I would do anything to keep him from it." A smile unlike any Catherine had seen lit her face. "Is that love, do you think?"

"It can be naught else."

But Mary's smile became a look of alarm. "How foolish I am," she complained. "How little it matters if I love him. I am not worthy of him. I am worthy of no one. And suppose I cannot always be good? Suppose I only cause him to suffer?"

Catherine took her by the shoulders and shook her. "Listen to me," she ordered. "The past is over, gone." It almost seemed she was lecturing herself. "What matters is who you are now, and you are worthy. God's blood, Mary, you are worthy. William is no fool. He knows of what is past, yet he has been your champion." Catherine's voice died away. Champion against Daniel's harsh criticism, she realized too late, wishing she could take back the ill chosen word.

It remained in the air, bald and pointed, but Mary did not seem to grasp its significance. She seemed to hear only that William defended her, and her face brightened again.

"He knows?" she questioned, as though to make sure. "He knows and yet is my champion?"

"He knows, and he has seen through all the troubling past to the true person, the good person who has been there all along, distorted by false teaching, now emerging like a butterfly from its cocoon."

"You speak truly?" Mary's smile was wider than it had been before. "Oh!

I do not deserve it, but were it so, I would be so grateful."

Catherine wanted to smile every time she thought of Mary and William together. And now her beautiful Mary had ceased making demands for herself and begun to concern herself with the welfare of others.

But such thinking inevitably led her mind back to her own dilemma.

"You are my world," Daniel had said. There was joy in hearing those words just as there was joy to be clasped in his arms. But Catherine did not trust the joy. She told herself that to be led by joy alone was to falter and to fall. He would not always speak so enticingly. He would, at times, revert to the wild-eyed Daniel she had seen too often, the man from whom sense had flown.

Catherine told herself that some day she would have to marry, that no man was perfect, that Daniel was surely better than most. It was his ability to hurt her that was so troublesome. Another man might shout at her, and she would get angry and shout back and be done with it. But not Daniel. Angry words from his mouth were arrows that pierced till she bled. No, marriage to Daniel would never do.

But after Daniel, neither would marriage to any other man.

Life was never easy, but she must not delude herself. There was nothing for her to do but to avoid being alone with him. For this reason, she refused to allow herself to be without company in the house, and she made certain that whenever she ventured out of doors, it was in the presence of Martha, Mary, or one of the twins.

Oh, Daniel had tried to approach her many times, to draw her away from the others, but she kept her distance. She even made certain she was the last to the table and the first to leave so that she would not be seated where she could look upon him or he upon her. On the occasions when her tactics failed to work, and she found herself under his sad gaze, she could not look up from her trencher nor stomach the food. To glance at Daniel was to long to reach out and comfort him.

Once, as he walked past, he said softly, "Am I never to be forgiven my sins?"

She was glad he did not wait for an answer; she could not even answer it for herself.

Chapter Twenty-four

The weather was invigorating, the sharp blue sky washed clean of summer haze. The only disadvantage, Catherine found as she and Martha walked to town, was the activity of the bees, which had ceased minding their own business and begun to mind hers.

She swatted a bee that was hovering about her forehead, then feared that it would retaliate. It merely began to harass Martha, who sent it winging back to Catherine.

"Miserable beasties," Martha complained. "It will be good to hev frost and be quit of them."

Catherine flicked a bee from her forearm, wishing she could roll her sleeves all the way to her wrists, but the fabric was too worn. In fact, there was little of her skirt or bodice that was not worn almost to uselessness. She would be an object of pity in town if anyone cared to notice, but today's errand was important. Daniel was unable to carry it out because the men had rushed to rescue Giles Watkins, whose tobacco barn had collapsed on him.

"We repaired his shed and his house," Daniel had complained, "but there was no tobacco, so we ignored the barn. What the devil was he doing there anyway?"

Martha began to chuckle to herself. What was there to laugh about, Catherine wondered. Her own anxiety lest the court reject the petition she carried, to return Mary's indenture to Daniel, made levity seem out of place.

"What is funny?" she inquired.

"Mary," Martha answered mysteriously, and then took her own good time to offer an explanation. Finally, she continued. "It is Mary. I heard her ask Judith and Jonathan to teach her the letters."

Catherine had to smile. "It was most clever, was it not, since she is to make certain they behave while we are gone. Did they seem pleased?"

"Judith was. Mary has near won her over. But Jonathan? Ye best ask

Mary what she hev learned when we get back. The Lord alone knows what nonsense he will try to feed her." Martha brushed a bee from her shoulder. "Damnation!" she exclaimed.

The closer they came to town, to the abundance of fruit trees and kitchen gardens, the worse the bees plagued them.

As the two followed the path beside the inn and rounded the corner, Catherine felt a sting on her ankle and, with a squeal, lunged forward to rid herself of the offending insect. She did not reach her objective, however, because her head met rather a soft resistance in the form of a man's stomach.

She heard a grunt and straightened quickly, only to see papers scatter as she was roundly cursed by an angry gentleman who wore the elaborately curled wig and fine clothes of a wealthy Englishman.

"It is but morning, and you are drunk already," he accused as Catherine and Martha tried to gather his papers.

"Not drunk, bee stung," Catherine retorted sharply as she scrambled about, hoping he might soon be similarly afflicted.

He stood stiffly, not even bothering to retrieve the sheet that had blown against his leg. When the papers had been returned to him, he counted them, certain, Catherine supposed, that these ragamuffins had kept several for themselves. Finally satisfied he had them all, he looked up at them with scorn.

"And who might you be?" he demanded to know as though he would cause them to be punished.

"This is Martha, and I am Catherine, servants to Daniel Falconer..."

The gentleman immediately roared her to silence. "Daniel Falconer is it?" he shouted so loudly that Catherine backed away. "Then you are party to a hoax most foul!"

"What do you mean?"

"Daniel Falconer is dead." The man lowered his voice to a level that was almost sinister. "Anyone who claims that name attempts to rob the true heir of his inheritance."

For a moment Catherine was speechless.

"It is nonsense," Martha hissed.

"Hush," Catherine cautioned her, raising her shaking hand, palm outward, to strengthen her warning to be quiet. Then she marshaled the courage to say, "You are mistaken, sir. He is very much alive."

"It is clearly an imposter who is very much alive. I have it written in a reliable report that Daniel Falconer has perished, he and his brother William."

Hook's report! The one she had heard Hook discussing. Catherine took a deep breath and inquired with all the courtesy she could manage, "Tell me, I pray, kind sir, who is the true heir?"

"One Josiah Hook, who would be cousin to the true Daniel Falconer. I am about to visit him now."

All the mystery about Daniel's misfortunes had been solved in a few short words. Catherine wanted to run to Daniel and fairly babble about what she had just learned, but she must not babble now. She was silent as she tried to think what she must say next, but the man was impatient.

"Out of my way, bawd. I have business to transact. Inform your master, whoever he truly is, that such behavior as his is criminal, that men are hanged for fraud."

Catherine could feel her face warming with anger at the terrible injustice, not only of what she had just been told, but also of the man's intemperate speech. She fought to control her voice.

"Please, sir, would you consent to talk to the man you are accusing of fraud? Unless his mother told him lies, he is truly Daniel Falconer, and I assure you he knows nothing of any inheritance, neither he, nor his brother William."

"You speak well," he said suspiciously. "You are well bred. How do you come to be servant to this man?"

"My father, Charles Quentin, a ship-owner, was lost at sea and with him his ship and all his wealth. My sister and I signed indenture papers when life became too desperate. Daniel Falconer bought them at auction."

"I see, I see," he said. "And what makes you so certain this Falconer is no cheat?"

"I have been with him since late winter, and he has worked very hard to make his freehold prosper. He has had great pride in it. He is not a man waiting for an inheritance to drop from the sky. His ancestors were wealthy, it is true, but his own family was disinherited long before his birth because his mother was papist."

He gazed at her, his brow knit, his well-manicured hands rubbing his chin. "If he has worked so hard to prosper, why do you, his servant, appear in such rags? You appear to be anything but prosperous."

"It has been a year of much misfortune," Catherine said, "but though we have not had the tobacco to afford us new clothing, we are otherwise provided for in a well-run household."

He looked from Catherine to Martha and back to Catherine again as though assessing the truth of what she said. "What do you know of Josiah Hook?"

he asked finally.

Hearing Martha suck in her breath, Catherine was afraid at first to answer. The man waited expectantly, though, and she knew she must say something, though only what was proven true, nothing of the suspicions about Hook's wrongdoing.

"His land is not far from ours. He is prosperous. He has caused us many problems. He seduced my young sister, bought her indenture without Daniel's permission, and then beat her very badly. She is back with us now, but I go today to give the court a written petition to return her indenture."

The man raised his brows. "Indeed! Why did Falconer not come?"

"A barn collapsed on a neighbor, and he went there to help. After this session, the court does not meet again for many months. Daniel desires that they have the written request before he appears in a day or so.

"Daniel, is it, not Master Falconer?"

"Yes. It is the way here in Mary's Land except for the wealthiest."

He went silent again, still frowning, and began to push the edges of the papers he held into a greater semblance of order.

"Perhaps I will visit this Daniel Falconer before I approach Hook," he said.

"I am sure he would be most grateful," Catherine said. "Of a certainty, I would." She had to struggle not to laugh nervously at her own audacity.

"And how might I find him?"

Catherine pointed. "Follow this path to the river. Go along it to the place where the shoreline bends sharply to the right. There take the path through the woods. The second freehold you come to will be ours."

"Ours?"

"Daniel's. But if you go now, there is not likely to be anyone there save my sister and Daniel's two children. Could I but have time to deliver my petition and then walk back to fetch Daniel, you would have less time to wait."

"And you would have time to prepare him for my visit. I mislike that plan. I will go there directly and wait for him."

"It would be fine, sir. If you do not frighten my sister, I am sure she will serve you food and drink as you wait. Then, too, if Daniel has not returned home, you might save yourself time by riding on to the next freehold where he went this morning."

He nodded a farewell with something resembling a smile. Catherine hoped it was a sign he believed in her honesty. Then she watched briefly as he strode toward the stables. As she and Martha scurried toward the courthouse, she found herself agog with excitement.

Martha was muttering, "It is not to be believed."

"Hook was trying to kill Daniel so his lies would become truth or to force him to leave so that his presence would not expose those lies," Catherine said. "All those injuries, all those wounds, all because a rich man wanted more. It is so evil, Martha. It is so incredibly evil." But a blade of fear pierced her. "Could Hook still have his way?" She could feel the panic in her voice. "Could he convince the man it is Daniel who is evil?"

She stood for a moment as the clattering of hooves suggested the man was already on his way, he who held Daniel's fate in his hands.

Chapter Twenty-five

If Martha had been able, Catherine would have run to the courthouse and then run most of the way home. But Martha could not have done it, and Catherine would not leave her alone.

Still, they delivered their petition and walked as fast as they could, rendering Martha so breathless they had to stop at the river's bend. A large canoe had edged close to the shore, and a man shouldering a pack with his boots tied to it, rose carefully and eased himself over the side and into the shallow water. As he waded ashore, Catherine wanted to shout with glee. It was William!

"Aha, you have come to meet me and to make sure I do not get lost," he joked as he sat on the gravel bank and pulled on his boots.

"You will not believe what has happened," Catherine began.

"And you will not believe the realization that has come to me," he countered.

Curious, Catherine decided her news could wait. "What realization?"

"Why Hook is so familiar. He looks like Daniel. That is why! I cannot imagine why it was not clear to me immediately."

Catherine laughed as William secured the straps on his boots. When he stood, she looked up at him, fairly bursting with her news.

"You laugh at me, but do you not see the resemblance?" William questioned.

"Now that it is pointed out. He looks like you as well, William, and there is good reason. Hook is your cousin…"

William interrupted her with a guffaw. "Catherine, I refuse to call such a worm cousin."

She put her hand on his arm to silence him. "Listen to me," she commanded. "He has written to family representatives in England that you and Daniel are dead and that therefore he is the one true heir to the family estate."

"It is all fish piss," William chortled. "We were disinherited years ago. Hook a cousin!? And for this he has attempted to destroy us? The court is in session now, is it not? If he has indeed made such a claim, we have reason to

206

bring the matter of that and multiple misfortunes before the court."

"The representative of the Falconers is at the house now waiting for Daniel or talking to him if he is back from Watkins' holding. Watkins was injured this morning," Catherine explained.

She was grateful for William's long strides that forced Martha to trot along faster than she might otherwise have done. Periodically, he would shake his head in wonder. "We have been in a war over family property and not even known it," he said once. Another time he exclaimed, "A war over an inheritance we are not even entitled to. How foolhardy!"

When they reached the house, they found pungent tobacco smoke filling the room. It was so thick, Catherine almost choked on it. A mug of ale and a trencher of honey-cake before him, the Englishman sat at the table with Mary and the twins. His attention was obviously so riveted on Mary, he did not see the newcomers.

Mary had been speaking, but stopped mid-sentence when she saw William. She stood as though to run to him, smiling more broadly than Catherine had ever seen, then halted, obviously unsure whether to greet him thus was appropriate.

Assurance had to have returned to her almost immediately because he fairly leaped across the distance between them and kissed her hand.

"Mary!" Catherine heard him say, "How I have missed you."

Meanwhile, seeming to assess the scene, the visitor looked from Mary to William to the children, wriggling with excitement. He cleared his throat, and the startled look on William's face told Catherine he had forgotten the visitor altogether.

"My apologies," William said as he turned his attention away from Mary. "I am William Falconer at your service. I have heard a little about your business here and wait to hear more."

"It would be difficult to heed the presence of a mere stranger with such a lovely lady awaiting you," the man commented dryly.

He was about to say more, but the figure of Daniel in the doorway interrupted him.

Daniel's eyes went immediately to Catherine. "Petition delivered?" he asked.

"Done," she said. "And Watkins?"

"Bones broken, but he is in good hands and will…" His speech halted as he saw William.

"Brother!" he exclaimed. "Back so soon? It is a good thing. You have been sorely missed. Is the business completed?"

"My wealthy neighbor, who is more generous than yours, will buy my land if I but give the word."

"Well done," Daniel complimented. "Most well done."

Then Martha moved a little, and Daniel saw the visitor, who had been blocked from his view.

"And who are you, sir?" he questioned.

"James Morris, representative of the estate of Lord Hillridge, the late Henry Falconer." He stood as Daniel approached.

For a brief time, Daniel seemed to be speechless, but then he managed to say, "Welcome to my house, but I do not see what you could want of me." My father was disowned, had no family at all when he died fighting Cromwell, no family who would claim him save my mother, my brother William here, and me."

There was silence as Morris sat back down on the bench, carefully adjusted his legs, scratched his ear, rubbed his chin, and looked down at his empty mug. Finally, he spoke.

"The deaths of Daniel and William Falconer have been reported to me, and when I heard your name from your servant Catherine, I believed you to be imposters."

"Why? " Daniel asked.

"Wait." Morris said with authority. "Let me finish. I find myself unsure that my information was accurate; therefore, I am going to describe the current situation. Lord Hillridge, Henry Falconer, son and heir of one Charles Falconer, has died without issue. There are no immediate heirs. He stipulated in his will that the estate, which was not entailed, should be divided, one third to go to Josiah Hook, son of his sister Elizabeth, the other two thirds to Daniel and William Falconer, sons of his late brother James, whom he believed to have been unjustly treated."

Catherine realized that she had been holding her breath and released it as she looked to see Daniel's reaction. His face had gone pale, and he seemed to be swaying. She went to him and put an arm around him, pushing him down on to the bench. William's face, on the other hand, was mottled with red.

"It is a shame he did not decide my father was poorly treated in time to save my mother's life," he said bitterly.

Morris ignored William's comment and went on with his explanation. "Last Michaelmas, Josiah Hook's agent sailed with one Captain Hudgins carrying a letter informing Hook that I had been unable to locate Daniel and William Falconer, and unless they were found within the twelvemonth, the entire estate would be his."

Captain Hudgins! It was his ship that had brought her and Mary, Catherine realized, and at the same time it had brought most of Daniel's troubles. She began to think she had better sit down herself, and sank onto a stool beside Daniel, who reached for her hand. She remembered that the first damage to his fences was done the day after she arrived.

Morris looked from Daniel to William and back to Daniel. "I take considerable responsibility upon myself to tell you this without verifying your identity because there is a slim chance you are not whom you claim to be. If that is the case, you are diabolically clever because your innocence of any of this intrigue has seemed so sincere. I wish to speak to Governor Calvert and to seek further proof..."

"That we are not dead," William quipped.

"...Of your identity," Morris went on as though no jest had been made. He was obviously not amused. It occurred to Catherine that he would probably be detained in Mary's Land longer than planned because, if he were the honest man he seemed to be, his task had just grown in size.

"When did you arrive on these shores?" he asked.

"1654," Daniel and William answered simultaneously.

"But I was sent to Virginia," William said. "And Daniel to Mary's Land. There are court records..."

Morris' brows went up. "The court sent you?"

Catherine wanted to cry at the emergence of what sounded so shameful.

"We were caught stealing," Daniel said quietly. "The war had reduced my mother's family to poverty."

"So I have accepted the word of felons, have I?" Morris mused. "Now I find I must inquire into your character on top of all else."

Catherine thought of Daniel's attack on Watkins and wondered what that would tell Morris of Daniel's character.

But the man was sighing. "Still, there is some stubborn part of me that continues to believe you. What I have heard from everyone here is too consistent, your initial belief that I could not possibly have business with you too convincing. Moreover, there was talk in London that wrongdoing had caused Hook to flee to the colonies.

Was this the same man who had accused Martha and her of being drunk this morning, Catherine asked herself.

Then, as though there had not been enough confusion in the day, the doorway darkened, and she looked up to see Eleanor standing there. Her appearance was frightening. Face, hands, clothing, all were covered with black streaks. Runnels through the black on her face spoke of tears, and she leaned heavily against the door post with one arm, while the other arm was thrust beneath her belly, now greatly swollen with her child.

She did not seem capable of seeing all the people in the room. She looked only at Catherine.

"Can ye hide me, Catherine?" she asked. "Hook locked me in somewhere. Phoebe hev let me out."

A succession of random thoughts ran quickly through Catherine's mind. Eleanor's coating of soot suggested she had been locked in the smokehouse. Did Hook mean to leave Eleanor locked in and smoke her, too? Phoebe would suffer for letting her out. Hiding Eleanor here would not be particularly secret since eight people had just heard the request. All but Morris could be trusted to mean to keep such a secret, though in practice, it might not be so simple. Only then did the pain of Eleanor's plight penetrate Catherine's reeling mind.

"Of course we will care for you, Eleanor, but why? Why would he do this?"

"It is a busy household," Catherine heard Morris comment. "Does the world bring its troubles here?"

Catherine did not hear what answer anyone might have made. She heard only Eleanor's jumbled reply, her voice breaking each time she had spoken several words.

"I am so confused…I think it is a threat Hook hev made to Hammet…that I will come to harm, I and my babe with me…if Hammet should say something…or not say something…I know not what…and I was told long ago, Catherine, that I must not speak to you."

Catherine put an arm around Eleanor and led her to the bed, on which she sank with a groan. Catherine knew the bed would be stained with soot because Eleanor was so coated with it, but she did not care. She understood what the girl had been through locked in the smokehouse, and it was scarcely to be borne. She scooped water from the pail into a wooden basin, took a cloth from the peg, and began to wash Eleanor's face and hands. Behind her, Martha was coaxing coals into a flame, most likely to make a soothing tea.

Morris stood, approached Eleanor, and stooped down before her, but she whimpered and pulled away from him in alarm.

"There is naught to fear," Catherine said softly.

"I wish you no harm, but tell me, young woman, have you any notion at all about what…your husband …must not say?"

Eleanor's face reddened. "I thought it was to do with Catherine and Mary and Daniel, but I was not full sure. Mayhap it was that Hook foul treated Mary…and Catherine, too, when she came unbidden to seek her."

"What business does your husband have with Hook?" Morris asked.

At first, Eleanor seemed puzzled about how to answer, then she said, "Hammet is Hook's overseer. He does his bidding, though he often mislikes it."

Suddenly she wailed. "Hook must not know I am here. I have been sore troubled in my life, but never so frighted."

Morris patted her reassuringly on the shoulder despite its effects on his hands. "No one will hear from my lips that you are here. I promise you that." He smiled, and Eleanor gave him back a hint of a smile.

"I believe I have heard enough," Morris said, standing and hitching his shoulders back as though to clear the stiffness away.

He turned to Mary. "Thank you, pretty maiden, for the food and drink."

To Daniel and William he said, "I find myself hoping you will indeed be entitled to this inheritance."

To Catherine, he murmured, "My deepest apologies for my rudeness today. You have given me only courtesy in return, and for that, I am most grateful."

He walked to the door saying , "God be with you." Then he was gone.

Everyone in the room sat in silence as the hoof beats of his horse faded into the distance.

Chapter Twenty-six

Slowly, as darkness became more complete, Daniel, knife at waist, club in hand, circled the house. He regretted that it had become a fortress for fear of Hook's desperation. Inside, the women still slept upstairs, but now all the men rested downstairs, weapons at hand, alert to any unusual sound. Daniel had been reassured about their response the first night of the vigil when a sneeze from Ezekiel had brought them immediately out of the door, ready to do battle.

Daniel's mind wandered to the problem of Eleanor. No one had come inquiring about her. Why not? Had the woman been Catherine, Daniel would have been half crazed at her disappearance. But then Eleanor was no Catherine. Daniel speculated that there could have been several reasons: that Hammet suspected where she was already and deemed her safe or that he'd been told Hook had her hidden away and believed it. At any rate, if Hammet attempted to tell lies in court, Eleanor's whereabouts might be a very useful tool.

Daniel's head began to ache, and he found himself grinding his teeth with anger. How tired he was of this ridiculous game that was none of his doing. He wondered if the inheritance, when debts and fees were deducted, would be large enough to compensate for the pain it had caused. Perhaps it would be some paltry sum, not even worth considering. What a cruel twist of fate that would be.

Something moved by the side of the tobacco barn. An animal? A man bent on harm? Daniel kept to the shadow of the trees and crept closer to investigate. Just as he stumbled on a root he would not have expected to find there, a blow landed on the back of his head.

It was not heavy enough to knock him senseless, so he was able to shout and to fight back as more blows were aimed at him. Someone attempted to jam an arm into his Adam's apple, but Daniel grabbed the arm to swing the fellow around with such force that he collided heavily with a co-conspirator, and both went down.

Daniel heard them thump, grunt, and curse, and immediately after, there came the sound of William calling his name and of footsteps pounding in his direction. His assailants scrambled to their feet and ran.

"Here, William," Daniel shouted. "I think they are running toward the barn. With this, he dashed after them, heedless of obstacles that might trip him in the dark. He had seen a flicker of light; someone was trying to torch the barn.

In what seemed an instant, a flame licked up the side of the structure. It was empty, but nearby buildings were not.

Daniel, Edwin, and Ezekiel streaked around the sides of the barn to try to catch the villains, but returned empty handed. Daniel's rage turned to fear at the realization that, if the wind changed, the fire might spread to the house, and he next ran to warn the women to leave. But he found Catherine and Martha and Eleanor hurrying across the yard in his direction carrying pails and pots and basins. The twins were just behind them, as was William with a steadying arm around Mary.

Edwin and Ezekiel grabbed the containers and hastened with them toward the stream.

"Form a line to pass the water," Daniel ordered, and within minutes, all but the twins, who were not yet strong enough, and Mary, who was not yet mobile enough, were toting containers from person to person and thence to Daniel, who dashed the water onto the fire.

The wind was light, but still a distinct danger, sending searing heat and burning cinders his way. Still Daniel faced it, thereby he hoped, preventing the spread of the flames even though it was beginning to be obvious that the barn was lost.

When the moon rose, it shone on the smoldering ruins. Daniel was still pouring water around the edges as a precaution when William tapped him on the shoulder.

"It is out, Daniel," William said gently. "You can leave it now."

Daniel nodded, though exhaustion made an effort of something so minor as a nod and a walk to the house behind his weary troops.

As Mary handed him a tankard of ale, she frowned.

"What troubles you?" he asked. Silly question. What indeed?

"Your brows," Mary answered. "They are gone, and your hair is mown in front like a scythe has cut it."

Catherine had dropped to the bench, sure she would be unable to rise again, but she peered at Daniel with horror. Were they all too stupefied to see? Blood ran through the soot on the back of his neck and from his hairless brow along the side of his face. His shirt was a mix of black and red.

"Daniel, you are hurt," she gasped as she went to his side.

He looked puzzled for an instant and then slowly put his hand to the wound on his brow. "Yes, they tried to eliminate one heir with a blow to the head," he said, "and I suspect to burn the house and all who were in it."

This realization seemed to have told his body to weaken still further, for suddenly he sank down on the bench, and Catherine suspected would have fallen had she not held him.

Eleanor brought water, and as Catherine began to wash Daniel's face, she could see Martha reaching for the herbs and the fat she would mix to make a healing salve. Under the soot, his face was burned and red in spots, and she could see that her touch, gentle as she tried to make it, pained him.

When Daniel's face was cleansed, before the salve was ready, Catherine found herself wanting to continue to sooth his face as though because she cared so much there would be healing in her touch, but she knew it would only bring greater pain. Still, she put one hand lightly to his temple, and he covered it with his and moved it around to his lips, kissing her palm and sending her into that realm of feeling she both desired and feared.

"We must get up to bed and leave the men to wash themselves and rest," Martha announced, and Catherine looked up, unhappy to find she must leave Daniel now.

"Let me apply the ointment," she said. "And then I will go."

"Gentle Catherine," Daniel murmured. "Thank you, Catherine."

Pleasantries done with, James Morris leaned across the table toward Daniel and lowered his voice. "My ship sails on the tide, and I regret that I cannot be here when you present your case in court. Please remember that the court records confirm your identity, and that the governor does as well.

"In my questioning of Hook, I heard him contradict himself on many points, certainly enough to prove you are who you say you are, and the fact that he has attempted to prevent your receiving your inheritance confirms it.

"When I return to England, the Falconer estate must be sold since neither you nor Hook can buy the other out. After the costs of settlement have been deducted, your share will be brought to you in credit and goods by a courier I trust. If all goes well, your portions should be worth about 5,000 guineas for each brother."

Daniel found himself shaking his head in disbelief. And he had suspected the sum would be paltry. This was wealth beyond imagination for him, whose needs had seemed so simple. He wondered if he would be corrupted by it and looked at William, whose mouth was open, his eyes shut. But Morris was continuing to speak, and Daniel brought his attention back to the man.

"I have found, by the by, that Hook's holdings here have not supported his lavish spending, and he has long since squandered the monies from his father. It is why he has been so desperate to have all the Falconer riches, both yours and his."

Amazed to the point of breathlessness, Daniel asked, "He told you all this?"

"I knew his father's funds were gone, and I saw his overblown style of life. Catching him in several lies as well as his attempt to bribe me told me the rest."

"It is amazing, the fortune that has sailed into this port, good for us, but boding ill for Hook," Daniel managed to say.

"There is information I must have from you before I sail," Morris added. "Do you wish to remain here or return to England?"

"Remain," Daniel answered without even a glance around to see how the others felt. A belated glimpse around the room, however, revealed agreement from William and Catherine.

"Then have I your authorization to find you an agent in England who will exchange guineas for goods to be shipped to you and for credit here in Mary's Land?"

Daniel nodded to William, who answered.

"Yes," he said. "You have our permission."

Morris drained his ale and rose from the table. "Be warned," he said. "Hook will have damaging accusations, lies, and half truths you may have to face as he tries to prove in court that you are frauds. Take with you those who will vouch for your identity and testify to your characters. Should the court find you guilty of wrongdoing, you could still be forced to forfeit your inheritance. I have here a letter explaining my conclusions in the matter, but there will be an attempt, of course, to impugn my character."

"Of course," Daniel repeated. "Fortunately it is clear your character is to be envied. I wish you Godspeed, sir, and I thank you for the fairness you have brought to this matter."

Morris nodded to the women, who were already beginning to chatter excitedly about the news he had brought, and Daniel and William walked with him to the hitching post. William loosed the horse as Morris mounted.

"May God guide the court and strengthen you." Morris inclined his head, smiled, and flicked the reigns to start his horse on its journey to the ship.

Daniel stood idly by the fence, gazing across the field at the expanse of dead plants, those for which he had worked so hard and held such high hopes. He wondered if plowing them under would strengthen the soil that they had so quickly depleted. He would be glad to undertake such a task as soon as possible because he did not like this feeling of having almost nothing to do, nor did he like the prospect of the court proceeding he faced the next day.

A cheery voice startled him. "Good morrow, Daniel."

Daniel spun around. "Father Thaddeus! How glad I am that you could come."

"Your need for me has surpassed all other considerations. It is good to see you though I cannot say you look well. What, pray tell, has happened?"

"Come Father, let us refresh ourselves, and I will tell you a very strange tale," Daniel said in response.

Shortly thereafter, they walked slowly to the edge of the woods as Daniel related the events of the past several weeks. At first, Father Thaddeus exclaimed at each new detail, but soon he merely listened in silence. The two men sat on logs as Daniel completed his story.

"So I am most grateful that you will appear in court to remind the good gentlemen that William and I are who we say we are and that we are worthy fellows after all.

"Of course, they will say I am a maverick, a defrocked Jesuit."

"Who is known to all for his good works," Daniel finished for him.

Father Thaddeus sighed. "If that were true, it would be of help to you, but I must admit I am surprised I have not heard from you on another matter."

"Another?"

"The sacrament of marriage, Daniel. Have you forgot so soon?"

"Not forgot, Father. All but given up. Catherine has rejected every overture but one, and I managed to ruin that opportunity." Daniel picked at a piece of gray matter on the log. "One moment she seems to respond to me with affection, and more, and the next moment she turns cold as snow. It is painful to be pushed away again and again. I think I must count Catherine one more loss atop so many others."

"Daniel, I am angry with you, both of you stubborn children. You are going to talk to her and tell her what you have been feeling, specifically why you once hurled such angry words at her. I swear to you, if you do not do this within the hour, I will truss you up like hogs, both of you until you do. And then I will ask God to forgive me."

Daniel almost smiled at the image. "She will not talk to me. She avoids me with great skill. I would have to hog tie her to make her listen."

"She will listen," Father Thaddeus said. "I will fetch her now, and she will listen. Stay right here and wait."

"How can you force her to do that? "

"Trust me. I can. You have but to explain the source of your angry words. Do not fail to do that." And suddenly he was walking away from Daniel, a determined man with a mighty task.

Catherine saw him as she carried a pail of water from the well. Sitting it down, she ran to greet him.

"Welcome," she said, smiling, as he took both her hands in his.

"My dear Catherine, you are lovelier than ever, but you have wrought great pain on my friend Daniel. Do you know that?"

Catherine recoiled. At a loss for words she merely stared at the priest. What gave him the right to interfere in so private a matter? She could not allow such interference to weaken her resolve.

"Do you think I am blind?" he chided. "I have seen the strength of the bonds when you two are together, and I have heard of your avoidance now."

"Daniel had no right to complain," she said.

"Be quiet! Listen!" Father Thaddeus commanded. "Catherine, you love this man, and he is full worthy of your love just as you are of his. I know why Daniel spoke cruelly. I know why you fear him. You are going to talk to each other about those very impediments and stop playing the woodenheads."

Catherine could not believe what she was hearing. Fear mingled with anger.

"What right have you…"

"I have every right. Both of you have confided in me, and I have seen your need for each other." He took her hands again, diminishing her anger a little "Has Daniel continued with those harsh words you told me of?" he asked.

"No, but…"

"Catherine, if God forgave us our sins as poorly as you forgive Daniel's, it would be a sad day for mankind."

"But I am afraid…"

"Does your heart tell you to forgive?" The man was relentless.

217

"It is my mind that refuses…"

"Listen to me, dear woman. The heart is not always the best measure, but often it is. Let your mind heed what is true now, with what kindness Daniel treats you. Let that join with what your heart tells you." Father Thaddeus' voice softened to something less commanding. "It is not like you to be afraid, Catherine. You have risked great danger for Mary, but you will not risk the small danger that Daniel will hurt you again."

Catherine turned her back to him, but he put his hand on her arm and gently turned her to face him again.

"We humans hurt each other, men and women in their closeness perhaps worst of all. Daniel will hurt you again, and you will hurt him. The very ability to be hurt is a measure of the depth of your feeling."

"Stop! Stop!" Catherine cried.

"I will not stop until you two have had honest discourse on what you have been feeling, and you will have it right now."

He took her hand and pulled her along the fence toward the wood where she saw Daniel waiting. "He has something to tell you, and you are to be sure to tell him why you stopped speaking to him after his betrothal to Mary. Do you understand me, Catherine? Unless you do this, I will break my vow to keep confidences and tell him myself. You would not like such a sin on your hands, now would you?"

His grip on her hand was like iron, his progress toward Daniel against her tugging surprisingly strong. She was shaking as he swung her around to face Daniel, who looked as stricken as she felt.

"Now talk!" Father Thomas ordered. "Tell each other the truth, you, Daniel, the source of your anger, and you, Catherine, the reason for your withdrawal."

With that, he turned and strode away. Catherine was speechless, staring at Daniel, as he at her.

He finally broke the silence. "It seems we are ordered to speak. I am directed to tell you why I was so cruel."

Catherine made herself study the ground at her feet.

"I did not know myself why I said the foul things I have since so regretted," Daniel began, "until I remembered that the sinner comes to hate the innocent."

"You hated me?" Startled, Catherine looked into his eyes.

"No, no, it was my sin I hated and because of that your innocence. Nor did I come to see until it was gone how I cherished your friendship."

These words disappointed Catherine. She did not want mere friendship, but he was continuing to speak.

"You withdrew that friendship, would not even speak with me after my great sin, and I could scarce abide your judgment, or myself for that matter."

At first Catherine did not know how to answer. She had judged, but her withdrawal had been for a greater reason. She reached for Daniel's hand.

"Oh Daniel! I did judge, just a little, but it was not why I avoided you. It was hurt, disappointment, and sadness that you were lost to me. Until I knew you, Mary was my only true joy, my reason for being, and just as I learned there was so much more, it was gone."

Daniel's eyes widened, and a smile hovered about his mouth.

"You speak truly?" he said, belief seeming to war with disbelief in his expression.

"Truly, Daniel. I could not imagine why you would prefer me to Mary, but it seemed to be so, just as it seemed you disliked her."

Daniel reached for Catherine's other hand. "One thing that is appealing about you is that you are not even conscious of your own grace and beauty."

"Then why did you bed Mary?" Those words had been difficult to say. She searched his face for an answer.

"Ah, Catherine, it is to my great shame, but I was fair starved for a woman's body, and hers tormented me unmercifully while she did all in her power to keep me inflamed. It is why I sought to sell your indentures, but I could not lose you."

"Why did you not sell hers?"

I had suffered too greatly at being separated from my brother, so I could not make you part from Mary."

Catherine thought of losing Mary and felt her eyes fill with tears.

"You were right. I did not like her," he went on, "which made my deed all the more despicable. I have only myself to blame, but she provoked me at a time of great weakness."

"And that is why you have found it so hard to forgive her."

"You see, Catherine, there she was in all her ripe beauty and terrible selfishness, and you, who were caring and full of joy were but a…a…"

"Skeleton," she finished for him.

"And by the time your comeliness had caught up with the beauty of your soul, I had already sown the seeds of my downfall."

"For my part," Catherine told him, "I tried to make myself stop feeling anything. If you but smiled at me, it was like a sword point. I feared it would pierce me, and all I wanted but could not have, would rush forth for all to see. And though now you have tried to woo me, I have been so afraid that at any moment you would turn back into that venomous creature who hurled accusations so wounding, so unfair. Daniel, I could not bear that."

"When all along, the true object of my venom was myself, never you. Catherine, please forgive me. Please let me prove to you the height of my regard, of my devotion. Do not hide from me."

He reached out and pulled her close, and she went willingly into those precious arms, no longer reluctant to feel the surge of physical longing, no longer afraid to trust herself to him.

"I love you, Catherine, with a love that threatens to overwhelm me," he said before his lips sealed hers.

She had to pull away ever so briefly so that she might say, "Oh Daniel! and I love you. It seems I have loved you forever."

And then in his embrace, with his kisses, she was lost in a whirl of feeling so great she feared she would swoon.

"And we will wed as soon as the notice can be posted, will we not?" he asked.

"Oh! yes, Daniel. Oh! yes," she answered.

Chapter Twenty-seven

Catherine watched dust particles dance in the fall sunshine, which shone brightly through the glass windows. Then she placed her attention on red faced, bewigged Weston Ellis, Justice of the Peace, who surveyed the courtroom from behind a table. Beside him were his scribe and an assistant.

Rows of benches filled the room and were broken by a center aisle, which separated the opposing parties. In the first row, Catherine sat between Daniel and Mary with William on Mary's far side. Behind them were Edwin, Ezekiel, Father Thaddeus, and Watkins' man Amos. Across the aisle, fidgeting and shifting about uncomfortably, Hammet sat behind Hook and his agent. The occupants of the other benches were unknown to Catherine.

Mixed with the fear that today's proceedings would not go well for Daniel were surges of joy at the memory of yesterday's reunion. Catherine had to push aside the desire to throw her arms around Daniel and to feel again that deep, burning connection. She told herself she was being a silly woman to allow such fancies to break into her concentration when so much was at stake today.

Glancing at the strangers in the back of the room, Catherine noted that most had fastened their eyes on Mary. Though she still walked with the aid of a stick or of someone's arm, her face had recovered from the beating and, if it could be believed, was more lovely than ever, particularly when William was present. Daniel, on the other hand, still wore the burns and bruises of the night attack. Catherine thought about Eleanor, another of Hook's victims, safely hidden away with the twins in the house of a friend nearby, ready to appear in court if she were needed and if it were deemed safe.

Ellis rapped his gavel to open the proceedings and began to speak. "The task before us this morning is to examine claim and counterclaim, those of Daniel Falconer and of Josiah Hook, to determine which man has the right of it. I have here three documents with which to begin the session." He cleared his throat and picked up a paper that lay before him and began to read.

I, Josiah Hook, do claim with honesty before God that two men who claim falsely to be Daniel Falconer and his brother William seek to usurp a large portion of an inheritance, which should, by rights, be mine.

Catherine saw a bitter smile flit across Daniel's lips as Ellis took up the second sheet.

I, Daniel Falconer, do claim that Josiah Hook has informed the representatives of my uncle's estate in England that I and my brother are dead, and further, that said Josiah Hook has used a number of measures to force me to leave the colony before that agent should appear and learn the truth. These measures include the destruction of my fences, the trampling of eight acres of tobacco, an attack on my servant Ezekiel, and the seduction of a servant indentured to me and betrothed to me. Furthermore, without my permission, her indenture was sold to him, and he later did her physical harm, breaking her leg and beating her about the face. Just two nights ago, he was responsible for burning my barn. Had the fire not been stopped, my house and all in it would have burned as well.

There was stirring and muttering in the room. Ellis looked up and squinted at the gathering before him. "I have, in addition, a letter from one James Morris, representative of the estate of Henry Falconer, Lord Hillridge, which is as follows:

I, James Morris, journeyed to Mary's Land to meet with Josiah Hook, whom I believed to be the sole surviving heir of Henry Falconer, now deceased, and to determine the nature of his wishes in regard to the disposition of the estate. I was surprised when I stumbled upon men who claimed to be Daniel and William Falconer, the other heirs, whom Josiah Hook had claimed were dead. I met with them, investigated court records, and interviewed people who have known Daniel Falconer since his arrival in Mary's Land in 1654 and who vouch for his good character. I can only conclude that these men are indeed the other heirs entitled to a portion of the Falconer property, and I return to England to act on that information.

The buzz in the room was louder as Ellis peered in Hook's direction. "Now sir," he said. "Since there has been so much already stated on behalf of your opponents, I wish to hear first from you."

Hook stood, and Catherine saw again that flash of a resemblance to Daniel. He was a handsome man if one could separate his character from his appearance. He was impeccably dressed, though not in the opulent clothing she had seen him wear in the past. One thing was certain: even clothed more humbly than usual, he outshone all but William on this side of the room. Daniel and his household were garbed like paupers.

Hook began to speak. "You have my word against that of a known felon, convicted in England and transported to these shores, and that of an unknown Englishman, who may or may not have been bribed by this felon to settle the estate on his behalf. Furthermore, Daniel Falconer's behavior has come before this court in the past because he physically attacked a neighbor without provocation. This man, this Falconer, is not competent to keep his fences mended, and he fixes the blame elsewhere, now principally on me. Before I am accused, I ask for proof of that and also proof that I attacked his servant or burned his barn. In addition, the indentured servant, who came to me of her own free will, had been foul used by this man, which is why I sought to secure her indenture. I was later forced to punish her for theft."

Over the hubbub that arose, Catherine heard Mary gasp and considered the impossibility of having her tell the court the damning truth about her role in all of this. She had stolen, but before she went to Hook, not after, or were there other thefts? Catherine bit her lip and glanced at Mary, who was shaking her head as though in answer to Catherine's question.

Hook was continuing. "Now, you look upon people who are dressed disgracefully, aiming to appear as poor men and women due to the ills I have caused them, and I would point out to you that this is but a sham."

As Hook went on, Catherine turned a little and peered from the sides of her eyes so she could see Hammet without being obvious. He looked like a man in pain. He would look briefly at Hook, then away, stare at his lap, then squint toward the window as though he wanted to climb through it.

The Justice of the Peace wore a dark frown. Catherine imagined he had been inclined toward Daniel, but Hook's words had sounded too logical, a clever blend of truth and falsehood that made Daniel look quite bad.

"Goodman Hook," Ellis said. "What do you make of records sent by the English court when these men were transported? The name Falconer does appear in those records."

"I make of those records that the conspiracy is an old one, that these two men as raw youths in league with others planned to claim this inheritance, that they gave the court false names."

Catherine breathed out sharply. Such an accusation sounded far-fetched. The justice could not possibly believe it. She looked at Hammet again. His face was red, she believed from anger. Mary made a motion that suggested she was about to stand and refute some of Hook's lies, but Catherine grabbed her arm.

"Wait," she whispered. "Daniel, we must get Eleanor."

"I hate to do it," he whispered back, "but I think we are lost unless Hammet tells the truth. Christ's blood, I hope her presence will free him to do that, else we will have delivered her into danger." He turned around and bade Edwin fetch the woman.

Then Amos was standing. "I hev a word fer the court, if ye please," he said.

The justice nodded.

"I be Amos, servant to Giles Watkins. It was not long ago, Daniel came to our holding and 'pologized for breaking my master's nose 'cause he thought my master had done him damage, but he learned different. He and his men raised our storm smashed roof and fixed a shed, and later, he helped when my master got trapped 'neath a fallen barn."

Hook was on his feet without a say-so from the justice.

"Clever, was it not," he sneered. "To regain the support of a man he had injured in time to back his claim before this court?"

Ellis looked toward Amos.

"When did he first apologize?"

"Oh, mebbe three, four days after the storm."

"Well before the representative arrived from England," Daniel added.

"When the man's arrival was imminent," Hook amended.

Father Thaddeus stood. "May I address these proceedings?" he asked.

Ellis, who was obviously a man of few words, nodded again.

"I have known William and Daniel since they were children," he said. "They are, beyond all doubt, who they claim to be. I was confessor to their mother."

"And now are stripped of your priest's status," Hook interrupted again. "For what reason did the Jesuits expel this man? It could have been for gross dishonesty," he said to Ellis.

224

"Why?" said the justice, addressing Father Thaddeus.

"Doctrinal disagreements," said Father Thaddeus, "and they did not expel me. I departed from them. We did not agree about the nature of human virtue."

Ellis, his chin sunk on his chest, peered at Hook. "Tell me, Goodman Hook, are you Catholic?" he asked.

"No, I am of the King's church," Hook barked defensively.

Ellis frowned again. "It is somewhat odd, is it not, to cast accusations at a man who is in disagreement with a church with which you yourself disagree."

Hook opened his mouth several times, but could obviously find no answer, so the justice sat back in his chair and looked from Hook to Daniel and William.

"Daniel Falconer, there is little doubt of your identity or that Josiah Hook conspired to cheat you of your inheritance, and this colony will in no way impede the distribution of the funds to either party unless the will stipulates "men of good character", and I doubt that it does. However, the question of damage done to you by Hook is an area of considerable doubt since there are no witnesses, no proof, only suppositions."

For the first time, Daniel stood to address the justice. "Sir, may I request a very short break. I have nearby one who might shed more light on this final issue, and I have sent someone to fetch her."

Catherine saw Hammet's head snap up as though he seemed to know who Daniel referred to, but his expression was unreadable. Relief that Eleanor was safe? Anger that she was to be put back in harm's way?

Most sat quietly except Hook, who was whispering to Hammet, and the scribe, who was softly asking the justice a question.

There was not long to wait. Soon, Eleanor, head bowed, limbs trembling, and seeming to be very conscious of her swollen body, entered the room. Catherine looked at Hammet, who was suddenly smiling broadly, and when Eleanor saw her husband, she gave a hint of a smile back.

"Sir," Hammet addressed the justice. "I would like to speak, sir, if I may."

"I believe we should hear first from this woman for whom we have just waited," Ellis said.

"It is not now needed," Hammet told him. "She is my wife, and she is safe, and I am now free to speak."

The brows of the justice rose. "Oh? Well, then, man, do go on."

"I am a free man employed by Hook," Hammet explained. "And he hev told me he hev my wife hidden away lest I tell you what I know. He hev threatened to hurt her."

Hook jumped to his feet. "He lies! He is in Falconer's pay!" he shouted, his calm air of superiority now become one of desperation.

Ellis rapped the table with his gavel. "According to you, the whole world is in Falconer's pay," he said sarcastically. "Please be seated."

Hook reluctantly sank to his seat, muttering something to Hammet.

"What did you say?" Ellis asked.

"Nothing," Hook replied.

"Well, from now on please say nothing more discreetly." Ellis then nodded at Hammet. "Go on," he said.

The room became absolutely quiet.

"Hook hev told me Daniel Falconer is a fake after his money and that we must make sure he leave the colony. I have directed servants to break fences, trample the crop and…" He hung his head. "…attack Ezekiel, though there was more harm done than I meant. I am guilty of wrongdoing, and there be penalty to pay, but I will not sit here longer and hear Hook's lies now. I know my wife is safe. I have even heard talk of false papers, though nothing more than that."

"And the fire?" the justice questioned.

"It was none of my doing. I knew naught of it." Hammet turned to address Daniel. "Daniel Falconer, I am full sorry for the ill I hev done and grateful ye hev cared for my wife."

He faced the table. "That is all I hev to say."

"And you have thus resolved my further doubts," Ellis said. "Josiah Hook, there will be penalty for the numerous attempts to do this man harm. The court fines you 20,000 pounds tobacco or the equivalent in credit to be paid forthwith."

Hook was on his feet again. "I cannot pay until the inheritance comes. I have no tobacco credit left at this time."

"Ah, but you have possessions and servants," Ellis answered. "Therefore, I appoint Neville Forester here at this table to put value on each good or service you provide Falconer. First, the indenture of his female servant will be returned to him. Second, your servants will labor to rebuild his barn and provide any other structures he might need. Further, you have land, servants, livestock, household possessions, beverages, and farming equipment that might go to make up for this sum. In addition, his debt to you, the one you purchased, will be canceled."

Hook looked startled. Catherine could not recall mention of the debt.

"Oh, yes," Ellis said. "We prepare well in this court. We know of the debt."

"A cow," Mary was whispering, "and horses and cloth. Oh! Catherine, he has much cloth in his house."

"And books," Catherine whispered back. "Books for the children and for me."

"Now." Ellis was still addressing Hook. "You had better hope that not even an unknown party commits further mischief against Falconer or against Hammet and his wife because it will be laid at your door, and you will forfeit to Lord Baltimore all holdings in this colony and leave it immediately. Such a measure will also be in place should you fail to meet within the month the conditions I have just laid upon you."

Hook stood and kicked over a bench.

"Further display," added Ellis, who had not even taken a breath, "will result in a fine paid to this court." He leaned over the table and addressed Daniel. "Daniel Falconer, since you have no more debt, you will not be required to relinquish your holdings in this colony, and the court wishes you well."

He directed a smile to Daniel, but Catherine had the distinct impression it had moved immediately to Mary, where it lingered until he seemed to remind himself that he had other matters to see to. Then, he rose and left the room.

"I cannot believe it," Daniel said, grasping Catherine's hand. "We are gone from poverty to wealth in just a few short weeks. Catherine, I can give you all the good things you deserve, and William, we can establish a home anywhere, do anything we want. It was not even to be imagined."

Catherine remembered Eleanor and looked around to see her in Hammet's arms. The two pulled reluctantly from their embrace and approached.

"I do not know if ye will forgive me," he said to Daniel, "but ought I can do to make up fer my blindness, I will do it."

"Will you be well on your own without Hook's patronage?" Daniel asked.

"It will be something hard, especially after the storm, but no, we will not fare too poorly."

"Should all go as we hope, we Falconers can be of assistance if you need it. We have you to thank that so much is restored to us. With the telling of the truth, you put yourself in legal danger, though not, I think, unless we make a claim in court, and we would not do that."

Hammet and Eleanor followed Daniel and his household as they attempted to leave the room, but Hook blocked the door. Mary turned quickly away, and William held her close.

Eyes narrowed and threatening, Hook thrust his face into Daniel's. "You win, cousin," he hissed. "For years, all my life, I did the bidding of our sour uncle, smiled in the face of his cruel judgment, and laughed at his pitiful attempts at humor. And still he did this, robbed me of two thirds of what is mine. Of all the places in these colonies you might have gone, it had to be here, and on land adjoining mine yet. Despite your name, I never suspected until I got the letter that you were my cousin, and now you walk away with treasure you do not deserve. May it choke you, destroy you as the Puritans claim riches will do, and may a hot part of hell be your reward."

He turned and stalked down the path.

Catherine fell to considering what strange thinking it was that Hook could wish on an innocent man the fate he had already drawn to himself. But she could sense that every part of Daniel's body was stiff with outrage. She took his hand and ran her fingers along his wrist. "God has given you justice today," she said. "His blessing is enough to melt the ice of such a curse, and from a man whose own reward will likely be a hot part of hell."

Daniel took a deep breath, looked down at Catherine, and felt the tension flow away.

"You are the greatest blessing God has given me," he said softly as he drew from the pouch at his waist two marriage licenses issued by the county clerk.

Chapter Twenty-eight

Catherine pulled her cloak about her as she sat on the log by the edge of the woods and watched the autumn sunset proudly display its most festive orange and gold.

She needed to be alone, to give thanks for the blessings that had suddenly been showered upon her, upon Daniel, upon Mary, upon so many.

She was relieved that Hook had embarked for Virginia shortly after the court session which revealed his villainy, but that, abiding by the ruling, he had empowered his agent to make all due transfers of goods and services ordered by the court.

Catherine heard the lowing of the cow and knew that Mary, so thrilled to have milk and cream and cheese, would be milking the animal soon. Outlined against the sky were the new barn built by Hook's servants, the two horses, which would replace the missing mule, and the two additions to the house, rooms which would afford privacy for the newlyweds until all were ready to move. Contained in the bedchamber, which would be on the morrow hers and Daniel's, were special treasures, books. There was a *Bible* and a book about ancient Romans by a man named Plutarch and a book of English history. She would improve her own reading and help the children to improve theirs, all the while learning about wondrous things.

She ran her hand along the fine fabric of her skirt and bodice, fabric which had been stored in Hook's house. While the men had been occupied with building, the women had been sewing in every spare moment.

The women! How it had all changed. She and Mary were freed from their indentures, and Daniel had been given Phoebe's indenture papers as part of Hook's payment, so she was now safely enfolded in the household, free of Hannah's punishment and flushed with happiness.

Eleanor's indenture was ended, bought by Hammet, who would purchase Daniel's house and some of his holdings as well when the time was ripe.

Ezekiel's indenture was over also. He and Martha would wed on the morrow. Father Thaddeus was here for the sacrament, nay three sacraments of marriage. Catherine saw the ceremony in her mind's eye. Mary in her lovely green fabric that set off the color of her eyes. William with his ready wit and steady allegiance. Plump Martha in skirt and bodice the color of the first yellow flowers of spring, bald Ezekiel beside her smiling with delight. She herself, clad in blue the color of a robin's egg, and most important, dear, sturdy, serious Daniel at her side, trembling, as she would be trembling, with the import of the day and the promise of the night.

Her love reached out to Father Thaddeus, wise Father Thaddeus, who had understood her dilemma so well and then brought healing, reunion. She smiled as she remembered his lively face intent on pushing her to risks she did not want to take. Even as she and Daniel and all the household set out to establish a new home, they would promise to make contributions for a lifetime to his mission. They were to be married by a papist, she reflected, one whose church she had been taught to scorn. She could see now how foolish that was. Such a label meant almost nothing here. Imagine fearing Father Thaddeus with his great love of God and of his earthly flock.

"I send you to worship God at another altar, and I mourn the loss to me, but it is time for you to leave this place," Father Thaddeus had said to Daniel. "The rewards for faithful stewardship are not always earthly. Yours are; therefore, you have been doubly blessed.

Where would they go after Morris' agent arrived with the inheritance? And when? There were so many opportunities that the question was not a source of anxiety, but of excitement, adventure. Settlements had spread up the Potomac River, across the great bay, and north to a river called Severn. Everywhere there was good land if you could pay for it. Daniel and William would seek out a likely site and request to purchase a land grant from Lord Baltimore.

Catherine reflected on perhaps the greatest good fortune of all, that the household would stay together. Daniel could now give Ezekiel what he needed to establish a holding, and Ezekiel would claim the acres due to him as he left the indenture. All were agreed that those acres must border Daniel's and William's.

Now Phoebe, brave, good-hearted Phoebe, who had risked so much to help the sisters, would bring her magic with food to the new home and be valued as she deserved. Already, Martha was passing along the knowledge of everyone's likes and needs and of the growing and use of her healing herbs. Moreover, Martha would be nearby to help as the families grew.

Catherine watched geese flying in their customary vee, a community on the move, their raucous calls heralding the end of summer, and there came to mind the possibility that even Phoebe and Edwin would wed, and that all four couples would move as a community to the land they had chosen, they and the children, and new, very fortunate indentured servants with them, though none would be as fortunate as she had been.

The reverie was broken as Mary sank down beside Catherine and took her hand. "I have been grinding corn, and I am so tired," she said.

"Just think, Mary," Catherine replied. "Soon we will have a quern to grind it."

"And someone else to do the grinding," Mary countered quickly, "and to plant the crops as well."

Catherine smiled. "What else that has seemed so impossible? A flatboat of our own perhaps to ship crops and visit neighbors."

"Bread of wheat, not corn," Mary added.

"Featherbeds for everyone." Catherine laughed at the thought of such a luxury.

"Curtains to surround the beds." Mary suddenly went quiet. Her hold tightened on Catherine's hand, and Catherine realized she had begun to shake.

"What is wrong?" Catherine asked.

"I am frightened, Catherine,"

Catherine was surprised. "Of what?" she asked.

"That I will not always be a good person, a good wife to William, that I will go back to selfish ways in time of trouble."

"But Mary, we fight against selfish ways, all of us. None of us are saints. It is a choice you have, which way you will go, and you already know what you choose."

"And I am afraid of being bedded tonight. I have known two men, and it is no pleasure. Oh! Catherine, suppose I am but a stone in William's arms."

Mary's dilemma was difficult for Catherine to imagine, so badly did she want to lie in Daniel's arms, skin against skin, an anticipation that filled her with immeasurable pleasure.

But she took Mary by the shoulders and looked into her eyes. "Do you feel like a stone now when he holds you, touches you?"

"No, it is a joy, but when there will be more, will I turn cold as I have already?"

Catherine put her arms around Mary and rocked her gently back and forth as she had when Mary was small.

"What do you think?" Mary asked into her shoulder, demanding an answer.

"I do not know the answer," Catherine said. "Perhaps if you tell him of your fear..."

"And remind him of what I have done? No, Catherine, I cannot."

"He knows already." Catherine reminded her.

"But I do not want to draw pictures anew. I have been so bad." Mary began to shake with her crying, and Catherine held her again. "I do not deserve the blessings that have come to me." Mary's voice was muffled as she spoke into Catherine's shoulder.

"Nor do any of the rest of us, I think. All we can do is be thankful. Trust William, Mary. Just trust him," Catherine answered, aware that she had only come lately to trust in Daniel, a trust blended with tenderness and desire. It was a potent brew.

"Yes." Mary gulped as her shaking subsided. "Trust him. Trust God. Trust forgiveness." She took a deep breath, then another and pulled away, holding Catherine's hand again as the two watched the fading sunset.

With one last look at his sleeping bride somehow aglow even in her slumber, Daniel reluctantly swung his legs from bed to floor and sat up. Pulling on his breeches, he considered life's strangeness. The temptress Mary, empty of desire for him, the god-fearing maiden, Catherine, meeting his every overture with a consummate joy.

He had anticipated the need to overcome the shyness and fear of a virgin, but she had shown a need that equaled his own. It was torture no longer, this demand his body made for that of a woman, but an invitation to fulfillment.

Wanting to crawl back into bed beside her, but deciding she needed to rest while every part of him was awake and singing, he kissed her forehead, watched her stir and smile in her sleep, and went into the main room. He had worried that William would find Mary as unresponsive as he had himself, but one glance at the reverent gaze Mary fastened on William told him he had worried in vain. He fought back a quick stab of jealousy that the girl had found him wanting and William obviously pleasing, but nothing could mar his joy this morning. He reminded himself he had done nothing for Mary's comfort or pleasure.

Nodding to the two of them, he went to help Edwin care for the animals. Ezekiel was otherwise occupied this morning.

Catherine stirred and reached out for Daniel. She was disappointed when she found him gone. But not for long. The animals did not care that she missed Daniel already. They cared only to be fed, and she did not think that Daniel had directed anyone else to do the task. There was comfort in knowing that he was faithful to the needs even of animals and that he had not wished to mar yesterday's joyful celebration by assigning new chores to other members of the household.

As she moved to sit up, she felt a telltale soreness and reflected that never before in her life had she been happy to be sore. Her mind went back to the ecstasy she had experienced during the night, to Daniel's blend of love and desire that had sent her into a world of sensation and adoration she would never have believed. As she pulled on her clothing, she would pause now and then, close her eyes, and call back the lovemaking. Now she knew why some women had more children than they knew what to do with and wondered how she might prevent an overburden that would mean difficulty for those children. At the moment, saying no to Daniel was not even a possibility.

She realized as she entered the main room and saw Mary that she had been so enfolded in her own rapture she had forgotten about Mary's fears. But one glance revealed her sister with eyes full of wonder, a smile playing about her lips as she looked at her husband. God be praised, all was well.

It seemed strange that Martha was not yet stirring. It was stranger still to see Mary hasten to prepare breakfast, William's eyes following her with pride and admiration.

Catherine was about to help her when thumping in the loft above gave way to clattering feet as the twins descended the stair and pulled her onto the bench at the table, settling down beside her. They threw their arms around her, and she reached out to pull them even more tightly against her.

"You are our mother now," Jonathan declared proudly.

Then, Daniel was behind the three, arms reaching around the children, his cheek pressed against hers.

"Good morrow, beloved," he whispered in her ear.

And she knew that this morning, this room abloom with love between those she cherished most, was an image she would carry with her into eternity.

Printed in the United States
19375LVS00002B/94-96